µ0

PATTERNS OF LIFE

Recent Titles by Janet Wright Matthews

PATTERNS OF LIFE

Janet Wright Matthews

This first world edition published in Great Britain 2000 by
SEVERN HOUSE PUBLISHERS LTD of
9–15 High Street, Sutton, Surrey SM1 1DF.
This first world edition published in the USA 2000 by
SEVERN HOUSE PUBLISHERS INC of
595 Madison Avenue, New York, N.Y. 10022.

British Library Cataloguing in Publication Data

Matthews, Janet Wright
    Patterns of life
    1. Military deserters - England - Fiction
    2. Cornwall (England) - Social conditions - Fiction
    I. Title
    823.9'14 [F]

ISBN 0-7278-5585-9

Typeset by Palimpsest Book Production Ltd.,
Polmont, Stirlingshire, Scotland.
Printed and bound in Great Britain by
MPG Books Ltd., Bodmin, Cornwall.

To my mother, Newlyn born and bred, who still thinks it is the best place in the universe, and to Norman, who deserves more thanks and appreciation than I can ever express.

One

"You'll be the death of me."

The words dropped into a pool of silence, their literal truth echoing round the small stuffy bedroom. Walter Harrison felt his throat tighten with fear as the images he had tried so hard to suppress invaded his mind: the soldiers, the pointing guns, the anxious padre, the white handkerchief pinned over his heart . . .

"Don't do it, Elizabeth. Please, don't do it." His pulse hammered in his ears, drowning the sound of the blackbirds outside.

She smiled at her husband, her plain face softening with emotion. "I have to, love. For the sake of our baby. I have to see the doctor."

Their baby. Last November, the glorious news of the armistice, the eleventh hour of the eleventh day of the eleventh month. And he and Elizabeth – the relief, the joy, the knowledge that there was an end in sight to his long period in purgatory – how could they have forgotten themselves so? Now, six months later, with the peace treaty signed at last, with safety so close he could reach out and touch it – now, she was going to betray him.

"Elizabeth. Please." Walter could feel the nervous tic in his cheek start up again and he slapped it lightly to put an end to it. "Elizabeth. Think."

In the dim bedroom, behind the permanently closed curtains, she smiled at him maternally. That was how she saw him now, he realised with despair – as another child. For two years she had made the decisions, paid for everything from the small annuity her grandmother had left her, arranged all their lives, while he had been forced to cower in this dim stuffy room. She had saved him – and in doing so she had usurped his position as head of the family.

1

As if to emphasise his subordinate position Elizabeth reached out and tidied back a lock of his hair.

"Don't worry, Walter. I know what I'm doing."

But she didn't. She hadn't thought it through. Walter could imagine how the news would fly around the little Dorset village of Affpuddle. Elizabeth Harrison, a middle-aged war widow, living in seclusion – pregnant.

How long before it reached the ears of someone paid to be inquisitive about these things? How long before they came for him, the hard-eyed men with shining leather belts and clipped moustaches? Men who had never had to face what he had.

He fought to control the rising panic. "You've had two children already!"

"Catherine is seventeen, Walter. Even Robbie is eleven. I am older now; it is more dangerous. And this is our baby, our hope for the future."

But not his future. His future would be counted in weeks if she went ahead with her mad plan. Her maternal smile maddened him.

"Please, Elizabeth." He knew real men didn't beg but now— "Please, Elizabeth."

She moved abruptly, turning away from him, automatically twitching the patchwork coverlet on the bed straight, lining up the jug and basin neatly on the wash-stand. "I have decided, Walter. I will not risk it." Her mouth was set in a mulish line.

He knew that look well. Once she had made up her mind nothing would change it. When she had decided to marry young Walter Harrison, her father's gardener, despite the fact that he was years younger than her, not even the threat of disinheritance would stop her. She had decided that Catherine was to go to college to be a teacher and nothing that Walter could say would persuade her. She had decided to hide him when he arrived, shaking and terrified, a broken man, a deserter, and she had kept him hidden for two years.

And now she was going to betray him.

Now, with the peace signed, with men already being released from the army, when, in a place where she was not known as a widow, they could have started a new life together – now, she was going to betray him.

He caught her arm. "Elizabeth. Wait two weeks, a week. We'll

2

go away, you can smuggle me out. In another town, where you are not known, we can start life again as man and wife. You can see a new doctor. There will be no danger then. A week, Elizabeth. Just a week."

The thought of going outside held a mixture of longing and terror. How often had he dreamed of the outside world, the world of wide horizons and sunshine that had once been his? As the nightmares of the trenches and mud and death had become less frequent, these other dreams had taken their place. The feel of wind in his hair, the smell of new-turned earth, the freedom, the limitless horizons . . . A thought too far. He slapped his face again.

"We cannot leave." The mulish look was more pronounced. "Catherine must finish her schooling here. And Dr Thompson knows me, understands my constitution. I will not risk our child with an unknown doctor." She turned, walked out of the room.

He followed her as far as the doorway. "Please." It was the barest of whispers. The thought that rose in his mind almost deprived him of breath. "Please, Elizabeth."

He loved her. He loved her so much. He had thought she loved him too – until now.

She turned briefly on the top of the steep flight of stairs. "You are being silly, Walter." It was the voice she might have used to Robbie. "You have nothing to fear." She turned again, reaching for the rail to help her negotiate the narrow flight with her already swollen body. She was going to betray him.

For the first time in two years he was out of his bedroom. Another step, a step too far, and he was immediately behind her. His hand reached out, made contact—

The scream she gave as she fell brought all the memories rushing back. Once again he could hear the sound of the mortars, feel the quake of earth as they hit, could detect the quicker, lighter sound of the German machine guns, was listening to the scream of the soldiers, of Robert . . .

The shaking was so great that he nearly pitched down the stairs after her. He clung to the wall as the cottage whirled around him. "No." He could hardly believe that it was his voice. "No. Elizabeth."

It had been a momentary anger. He hadn't intended this. He just wanted to stop her.

Clinging to the rail he began to go down to her, down the steep stairs he had never seen except for the time he had come up them to his refuge. "Elizabeth."

The small downstairs hall was dark. Her body seemed so small, crumpled on the tiled floor. She wasn't moving. His legs shaking, he climbed down another step, a third, willing her to move.

And then, in the dark hall, by her head, a sudden flash of scarlet.

Blood.

He backed away up the stairs, his cheek twitching rapidly. He couldn't. Whatever it cost him, he couldn't. Not blood. After all he had been through, all he had suffered, no one could expect him to go down there.

But why should they? He needn't have seen anything. He needn't have heard anything. He often slept in the afternoon; it was as good a way of passing the time as any. If he was asleep he wouldn't have known about it.

The moan was feeble but it brought back memories and he couldn't cope with memories. Not pain, not blood, not death. Elizabeth had known that. Elizabeth would understand. She would forgive him.

Leaving his dying wife huddled at the foot of the stairs, Walter closed the bedroom door behind him and lay on the bed, his face buried in the pillow, his hands covering his ears.

She would forgive him. She had forgiven everything else.

Suddenly, her happiness was too great to be controlled. With a skip more suitable for her eleven-year-old brother than a girl of seventeen who would be going to college in September, Catherine Harrison burst into song.

"Pale hands I loved, beside the Shalimar—" Her tuneless voice cracked on the high note and Robbie winced.

"Y-you sing like a crow."

"I don't care." Catherine grabbed her brother, whirling him around in the middle of the deserted lane, sweet with the scent of summer flowers and somnolent with bees. "I'm so happy I could dance."

"It's all right for you." Robbie pulled himself away and kicked at a stone disconsolately. "You'll be going away to college soon, but what about me? I shall be left here alone. With *him.*"

4

The word dropped heavy as a stone. Catherine stopped dead. Even though she knew that they were alone in the lane she could not help glancing back over her shoulder. After two years of constant warnings from their mother she found it difficult to even think of her father outside the confines of the cottage, let alone mention him.

She made an effort to lift the atmosphere. "I know, sweetheart, but it's only for a couple of years. Then I shall be a teacher and you can come and live with me and everything will be just as we planned it." She smiled at him. "It will go quickly, really, Robbie and – and anyway, *he* might get better soon, and—"

Robbie pushed her away. "You're stupid," he said disgustedly. "You're really stupid, just like all the other girls."

"Well, I may be stupid but Miss Rose said I paint like an angel."

Catherine still couldn't believe it. An angel! And she was going to take one of Catherine's paintings with her to London, to show an art dealer friend.

Her mood lifted again and Catherine burst out laughing out of sheer happiness. All her dreams were coming true. To go to college, to get away from the tiny cottage with its brooding, secret presence, to mix freely with other young people instead of being denied friends her own age, to even, possibly, have – oh, miracle! – talent.

It was the first time she had even dared to whisper the word to herself. Skill, yes; a gift, possibly; but talent . . .

Mother would appreciate it, she knew. Mother, who wanted so much more for her than a restricted life in a small cottage. Mother had married beneath her, had lived the life of a working-class woman, but she was determined that Catherine should rise above it, climb back up the slippery slope.

"Come on." She began to run up the road, holding her ankle-length skirts almost up to her knees so that she could run more freely, so anxious to get home that she almost forgot, for the moment, the brooding presence of *him* in the upstairs room.

Behind her she heard Robbie's angry shout as she left him behind, the pounding of his boots as he set off after her, and she ran faster, ignoring the fact that her high-piled chestnut hair was being jolted loose and was in danger of cascading down around her shoulders. No one would see, anyway. Very few people ever came up this deserted lane.

At the gate to the cottage she swung herself round the post and her hair gave up the battle. It fell in rippling coils down past her waist, but she merely laughed and shook it out of her eyes, racing up the path, throwing open the door.

"Mother. Mother! What do you think!"

And saw her mother's body.

"Mother." Catherine dropped to her knees beside the still figure, her happiness evaporating in the sudden shock. "Mother."

No answer. Just the crumpled heap lying there, unmoving.

Catherine felt the chill of fear. If she was dead—

The thought was so dreadful that it took all her courage to reach out and feel for the pulse in the limp, cold wrist. It was there, weak but definite. Her mother was still alive.

Pounding boots sounded on the garden path. She jumped to her feet and leapt to the door, barring the way with her body. "Don't come in, Robbie. Don't look."

"Wh-why?" He craned round her slender figure. "What's happened?" He pushed past her until he could see the silent figure on the floor, then stopped abruptly. "Is – is she dead?"

"No. But she is hurt." Catherine took a deep breath to steady herself and turned back.

Elizabeth Harrison lay on the floor, her head in a pool of blood that glowed scarlet in the evening light that streamed through the open doorway. She was not dead yet – but how long would she last, lying on a cold, hard floor?

"Robbie, go to the doc—"

"No."

The harsh voice from above made her jump and look up. At the top of the steep flight of stairs, made taller by the fact that she was staring up at him, her father loomed in the darkness. "No doctor. Not yet."

"What happened?" Catherine asked. "How did she do it?"

He shook his head. "I don't know. I was asleep. She must have fallen. She'll just be knocked out. She won't need a doctor."

Seventeen years of obedience to her parent's every word warred for a moment with common sense. She looked down at the pool of blood, the cold, hard floor. "You can't know that. She could be badly hurt."

6

"She doesn't need a doctor," he repeated. "It was only a fall."

"But – we can't leave her here."

He came downstairs, stiffly, as if his legs, after all this time in one room, could not cope easily with the steep pitch of the steps. His eyes were firmly averted from the figure on the floor. "I'll help carry her upstairs."

Catherine stood up and faced him across the still figure. "She needs a doctor."

"She'll be all right with rest." His cheek twitched and twitched again, hypnotically, and she turned her eyes away as he slapped it lightly. "I'll carry her head. You take the feet."

Catherine hesitated but knew that she had to get her mother off this cold, hard floor. "Very well." She bent, gathering her mother's sprawled ankles together. There was a worn patch in the heel of one of her stockings, and the sight of it made her want to cry. She glanced up at her father. "Ready."

He was not looking at the body. Eyes fixed on Catherine's face he reached down, fumbling, until he found his wife's shoulders. "Up."

You *could* look at her, Catherine said furiously inside her head. Whatever your problems you could look at her.

Elizabeth was heavier than seemed possible for such a thin body, sagging limply between them. Catherine gritted her teeth and panted and stumbled up the steep, dark stairs.

Walter backed into the small bedroom, jarring Elizabeth's body against the doorframe and dropping it on to the bed with a thud that made the springs creak. "Keep her warm. She'll do all right."

Catherine carefully lifted the skinny ankles on to the bed and pulled at the covers. There was an indentation where her father had been lying and she could feel the residual warmth of his body on the sheets. "Aren't you going to help me?"

He was already at the doorway and although he stopped he did not turn round. "I'm not well." The words were rough and she saw his hand move to his cheek where the nerve twitched incessantly. "I can't cope with illness. Your mother knew that. I'll – I'll go downstairs, get some food; you look after her."

Catherine watched him go, her hands trembling with anger.

After all that their mother had done for him; after the way she

7

had brought them up to respect his slightest wish, to show him nothing but honour and respect; to lug her upstairs without a glance as if she had been a sack of coal and not his wife . . .

Anger burned deep inside her, anger and the seeds of another, darker emotion.

Surely it couldn't be – hate?

"What good's that to give a man?" Walter Harrison demanded furiously.

"I-I-I-it's all I can d-d-do." Half expecting a blow, Robbie ducked his head protectively into his shoulders. "I c-c-can't really c-c-cook. Not like M-M-Mother."

"Dear God. What I have to put up with." Walter glanced up at the ceiling. "Has Catherine said how your mother is?"

Robbie shook his head, not trusting words. His stammer was always bad in his father's presence and tonight, upset by the shock of his mother's accident, it was worse than ever.

Walter sniffed, pulling his chair up to the table, and prodded the overcooked poached eggs with distaste. "Pass the bread and butter. I've got to fill up with something."

Robbie reached for the butter dish then remembered and changed hands. With father in this mood it wasn't a good idea to get too close. He leaned forward and the dish slipped from his fingers. It bounced on to the edge of the deal table, hovering a second. He leapt for it, heart in mouth, but his hip banged against the table. The jolt was the final straw. The tea in his father's cup slopped over on to his trousers, the milk jug splashed and the butter dish slid from Robbie's despairing fingers and crashed on to the floor. Shards of blue and white china ricocheted across the floor and the butter slid with a greasy thud on to the toe of his father's boot.

There was a moment's silence and Robbie felt his heart quail. His clumsiness could always rouse his father to fury – combined with a loud noise as well . . . Silent, scared, he stared up as his father rose to his feet, scarlet with fury, his dark, curly hair seeming to bristle with a rage of its own.

"You little . . ."

Despite himself Robbie flinched. It did no good – his father hated and despised any sign of cowardice – but his anger was more than the boy could stand.

With a sudden movement he ducked under his father's arm and shot past him. A brief struggle with the door and he was out into the overgrown garden, racing through the night, stumbling and tripping over the tussocky grass. He heard the roar of anger behind him, heard the shout – "Come back here, you little coward!" – but he did not hesitate. He had to get away.

There was a yellow flash of lamplight as the cottage door was pushed open again and Robbie felt his heart constrict with terror. He was coming after him! The man who had never come downstairs in the last two years was following him!

But this was a world he knew like the back of his hand, a world his father had never ventured into. And the summer night was moonless, even the stars covered by a thin film of cloud. The whole of nature was on his side.

Trying to stifle his nervous panting, the noise of his boots on the ground, Robbie moved along the hedge until he came to the well-known weak spot, just by the sycamore tree. A quick glance behind, a sudden surge through the bushes and he was free, running through the darkness to safety.

Standing at the window, Catherine was alerted by the shouts from below and saw the dark figure race across the garden. That was one worry off her mind; she really did not have time to intervene between father and son – not now.

She glanced over her shoulder at the figure on the bed. The pulse was weaker now, and although the head wound had stopped bleeding her mother had shown no sign of regaining consciousness.

Catherine gnawed at her lower lip, fighting with her conscience. Father had told her not to call the doctor but that was hours ago. If it was just a simple bang on the head as he had told her, surely Mother should be improving by now?

What if she died? God wouldn't let that happen, would He? But – a worse thought – supposing she died when she needn't *because Catherine hadn't the sense to get a doctor?*

Catherine turned back to the window and stared into the darkness. There was a larger figure stumbling through the garden. Her father. For two years he had refused to leave his room and yet here he was – in the garden! And all because Robbie had overcooked his dinner.

The triviality of it all was the final straw. Mother was possibly dying and Father, who would never go downstairs, was *out in the garden* because his dinner had been spoiled.

She glanced behind her at the still figure on the bed. "Mother?" she whispered.

No response.

She had washed the congealed blood from the red hair, now streaked with silver threads, which hung around her mother's shoulders. Surely, it was only the contrast with the hair that made her face look so green and sickly? Scared, she reached out and felt the wrist. There was still a pulse. Her mother was alive – but for how long?

Catherine knew where Robbie would be. He had a secret camp in the overgrown corner of a nearby field. Here he held great battles, fighting off pirates and Indians with equal fervour. He would have made for there, huddling into its scanty shelter, hiding himself until he had mastered his fear.

But he would do as she asked him; he wasn't a coward. He would go to the village in the darkness. Another glance at her mother, motionless on the bed, decided her. She had to get help, whatever Father said.

Catherine turned and slipped silently from the dying woman's bedroom.

"Don't you think you should forget it?" Margaret Random's tired pretty face was creased with anxiety. "The war is over now, Francis. It doesn't matter what happened two years ago."

"Of course it matters!" Francis Random turned on his sister-in-law. The black patch he wore to cover his empty eye socket only emphasised the whiteness of his face. "My wife died, Margaret. Jenny died – and I wasn't here to hold her, to comfort her . . ." His face, the face of a professional soldier, that seldom expressed any of the softer emotions, suddenly crumpled like a child's.

Aware of this, he turned his back on her and stumped angrily to the window, supporting himself on the silver-topped stick that his father had used in old age.

The loch outside looked cold and drear, even on this warm summer's day, the mountains behind piling high to the sky, as he had so often dreamed of them while he was in France.

Behind him, Margaret said tentatively, "You weren't the only one, you know. A lot of men lost people dear to them while they were away fighting, and couldn't get leave to come home."

He turned on her, his grey eyes blazing. "But I *had* leave, dammit! I had leave and I was on my way home – and some bugger stopped me."

"It's the past." She spoke as if she hadn't heard, her eyebrows lowered in a frown. "Francis, leave it be. It isn't good for you. You've been hurt and – well," she finished lamely, "you don't look well."

He knew he didn't look well. Come to that he didn't feel well. It had been that which had driven him to telling his consultant in Harley Street about it last month, when he had visited him about his crippled leg.

He had been told the prognosis yesterday. Cancer of the liver.

Six months. His first feeling had been of relief. In six months he would be with Jenny again. In six months he would be free for ever from the pain of his damned leg, free from the constant annoyance of having only one eye.

But, before that, there was something he must do.

He could not rest in peace while that man . . .

Margaret must have seen the determination in his face because she tried another track. "Revenge is not a nice emotion, Francis. It – it's corrosive. It eats away at you." She sighed, spreading her hands in appeal. "Leave it, please. Whatever happens, you cannot bring back the past."

"Revenge?" He gave a short laugh that caught in his throat. "This isn't revenge, Maggie. It's justice."

He turned, began to stomp around the cold, echoing room. In winter a fire burned on the great hearth. Above him, in the rafters, the tattered remnants of his family's flags hung, like coloured cobwebs. Would he ever see that roaring fire again? Six months. But that was a guess. And he would be incapacitated before the end. The doctor had not said so but Random had seen through his reserve.

He had so short a time.

"That man stopped me seeing Jenny that last time. He attacked me, robbed me, destroyed my eye, ruined my leg, left me for dead!" His voice rose. "Do you wonder that I want justice?"

"But that was two years ago," she protested. "Since then the casualty figures have been immense, and there's been an influenza epidemic that killed millions. He could be dead."

"The influenza might have killed him, but the Germans didn't." He snorted. "Think, woman. He attacked me as I was on my way to Dieppe to come home. He stole my uniform, papers and money, he left me for dead. He was a deserter, Maggie. A damned coward."

"But he might have been caught by now."

"I'd have heard. Not many got back across the Channel and those that did were questioned pretty closely to find out how they did it. They'd have had the truth out of him, one way or the other, and I would have heard. I made it pretty clear to everyone I came in touch with that I was to be informed if such a person was caught."

"Give it up, Francis. If he did escape, you'll never catch him after all this time. And if you do, what will happen to him? A few years in prison." She reached out and shook him lightly. "The war is over, Francis. I know the death penalty is still in force for desertion but it won't be used. People are tired of killing. Is it worth driving yourself like this just to lock some poor beggar up for a few years?"

He leaned the stick against the back of a tapestry chair and began to count off on his fingers.

"He deserted immediately before a big battle, when the orders were already out; he has been absent without leave, not for a few hours or days but for nearly two years, and in all that time he hasn't given himself up, not even after the armistice was declared last November; he attacked a senior officer, he caused me such bad injuries that the British Army lost my services as an active combatant for the rest of the war and I was reduced to pen-pushing until the Ministry decided in their infinite wisdom to release me; he almost certainly impersonated an officer to get across the Channel in my uniform."

In his mind, Francis Random added, *He took away my chance of dying in action, when that was the only relief I wanted from my grief,* but he kept this reason to himself. Margaret was distressed enough; the only way he could help her was to keep from her the diagnosis that had just been pronounced, and his longing for the death that it promised him.

He pointed a lean finger at her. "Any one of those reasons,

Margaret, would have got him shot as a traitor during the war. Add them all together, and you have a reason to carry out the sentence even if the war is over."

He gave her a sardonic grin that creased his lean cheeks and lit up his single grey eye.

"And I am not exactly a nobody, Margaret," added the Honourable Francis Random, MC, younger brother of the Earl of Loch Lour.

Two

The cool night air was a benediction, stroking his cheek with soft fingers, blowing with scented breath upon his cheek.

Brought to a sudden realisation of what he was doing, Walter Harrison came to a dead halt, standing stock still at the side of the road. Above him, a great tree spread its branches in a rustling roof but it could give him no real sense of protection.

He was out, out in the open air. Out of the sanctuary of his small room, out where anyone could see him, where there were no walls, where there was no *safety*.

He felt the world turn slowly around him and he staggered, stretching out a shaking hand to the great trunk of the tree to steady himself. The moonless summer night suddenly seemed as bright as day. He felt as if there was a spotlight trained on him, as if the countryside was full of people watching him, spying on him.

His knees shook as if they would collapse under his weight. Only the memory of his old sergeant in the West Yorkshires, a voice from a different life, kept him upright. "Don't crawl, lad." The Yorkshire accent was thicker than his own, but deeper, more confident. "The Boche, see, they train their machine guns at ground level to get as many of us as they can. If you're on yer feet you might get a leg shot off but if you lies down you'll get yer brains blown out for sure."

He shivered, the muscle twitching in his cheek. He could almost hear the noise of the guns, the great boom of the heavy artillery, the screams of the wounded, the soft suck of the mud, the tramp of marching feet . . .

"You all right, mate?"

It took him seconds to realise that the voice, the sound of footsteps, hadn't been echoes from the past, that they were real, here, now. He had been discovered. It was over!

14

Walter swung round, panting, staring at the man with wide, terrified eyes, his breathing harsh in his own ears. He was trapped. This was it. The end. He could see it all: the court martial, the sentence, *the firing squad* . . .

"Here, mate, sorry I startled you." The other man took a step back in the darkness, raising his hands, palms out, in a gesture of appeasement. "I didn't mean to give you a fright." Then, when Walter did not answer, he dropped his voice, glanced around. "Just out, are you?"

"What?" In his fright Walter could not follow this. Out of where? Prison?

"Demobbed?" the other man expanded.

"Wh— oh, yeah." Walter swallowed, trying to get air into his lungs.

"Lots about now," the other said, calmly. "And more coming. We'll be having old soldiers overrunning the place before we know where we are, and all of them expecting an easy ride." He suddenly seemed to realise that he wasn't being tactful. "Where were you then?"

"P-P-Passchendaele." He hadn't spoken the name for nearly two years, trying to forget, to wipe out the images, the memories.

The stranger whistled. "Bad show, that. No wonder you're a bit . . ." He tailed off.

"A bit what? A bit what?" Walter had thought that nothing would ever give him the power to move again, but this worked. "I – I'm not a coward. No one says to me that I'm a coward and—"

"Wouldn't dream of saying it." The man backed further away. "I only meant it wasn't a place that I would have wanted to be. But a great victory, mate, a great victory."

A great victory. Dear God. The mud, the guns, the bodies, despite himself, Walter felt tears come to his eyes. And Robert, his brother, his only brother . . .

The comfortable Dorset voice was droning on. "'Course, I was in a reserved occupation. I were lucky like that."

And so had he been. Walter clenched his lower lip with his teeth to stop its trembling. *He* had been safe – but Robert wasn't. Laughing, happy-go-lucky Robert, after whom Robbie had been named, called up to the front. And Walter had joined too. To be with him. To look after him. And then—

15

The living hell that had been Passchendaele – the noise, the smells – was all around him again. He turned into the rough comfort of the trunk, leaning his head against it, hiding the unmanly tears that flooded his eyes.

"Sorry, mate, sorry." The voice was vibrant with embarrassment. "Didn't mean to – there's a lot like you . . ." A long pause, then, more cheerfully, "Well, I'd better be getting along then."

And he was gone, rough boots striding down the lane, into the distance, away . . .

Walter stayed where he was, disbelieving. It was all a trick, surely it was all a trick. The man would turn in a second, come back, pull out a revolver. "Joke over, old man." Dorset accent gone, upper-crust accent in place. "Got you now, you nasty little coward."

But the steps faded away; the man did not return. The peace and the darkness were undisturbed.

Eventually he lifted his head. The night held only the quiet noises of the English countryside – the bark of a fox, the rustle of leaves and of standing corn. It took time for the truth to sink in. No one was coming back for him. No one was going to arrest him. He had spoken to another man for the first time in nearly two years – spoken to him face to face – and nothing had happened.

The truth wasn't carved across his forehead, it wasn't obvious to every chance-met stranger. The war was over now. The peace was signed. There were young men everywhere, strange men, back from the war. No one would notice him. No one would recognise him.

He straightened, breathing deep. For the first time since he had arrived in the trenches, nearly five years ago, he could dare to believe that he had a future. Time stretched before him, containing not fear and pain and death but life and laughter and freedom. He took another breath, feeling the cool night air filling his lungs, flooding his body with fresh energy and optimism.

It was over. The long nightmare was over and gone. They could move away, to a place where Elizabeth wasn't known as a widow, start a new life—

Horror gripped his spine with icy talons. He had forgotten Elizabeth. He felt sick again, all his pleasure vanished. What if she survived? What if she remembered? Blood was thicker than water, she was always saying, but would she still think that?

She had looked after him all this time, kept his secret, loved him. It had been Elizabeth who had taken him in when, shaking and crying, his stolen uniform spattered with mud, he had scratched at the door on that night two years ago. It had been she who had arranged their removal from the Yorkshire village where they were known to this distant Dorset cottage where they were strangers. It had been she who had explained the terrible workings of neurasthenia to the children, emphasising that visitors would set back his recovery so that it was better never to mention him – just in case.

She had done all these things for him, but . . .

But he was deep in her power. If she told the authorities what she knew, what he had wept out into her arms those first few, terrible weeks when he had lived and relived Robert's death – if she told, then he was a dead man.

The shivers started again, making his teeth rattle. But, she might not live. He hadn't dared to look at her as he had helped Catherine to carry her upstairs to the bedroom, but she had been a dead weight; there had been no groan or sigh. And if she died—

Again, the abyss opened at his feet. A sudden death, where there had been no doctor in attendance, always caused problems. And gossip. But he could go away . . .

The children might talk. He shivered. He had seen that look in Catherine's eyes, he knew what she was thinking. She was seventeen now, almost a woman. He knew that she was already beginning to wonder why he never left his room, why visitors were forbidden, but she must never learn that he was a deserter. She was never able to lie convincingly. Catherine would never question Elizabeth, of course; she had always loved her mother more than she loved him. They both did. They had loved their Uncle Robert more than they had loved him. He was the odd man out, despised, looked down on. Loyalty to their mother had kept them silent until now, but if she were dead, what then?

Robbie had no friends – who would want to be friends with such a runt, stammering and stupid, as hopeless at games as at lessons? Catherine was a different matter.

She would soon be going to college, would be moving away, out of his control. She would have new friends. She was silent now, but how long before she told them about him? And that stupid old woman, her teacher, who encouraged her in the ceaseless drawing she had done since she was a small child – how long before Catherine told her everything?

He had to get them away from here, away from the people they knew. Walter knew his own powers. He was a chameleon, could blend in anywhere. Let them go somewhere where they were not known and within weeks he would have an unassailable position. It would be easy to make sure that his story would be the one that was accepted – but he had to get the children away from here where they were known.

Walter breathed a sigh of relief. The future was settled and he would have his freedom at last. He walked back towards the isolated cottage that had been his refuge and his prison for so long. He would take the children and go, start a new life as a grieving widower. No one would be able to trace him, no one would be able to find him. For the first time in two years the terrible fear that weighed down his shoulders had been lifted. He had a future. He could be free again.

Lost in his plans for the future, Walter Harrison pushed open the back door of the cottage – and came face to face with the doctor.

"Traitor. You are a traitor to the Kaiser, to the land of your birth."

Despite being a prisoner of war, forced to dig like a peasant to grow food for his hated enemies, no one could mistake Heinrich for anything other than a Prussian officer, Gunter thought wearily as he rested on his shovel and prepared to defend himself.

"I am a quarter English." He had had this conversation so often he was saying these things in his sleep. He pulled off his cap and ran a hand through his fair hair, enjoying the feel of the cooling breeze. "It is no different for me to stay here in England now that the peace is signed than to go back to Germany with you."

"They are the enemy." Gunter sometimes thought that the Prussian officer class were given lessons in barking out statements. "You will be displaying the utmost disloyalty."

"The war is over," Gunter said wearily. "There are no enemies now. There probably never were. Just politicians and foreigners."

"These 'foreigners', as you call them, would have killed you a few months ago."

"And I, God help me, would have killed them. As it is" – Gunter slapped his left leg, stiff from the bullet wound he had received before he had been captured, as it would be for the rest of his life – "the man who did this might have been a relative of mine. Who knows? But he was just an ordinary man, not a devil."

"They tried to kill you!" Heinrich shouted. "You told me yourself. After they had caught you, three Englishmen wanted to shoot you. A wounded man. No danger to them. They are swine, pigs, uncivilised."

Gunter's blue eyes blazed. "Are we any different? When we had seen our comrades, our *brothers*, blown to pieces, did *we* not sometimes act wrongly, take revenge on some prisoner who was unable to fight any longer? Life in the trenches made animals of us all. And, although the Englishmen wanted to kill me, it was an English officer who stopped them, who risked his life later to drag me back to safety when our soldiers mounted a counter-attack."

"To drag you back to prison." The German spat. "They just wanted to humiliate you. And they have succeeded. Look at us. Proud sons of our country, warriors, forced to labour like peasants to provide food for our enemies."

"Food that we eat, also," Gunter said wearily. Nothing he said could persuade Heinrich that he didn't want to go back to Germany. Nothing ever would unless he told him the truth – and he would never do that.

And what was there left for him in Germany? Just reminders. Of his parents, dead of the influenza epidemic that had decimated the war-torn world last winter; of his wife: faithless, beautiful, dead also, killed in an accident beside his best friend. Even the silk business his family had built up was gone now, and there was no money left to build it up again.

"If there is another war—" Heinrich began.

"If there is another war I will not fight." Gunter said firmly. "There has been too much killing already, too much fighting." He almost smiled at the outraged look on Heinrich's face. "Sometimes I wonder if there is anything in life worth fighting for."

"You are a coward!" the Prussian shouted. "That is why you are afraid to show your face in our country of heroes."

"I am a businessman who is sick of war," Gunter said. "And I think" – he flashed a wry grin at the affronted Prussian – "I

19

think that perhaps it will take more courage to live in England now than to go back to Germany."

And that, he reflected, would certainly be true – if you forgot the ever-present ghost of Matilde.

"I'm not going." Catherine tried to sound firm and composed but her father's demand was one strain too many.

The dreadful coroner's judgement was over, with Catherine and the doctor as the only witnesses though the villagers of Affpuddle had crowded into the back room of the local inn with avid curiosity. Catherine knew with bitter certainty that there would be fewer attendants at her mother's funeral tomorrow.

To come home after that and to be faced with this demand from her father was too much. She took a deep breath and composed herself, her chin high. "I am not going to leave here. I am going to college in the autumn. When Miss Rose returns I shall be able to stay with her."

The kitchen curtains were drawn even though it was only mid-afternoon. In the dimness Walter looked taller than she remembered, his once strong body shrunken by lack of exercise so that his clothes hung loosely off him.

He stood between her and the door. "You're coming with me and that's the end of it. There'll be no college for you anyway. There's no money. Your mother had an annuity from her grandmother but it lasted only as long as she was alive. There'd be no money to send you even if I was prepared to waste money on rubbish like that."

"No college." Catherine gasped as if she had been struck. "But – mother said – it's all I ever wanted . . ."

"No college." She could swear that he looked pleased at the thought. "I'm a working man and you're my daughter. It's time you forgot these fancy ideas and buckled down like a good daughter should. Work is what you should be doing, my girl. When my mother was your age she had been working for three years already and was going steady with my father."

"But – she was a servant."

"And what's wrong with that?" he demanded. "She was honest and hard-working. Where's the shame?"

"N-none, but —" She stood on the edge of an abyss. Her future, her whole future, was being ripped from her. Three days ago it had been planned, settled, safe; so close that she could reach out and touch it and now . . .

She took a deep breath. "I have an education, Father. If you let me stay here I – I can probably get a post as an assistant teacher at my old school. I've helped teach classes there these last two years, when they were short, and the headmistress always said how good I was."

Even as she said it her heart sank. To be an assistant teacher, the lowest of the low, unqualified, paid a pittance, when she could have been a trained teacher with a higher position and pay, would be a dreadful comedown. But anything would be better than to be a servant, living in another's house, at everyone's beck and call, with no way out except marriage.

"You're coming with me. I need you to look after the boy – and me. I'm going to be keeping us all from now on and a working man needs his comforts." He pointed to one of her oil paintings that hung on the wall. "And there'll be no more of that foolishness. Wasting your time! There's clothes to mend and food to cook and plenty to keep you busy without that muck."

"But Miss Rose said—" Catherine began.

"Miss Rose said! A dried-up old biddy who's come down in the world, without enough intelligence to find herself a husband while she still had what few looks God gave her. Why should she say anything worth listening to?"

"Her father was a famous artist and she—"

"*She* says. No, lass. You're seventeen and I'm your father and you do what I say. And you'd better start packing. We're leaving here the day after tomorrow."

She gaped at him. "But – why? The rent on this cottage is paid for the rest of the quarter and . . ." If they could only stay here until Miss Rose came back from London. Miss Rose had little money and no husband but she was an adult and the only friend Catherine had in Dorset. She might think of a way that Catherine could persuade her father to let her stay.

"Surely we don't need to go so quickly," Catherine pleaded. "Think of your nerves. Surely it will be better to stay here a little longer, in a place that you know and are comfortable in?"

Father's "nerves" had ruled all their lives for so long. No sudden noises, no loud shouts and, in particular, no sign of blood or tears. It was no hardship for her but poor Robbie, with

21

his clumsiness, was always in trouble. He tripped or cut himself on a daily basis and Catherine had become adept at patching him up.

"My nerves are getting better," Walter said shortly.

Catherine almost gasped. She had begun to believe that they had got better long ago. True, her father's cheek still twitched uncontrollably at times but the nightmares that had kept them all awake for the first few months after they moved to Dorset had all but ceased.

"But even so," she persisted.

"Don't question me, miss." She could see his face darken and his Yorkshire accent grew stronger, always a sign that he was upset. He was like an actor, able to imitate any accent at will. While her mother had been alive he had spoken with her well-bred accent but already that was fading and the Yorkshire she remembered from her childhood was growing stronger. "We leave the day after tomorrow. In the meantime, I want all those paintings down. We'll burn them and all the other rubbish before we go."

She felt as if he had stabbed her to the heart. "Burn them? But – why?"

"You don't think we can carry them as well as our other luggage, do you? Right fools we'd look! They're to be burned."

She would more willingly have stuck her arm in the fire: she, who had always cherished her hands because of her painting. "If we just waited until Miss Rose returns . . . The canvasses and paints belonged to her and she should have them back." Catherine swallowed. "She might – she might want to paint over the canvasses herself." She knew that Miss Rose would not do that. She would keep them, surely, as a token of their friendship. They would be saved; Catherine might even see them again one day.

"We leave in two days' time. And I wouldn't let her have them anyway."

He turned and lifted the painting from the wall and she flinched as he punched at it with his fist, as if the blow had been aimed at her head.

"Please, no!" The cry came from her heart. "Please, Father."

He looked at her under lowered brows. "You're a working girl now and the sooner you recognise it the better. You've no time and no money to waste on trash like this."

He pushed past her and though she caught at his coat she could not stop him. The oil painting above the fire in the sitting-room, her best, was dragged down, kicked through. "It will make good kindling."

"Please." It was only a whisper. Those paintings were her babies, her life. They represented the life beyond this cottage; they symbolised culture and education and all the other things she aspired to. "Please!"

He reached for the third painting and her courage broke. With an inarticulate cry she ran from the room and threw herself on to her bed. He had destroyed her future and now he was set on destroying her past. Those paintings symbolised her happiest hours, hours spent by the river under the arching trees, watching the grasses sway in the shadows.

She paused.

The oils she could do nothing about. They were too big and cumbersome to hide, but the water-colours – surely she could save those.

She could hear his footsteps on the stairs. Catherine leaped up and pulled her most recent water-colours from the drawer where she kept them. With shaking hands she thrust them under the mattress and threw herself back on the bed before her father came in.

"You've got those small pictures too, I know. You mother used to show them to me." He clicked his fingers impatiently. "Come on. I want them."

Thank heavens she had not had time to gather them all up. Feeling like a traitor Catherine handed the others over, her heart breaking. This must be what a mother felt like when her child died.

A thought came from nowhere, a memory from long ago, from when she was a small child and Robbie just a babe in arms, when they had lived in Yorkshire in the cottage that laughing Uncle Robert had shared too.

It was always said that when Mother had married Father, she had been disowned by her family, but Catherine remembered that there had been days when her mother had dressed them both up in their best clothes, when she had taken them along a certain road.

And then the carriage would come past, the panels gleaming,

the uniformed coachman staring straight ahead, apparently indifferent. But, somehow, as it passed them, the horses would slow their pace and she could remember the face of an elderly woman peering out at them, turning in her seat to keep them in sight as long as possible.

Once past, the horse would pick up speed again, the carriage would disappear – and Mother would sigh and lead them home. Nothing was ever said, certainly not to Father, but Catherine knew, without it ever being stated, that the old woman was her grandmother.

Her grandmother would not know that her daughter was dead. That lady, rich as she was, missing her daughter, loving her despite the mistake she had made – surely she should be told.

Catherine knew that her father would never give her permission. He was a proud man who hated the fact that their mother had been disowned for marrying him. But her grandmother should be told. It was right and proper – it was *fair*.

Catherine believed in fairness.

Three

"I hate it here."

Robbie Harrison scowled at the Cornish sea in front of him, sparkling in the summer sunlight. "Th-th-they called me a German s-s-spy!"

He dragged a torn sleeve across his face, smearing tears and blood with an eleven-year-old's disregard for clothes. "A G-G-German!" After four years of war against the Kaiser the insult was unbearable.

"They're just ignorant." Catherine struggled to control her dismay. She had only left her brother for ten minutes – and this had happened! Set on by a gang of boys, just because he was a stranger and had a stammer. Her anger rose at the unfairness of it all. As if Robbie didn't have enough problems already. As if they both didn't!

"Didn't any of the grown-ups help you?" Usually children were considered almost as common property, to be comforted and chastised by any adult within range.

He sniffed. "There was only the old soldier with no legs selling wooden toys. He shouted at them, but . . ."

She stared at the long curve of golden sands that cradled the castle-topped island of St Michael's Mount. In the evening sunlight it should have been an idyllic scene; instead, the beauty of the place seemed to mock her. So much beauty of landscape – and the people were so horrible.

"Hell and damnation!" No lady would even use such language but she was too upset to care. Besides, being a lady was all behind her now; Father had made that plain. She could forget about her plans, her education, her upbringing. She was no longer the granddaughter, however poor, of the Tranters of Coombeside; she was his daughter, a working girl, a nobody.

"We c-c-could run away." Robbie was still preoccupied with his own problems. "I c-c-could live with you like we planned."

25

Catherine sighed. She knew how unhappy he had been, even before Mother had died. His very existence seemed to annoy Father, but in the boarding-house there was nowhere for him to get out of Father's way – and if he now couldn't even go outside for fear of being attacked . . .

Robbie sniffed once more, plumping himself down beside her, leaning his thin body against her arm for the comfort it gave him. "Why did Mother have to die?" His voice was plaintive, tears trembling only just below the surface. "If someone had to die, why couldn't it have been *him*?"

Catherine knew that she ought to tell Robbie off for such a comment but she didn't have the heart. It was the thought that had hammered through her brain every night as she had lain, unsleeping, on her bed, eyes staring blindly into the darkness as she tried to come to terms with her changed situation. And Robbie had suffered far more at *his* hands than she had. Father ignored her, despising her as a mere girl – too clever, too thin to be a real woman, with grandiose ideas about getting above the station in life to which she had been born – while Robbie . . .

Poor Robbie, called after their beloved uncle who had died in the war. Poor Robbie, stammering, skinny, clumsy, always dropping things, always in trouble. He had always been thin and small, but in these last two years since *he* had come back from France, Robbie did not seem to have grown at all. His face under the fiendishly red curls was paler and more pinched, his stammer worse.

Her heart went out to him and Catherine put her arm around him, pulling him close, providing what comfort she could from the warmth of her own body. It was a warm evening but he was still shivering from the shock of the unexpected attack. She would have to stop that before they went back to their lodgings or he would get a hiding.

She glanced down at him and stiffened. "Oh, Robbie! Your jumper . . ."

The hand-knitted pullover, the wool carefully chosen by their mother, was smeared with red where his nose had dripped blood down the front; the sleeves too were marked and as for his face . . .

"Give it to me, quickly. Perhaps we can wash the blood out in the sea." It was a warm evening, he would not get cold, and while the salt water would not do the wool any good she might be able to wash it out tomorrow, in Mrs Penrose's scullery. Anyway, it had to be done. If Father caught sight of the jumper covered with blood Robbie would definitely get a thrashing.

He pulled it off awkwardly, his mind still on the future he was dreading. "If we stay here I might have to go to school with those boys."

"I'll make sure that they realise before you go that you aren't a German." It would have been laughable if he weren't so upset. She gave him a last hug, took off her shoes and stockings and walked down to the water's edge.

It was a calm day. Little ripples, edged with white lace, ran lazily onto the sand. Catherine pulled her skirts up to mid-calf length, reminded suddenly of the shocking young women she had seen in Exeter as they crossed to get on to the Great Western line. Their skirts had been this short, showing their legs clad in silk stockings, the dresses amazingly different from her own full skirts. They almost looked, to her astonished eyes, as if they were wearing a grown-up version of children's clothes. But they had been rich, she had realised immediately, noting the quality of the material, the jewels. The rich could do those sorts of things. She was poor and had to conform.

She dumped the jumper into the sea, watching the ripples run red as the blood washed out. Poor Robbie. He had suffered enough already in his short life. No friends, constant bullying, his clumsiness and stammer the butt of jokes.

Catherine had had an easy life compared to his, always top of the class, always popular with her fellow pupils. Her mother's death was the first bad thing that had happened to her.

She glanced back at the thin, red-haired child sitting forlornly on the deserted beach, hands clasped around his bare legs.

Whatever happened to her, she was determined that Robbie's life was going to get better.

Walter Harrison paused outside the door to the Star Inn, the familiar fear hammering down on him.

It was almost dark but he felt as if a searchlight were trained on him, as if he were standing alone on the edge of the trench with no cover, no protection, with every machine gun the Boche owned trained on him alone.

27

This was it, this was part of his plan, the great plan that he had refined and honed all those empty, lonely days. This was the time. This was the place. He knew that he had the skills to make the most of it.

But still he hesitated, panting harshly, eyes darting up and down Market Jew Street, Penzance's main thoroughfare. If this went wrong – if he made a mistake here . . . The fear paralysed him. He had so much to lose.

The sudden burst of laughter from inside the pub made him jump. It was the sound of men happy together, enjoying each other's company; sounds he hadn't heard for years. Once he had been one of them, one of a close-knit male band, sharing laughter and privations. The loss of that comradeship was as great as anything he had suffered – except the loss of Robert.

The whimper was deep in his throat, so soft that it could not have been heard a foot away, but he felt as if he had screamed out loud, as though the pain was as new and raw as it had ever been. That day, that dreadful day—

"You waiting for your 'orse, are you?" The voice behind him made him jump like a girl but it brought him to his senses.

"Just going in, mate." Automatically, his voice began to drop into the local accent although he realised that he had the wrong idiom. Still, that would come. Give him a week and no one would ever know he was a Yorkshireman by birth. And, reassured by the thought, he pushed open the door and let the warmth and light and sound wash over him.

"Major!" The young officer behind the desk leapt to his feet, saluting, his face shining. "Good to see you again, sir."

"At ease, Captain." The words came out automatically and Random winced as he remembered that he was no longer in the army. So much he had lost.

He settled himself on the hard wooden chair, all the War Office allowed its visitors, and looked keenly with his one good eye at the man behind the desk. He remembered him from France, a bright young man, eager and intelligent – the sort that usually got themselves killed. Well, it made it easier if he had to deal with someone he knew. "I have to tell you, Captain, that I am here on – a personal matter."

"That will not be a problem, sir." Captain Walton leaned

forward. "You did so much for the men under your command. It will be a privilege to help if I can."

Random grunted. "It's about these injuries of mine."

"It was a damned shame, sir." The captain leaned forward, his face earnest. "The whole brigade was disgusted when they found out. To think that a sneak-thief would attack someone like—"

"Not a sneak-thief," Random broke in. "I believe it was a deserter."

"But, sir!" The young officer's face was horrified. "Surely . . ."

"Yes, I know," Random barked. "They covered that side of things at the time. Unfortunately, I could remember nothing of the attack but I know that, because my papers and travel documents were stolen, they assumed it was a deserter and set the wheels in motion."

"And?"

"And nothing." He jerked his head angrily. "They picked up one or two but they were what you might call 'the usual suspects'. Men who had got into a blue funk before the battle and drunk themselves into a stupor. You know the type as well as I. They turn up a day or so later with a thick head and a hangdog expression. At the beginning of the war, we might have shot them; by 1917, thank God, we had more compassion. Punishment, then back into their unit." He sighed. "Most of the poor blighters fought well after that. It had only been a temporary funk when things got too much for them."

"And you don't think that any of those were your attacker?"

"If they had been, why were they still in France? Why didn't they use my papers to cross the Channel? That would be the only reason to take them."

"But if the deserters hadn't used them—"

"I didn't say they weren't used. I said that the deserters the army found hadn't used them."

"So, who . . ."

"A deserter," said Random carefully, "who got away."

"But surely we would have known—"

"Would we?" Random leaned forward, rapped his silver-topped stick on the table. "How?"

"Well, there would be a man missing. And, besides" – he looked more confident – "hardly any of the deserters managed to get back across the Channel and those who did we picked up."

29

Random snorted. "I looked into this. With the right papers and a uniform, it would be easy to get across the Channel."

"But the man would still be found," Captain Walton protested. "We would know someone was missing; the police would watch his house, his parents' house. During the war papers were always being asked for, especially from a man of age to serve in the army."

"But if we didn't know he was missing?" Random asked. "You remember what the war was like. The shells would blow you to smithereens; the front line moved. We would capture the German lines, they would take them back again. How many men were killed who were never found? Thousands!"

"At the time, perhaps, but when things quietened down we went back. We found many bodies, gave them a good burial."

"Many" – Random seized on the word – "but not all. There are still people who we think are dead but whose bodies are still missing."

"You are asking me to make a search for men who have no known grave?" The young man's face was appalled. "That will take months. Major, I offered to help but I have work to do."

"I can narrow it down," Random said shortly. "Men who were presumed killed within, say, three days either side of my attack. And I have a further possible lead." He paused, staring down at the table. He hated having to say this but it had to be done, even though he felt that he was slandering a highly respected regiment. "I think I was attacked by a member of the West Yorkshire Regiment."

"You can remember that much? Then surely—"

"I can remember nothing," Random said shortly. "But the attack on me was no ordinary assault. I was knocked out and kicked so hard I lost an eye, I had boot marks all over me and internal injuries. My thigh was shattered so that—" He tapped his left leg with his stick. It gave off a muffled clunk.

"Perhaps" – the captain was battle-hardened, but he could not keep the shocked look off his face – "perhaps he wanted to kill you."

"If I am right, Captain, we are talking about a soldier," Random snapped. "If a soldier wants to kill someone he doesn't need to kick them to death." He took a deep breath. "I think that this was a personal vendetta."

He stared out of the window at the evening sun gilding the Horse Guards' parade. If the doctor was right, this was the last summer he would ever see. For a second he wavered. Why waste his last few months seeking revenge? Then he rallied. Right was right, justice needed to be done. His family had never shrunk from doing their duty whatever the cost to themselves. He sat up straighter.

"A couple of days before I was attacked, I was involved in a raid on the German trenches. There were men from two regiments involved – mine and the West Yorkshire. It was, for once, a success. We captured their front line against stiff opposition."

He paused, staring blindly out of the window, remembering the scene. The noise, the mud, the smell of weapons and wounds mixed with the deeper smell of putrefaction where the artillery bombardment had brought to the surface the buried bodies of British and Germans killed in earlier engagements.

"I came across three or four men of the West Yorkshire. They had captured a German. He had put up a fight before he was caught and had made his presence felt, even though he was wounded and the only man left alive in that part of the front line." He cleared his throat, hating the fact that he had to tell another man the next, shameful fact. "The men I found were preparing to kill him."

"But if he had surrendered, was a prisoner . . ."

"Exactly. But it happened sometimes, even though we pretended it didn't. Apparently the German had badly wounded – killed, in fact – the brother of one of the men. Quite legitimately, but it had been too much for the poor fellow. He went off his head and attacked the prisoner." Another, longer pause. "I rescued the German."

The captain asked no indiscreet questions. Random was brave and would have acted as he thought fit but he wouldn't boast about his actions.

The captain cleared his throat. "You reported the men, of course."

"No chance," Random grunted. "Another bombardment started up, the Germans counter-attacked. I told the men what I thought of them and then we had to retreat. I – managed to get the German back behind our lines."

31

The young man knew what that must have entailed. "You risked your life for a German?"

"I could do no less after the way those fellows had behaved."

"And you think one of those men was the one who attacked you?"

"I don't know." Random rubbed his injured leg. "I hate telling tales out of school, but that is the only reason I can think of for the viciousness of the attack."

The captain considered. "It is a manageable proposition. The casualties later in the war were not so horrific as in the first few months. If I find something . . . ?"

"Send the names and addresses to me." Random opened his gold card case and passed across a card.

"If I do . . ."

"I'll be tactful, of course." Random struggled to his feet with the help of his cane. "Good God, do you think I don't know that I am probably barking up the wrong tree? That these are almost certainly families who gave their sons and husbands for the defence of their country and now don't even have a grave at which to mourn?"

"Of course, sir. I apologise." The captain rose to his feet and gave a brief, un-English bow of apology and respect. "And if I find no one who meets these criteria?"

"Let me know that, too," Random said shortly. "Then I shall be able to give up the search."

Looking out at the evening sunshine of the last summer he would ever see, Random almost hoped that Captain Walton would not turn up any names.

Already his terror was dying.

Walter Harrison felt himself relax by infinitesimal degrees. His fears had been ridiculous, he could see that now. He had walked in feeling like a marked man, as if the mark of Cain was branded on his head. But life wasn't like that. All he had met with was the wariness of those who had known each other for years and to whom any strange face was a reason for distrust.

"My round." It wasn't money wasted, it was an investment. Even these surly Cornishmen would talk to a man who would buy them drinks. He came back, beer spilling from the handful of mugs, slopping on to the stone flags on the floor. He put them down harder than he had intended and the frothing liquid ran down the sides, puddling on the marked table top. *Steady*, he reminded himself, *you haven't drunk for two years, near enough. Keep your head.*

One of his drinking companions raised the glass to him. "Where you from, then? Not round here?"

Walter grinned. "Where do you think?" Already he was dropping easily into the Cornish accent, his voice deepening and growing louder like the voices around him. He owed so much to this ability – his wife, probably his life too – but now he wanted something else. A job. And he would have to angle for it as delicately as any fisherman after a trout, he knew that.

They laughed, ready for a game. "Falmouth – Truro – Bodmin."

He shook his head, laughing with them. "Nowhere that big. Just a small place."

They tried again. "Breage," one suggested, to the scorn of the rest.

"Brem sight further away than that, Nabbo. That idn't no Helston accent, nor anywhere near it."

"Somewhere on Bodmin Moor then," they guessed again. Walter drank and listened, smiling, shaking his head. Better not admit to any place in particular. It would never do to be proved a liar.

"Near there but smaller," he said at last, refusing to be forced into naming the village. They were indignant but satisfied. He was Cornish, at least. And Bodmin Moor was a long way away. Coming from somewhere that distance away would account for any oddities of accent that he couldn't iron out.

"So why've you come all the way down here then?" Nabbo was still curious.

Walter shrugged. "Work. I used to be a farm hand up there – until the war. But now . . ." He grimaced. "The young master's dead in the war and so are most of the men I worked with. The house is sold up for a school. Well, that's no work for me, cutting grass for a lot of kids to run over."

They nodded, understanding. "But why here?" Nabbo was not so easily put off.

Walter grinned. "Market gardening, that's why. This area, why, you can grow plants down here that come up weeks before anywhere else. You've got palm trees growing outside here which we used to have in greenhouses, and fuchsias growing wild as hedges, not potted and protected." He took a big gulp of his drink. This was where he made his pitch. These men were fishermen, he knew, but this was a small area. Word would get around. "I can do all sorts of work on the land but flowers and vegetables are my first love and down here everything is up weeks ahead of anywhere else."

As he had hoped, they were delighted by the suggestion that the far west of Cornwall was better than anywhere else in the country.

"There's Trengwainton, just a mile from here. Brem gert place that is and lovely gardens. Got trees brought back from all over the world. But they'd need a real gardener I reckon. The Colonel is dead set on his flowers."

Walter automatically crossed the estate off his list. Colonels would be too inquisitive about his war record.

"And Roswallow. Just a farm that is, up Newlyn Coombe, but he does a lot of daffodils and vegetables and such. Good and sheltered it is there."

"That's what I want, after Bodmin Moor. Likely to be looking out for a hand, you reckon?" He shrugged. "I know you could say I'm taking away jobs for local men but there aren't many experienced men left after the last four years."

"Well, 'tisn't as if you was a *furriner*!" Walter thought he meant a Frenchman or similar until he added dismissively, "One of they men from Plymouth, like."

Perhaps he shouldn't have claimed to be North Cornish. With men like this, anywhere east of Hayle river was probably considered beyond the pale. "No," he assured them. "I'm no furriner." His imitation of Nabbo's accent was so exact that for a second he was afraid they would take offence but no one seemed to notice. "Anyone you reckon I could see up Roswallow way about a job then?"

There was a general chorus, led by Nabbo. "Old Billy Bennet. He's the gaffer up there."

Walter tipped back the last of his glass. "And do I mention your name? Or would that damn me for ever in his eyes?"

They laughed at the small joke, joshing around. "No respectable man ever says he knows Nabbo! Even his wife do keep her maiden name."

Nabbo was affronted. "You tell 'im I sent you," he insisted. "Him and me – like that we are!" He held up a gnarled brown hand, thickened by a lifetime of pulling in nets, and crossed his first two fingers as a sign of their closeness.

"I'll take your word for it." Walter laughed, relieved that it had all gone so well.

And someone dropped a glass on to the stone flags behind him.

The sharp sound cut through the noise of the relaxed men, sudden as a bomb, and he was out of his seat before the flying shards had come back to land.

The laughter of the fishermen, the fuggy warmth of the pub: suddenly they were gone as if they had never been, and he was back in the trenches again, back to that dreadful day, with shrapnel bursting around him, the constant clatter of the machine guns, and Robert, his only brother, with his face and one arm blown off and tears – unmanly, shocking tears – pouring down his ruined face, mixing with the blood and shredded flesh.

He felt his mouth open in a scream, his pounding heart booming in his chest like the great howitzers—

A hand touched his arm, a voice soothed calmly, "'Tes all right, you. 'Tes only a broken glass. Just you sit down and relax now."

Walter felt himself come back to the present with a jolt that was almost physical, as if he had missed a step on the stairs. His whole body was shaking, tremors running up and down it as if he had a temperature and when he wiped a shaking hand across his face it came away wet with sweat.

Shame shook him. To act like that – like a coward – what would they think of him? He would have no respect. He would be a laughing-stock. He would have to leave here, the area he had spent long, lonely months working out to be the safest place for him. He would have to take the children and go.

Words began to percolate his chaotic thoughts, cheerful, pleasant words; as if he hadn't just showed himself the greatest coward on God's earth, as if he hadn't reacted like a child.

"Quick off the mark you were, then, Nabbo!"

And Nabbo, casually sitting down and taking up his pint as if nothing had happened, "Used to it, aren't I? Old Barney Pentreath was always going off like that. Right pest he could be. Mind you, in his case it were the drink."

"Surprised it idn't you with that problem, boy, the amount you do drink." The men's laughter rang out again, easy and relaxed.

"Here. My shout." Nabbo got up and pushed Walter back in his seat. "Can't let you buy all the drinks, now."

Walter had intended to go, hide his shame in the darkness outside, but no one seemed bothered and the idea of a drink was tempting. Besides, his legs were still shaking. He sank on to the stool Nabbo pushed under him, afraid to meet the other men's eyes, but they seemed unconcerned with his turn.

Only Nabbo, shoving a brimming glass in front of him asked quietly, "In the war then?"

"One of Kitchener's boys." Walter took a long draught, feeling his tight throat ease as the cool liquid poured down it.

"Duke of Cornwall's, were you?"

It was only because he had never fought alongside them that he had chosen this part of the world. Most men had joined the local regiment, whole families and groups of workmen volunteering together, fighting together and all too often dying— He dragged his mind away. Don't think. Don't remember.

"I was away when I joined up." Despite his shock he had enough self-control to stop himself mentioning the West Yorkshires. Thank God no one would know where he came from by his accent. Even if he forgot and dropped the Cornish burr, the years of living with Elizabeth had toned down his natural accent to an unrecognisable minimum.

Nabbo dropped the subject, turning to exchange a few words with the barman who was collecting the bits of broken glass from the floor. There was an exchange of loud joshing, which Walter was beginning to realise was the normal way these men communicated in a social situation, a light buffet on the shoulder – and a piece of glass slipped through the barman's fingers.

Walter turned his head quickly, so quickly that he was looking away by the time he heard the gasp, the furious expletive. As long as he didn't see the blood, as long as he didn't actually see it . . .

But he was shaking again, the strain of the evening getting to him. He pressed his hand against his cheek to hide the tic, and stared resolutely into his drink until the man had left, until the conversation had flowed on, until he had his nerves under control.

After all, he had made his first foray into society, had found the possibility of a job, had been accepted by these people without reservations. He had achieved more today than he could have hoped, he told himself, as the alcohol was absorbed into his body, warming him, soothing him, giving him confidence.

He had passed the first hurdle. What could possibly go wrong?

"Well, I don't know who or what you are and I aren't going to have you here." The Cornishwoman's red face was shiny with suspicion. "You can go and find somewhere else to stay. I'm a respectable woman, I am."

Gunter Steiner bowed slightly. "I assure you, Fräu—" He stopped hastily but he had already said too much. The woman's face tightened.

"Here, you was going to say 'Fräulein', wasn't you?" She reached for the door, ready to slam it in his face. "You – you're one of them there Huns." Her voice rose in fear. "What have you come here for? We beat you lot. You keep away from here."

"Fräu – Madame" – why didn't English have a properly respectful way of addressing a strange woman? – "I assure you, there is nothing to fear. I am myself partly English and I have been—"

"You get away from here." Her voice was rising, driven by fear and excitement. Already doors were opening along the rest of the small street, heads were peering out inquisitively. "You go back to where you belong! You're not going to eat any of *our* babies."

"Madame, I—" But the door was slammed shut in his face and as he turned, other doors down the street were also pulled shut.

Gunter sighed. "Baby eater"! But the Germans had said the same of the British, both sides blackening the name of the enemy so that the ordinary men who made up the armies would be able to overcome their repugnance at killing another human being. So much easier to fire the bullet or stab with the bayonet when the person facing you was not a baker or corn merchant, a father or husband, but a potential eater of your child or rapist of your wife.

And now he was having to live with the results. He walked

37

away from the street, with faces peering out of every window and down the hill to the harbour.

Penzance was a port, as was Hamburg. He dragged his mind away from the thought. He would never go back – *could* never go back. There was nothing to go back to. Better to stay here, put up with the antagonism, the hatred. It would pass, he knew it would pass. The wounds of war were too deep at present, too new. There were too many empty places beside the hearth, on the boats, behind the plough. But it would pass; it would all pass.

Four

Catherine bent down so that she could see her reflection in the small looking-glass that was the boarding-house's only concession to vanity, and skewered her hat to her piled-up chestnut hair with long pins.

Father had gone to look for a job and had taken Robbie as a visible sign of his respectability so she was free. Free to go where she wanted, to do what she wanted without having to justify herself to Walter or explain herself to Robbie.

She was going to go to Newlyn and look for artists.

She hadn't been able to believe it when she found herself here. She missed Dorset, of course, would give anything to be able to return there, but Cornwall . . .

Walter had not told them where they were heading until they were on the train and when he did, Catherine had to fight to disguise the excitement she felt. With his contempt for the arts Walter would never have heard of the Newlyn school of painters, but they were Catherine's favourites. Their very names made her pulse race: Stanhope Forbes, Harold Harvey, Augustus Farley, Lamorna Birch, George Grantham . . . To think that he had brought her here to Penzance, only one mile from one of the most famous colonies of artists in the whole world!

She thought guiltily of the watercolours and brushes she had hidden in the depths of the trunk she and Robbie shared. Her dream of becoming a teacher was finally at an end – without money she could never go to college – but she still had her painting. Her father wanted her to be no more than the working woman his mother had been but if she really did have a talent for art – could that be a way of lifting herself out of the slough into which they had all fallen?

For a second she allowed herself to dream. She would show someone her pictures and then – acclaim, fame, money.

With money she could afford to pay to go to college. With money she could provide a home for Robbie. Money, money – it all came down to money – and her art was the only way she might be able to get some.

She did not know if the artists of the Newlyn school actually lived in Newlyn but she was determined to find out.

With a last check that her hat was straight and her hair not falling down she ran lightly down the stairs and out into the sunshine.

The legless man was still on the street corner, with his tray of small carved animals. Old soldiers, too wounded to work, had become a common sight, despite the government's best efforts to find them alternative work. Wherever you went you saw them propped up on crutches, selling matches or singing on street corners, their blind eyes hidden from view. Catherine was grateful to the man on their street for trying to save Robbie. She gave him a smile and a cheery "good morning" as she ran past him down the street and into the heart of Penzance.

Excitement bubbled over inside her. She threw her head back, loving the feel of the sun on her face, the scent of tar and salt from the sea.

Her way lay along the Promenade. Although there were large covered swimming baths erected there, many people had decided to brave the sea itself. Uniformed nursemaids kept careful watch over small children playing in the waves or on the dark shingle below the Promenade, their broad sun hats shading their faces even though their legs were bare.

Catherine leaned over the railings to watch them, then turned her attention to the sea. How could you paint it? she wondered. It was never still, its surface showing a myriad of colours from turquoise to deep cobalt, the sun flashing brilliantly from the edges of the waves. But the thought of paint reminded her of her mission and she set off again to Newlyn to find out for herself if any of her heroes still lived there.

On the outskirts of the village she stopped, her mouth open. A granite building stood by the side of the road and across the front . . .

An art gallery.

Catherine felt her heart leap with delight. Here there would be people who would know. Here she would find the answer to her quest.

She leapt lightly up the steps and passed into the cool shadows of the hall.

"Got any references, 'ave 'ee?" The old man stared at Walter through permanently watering eyes.

"Not recent. I've been in the army." Damn it, surely he had done enough to prove he knew his stuff. He probably knew more than the old fool but half the time he had used dialect words or spoken with such an accent that it was difficult for Walter to follow him.

"Well, I dunno." The old man pulled off his greasy cap and scratched the bald spot on his head. "I mean ter say, 'tes different down here, like. We do things our way. And then again, are 'ee up to 'un? That's what I've got to consider."

Walter hadn't realised until today how unfit he was. Not surprising after two years of being stuck indoors, doing nothing, but he had really struggled with the work old Bennet had set him. The sadistic old fool had made him sweat in the sunshine for an hour.

"Well" – he shrugged on his jacket, feeling his muscles already start to stiffen – "don't consider too long. I might go back up-country." Already he was getting into the dialect of the area.

Bennet considered. "Where you living, then?"

"Boarding in Penzance," Walter said shortly.

"And yer wife?"

"Died earlier this year." No need to say when.

The old man took it as he had hoped. "Brem dreadful that there flu." He nodded to where Robbie stood by the gate, watching them, his red hair startling in the bright sunlight. "That yer boy?"

"That's him. And I've a grown-up daughter at home."

Bennet nodded. As Walter had hoped, the mention of a family swayed the man in his favour. Single men were unreliable, getting drunk, changing jobs, but a man with a family needed work.

Bennet nodded. "Got a place goes with the job, if yer interested."

Interested! "Near by?"

"Other side of the farm."

So it was further from Penzance, but he didn't mind that.

Crowds still made him feel nervous and the sight of a policeman made his cheek twitch and his heart race so fast that he
felt sick.

"Any jobs going that my daughter might do? She's seventeen,
a good clean girl, quiet, clever."

Bennet spat. "Can't abide they clever women. 'Tes against
nature, I say." He thought. "No job for a woman here but there's
a fish factory in Newlyn, always looking for girls, that is. Smelly
old job, though."

"That won't worry her." Walter grinned to himself. "It'll be
right up her street."

Gunter Steiner stared at the building on which all his hopes for
the future rested. It did not look encouraging.

Before the war, he had been a young man with a secure future,
heir to his father's silk factory in Hamburg, trained in design and
married to a beautiful woman. It had been of no consequence
then that his grandfather had brought his dying wife back to her
native Cornwall and set up a tiny silk printing factory "to keep
himself busy".

Now, he had nothing, a hated stranger in a strange land whose
only ambition was not to have to go back to Germany where his
property was lost for ever and his wife's betrayal was common
knowledge. Only this small factory, a remnant of his grandfather's
concern for his dying wife, stood between him and penury.

At the outbreak of war his grandfather had escaped internment
because of his age, but the authorities dared not let a German
national live so close to the sea in case he signalled information
to passing ships. They had forced him to close the factory and
move to the centre of England. Now he was dead, and the building
showed all the signs of four years' neglect. The paint on the once
blue door was grey and peeling, the lock and hinges rusty. The
key stuck and screamed, cutting into his hand as he forced it to
turn. Gunter took a deep breath and pushed the door open.

Inside it was dark except for the light that came through the
open door. Gunter moved slowly forwards, brushing the long,
dusty tentacles of unseen cobwebs away from his face with an
impatient hand.

As his eyes became accustomed to the gloom he could see the
faint outline of shutters over windows on the far side of the room.

He wrestled them open and the light that flooded in allowed him to take stock of his sole inheritance.

The building had obviously been converted from some other use. Through the windows he could see that there were more buildings surrounding a courtyard, some with strong padlocks that looked like storerooms.

He forced his way through into the yard, opened the locked doors. Gunter had half expected that the prevalent anti-German feeling would have led to the building being vandalised; at the very least he had expected his grandfather to have sold off all the stock and furniture, but it was all here, he realised.

Piled in the outbuildings, with their windows protected by iron bars and closed shutters, was all the paraphernalia of a silk printer's. Trolleys for use by the "wipers", as the printer's assistants were known, the thick ply blocks of wood from which the printing blocks would be carved, the cutting tables and treadle machines on which the machinists would produce the finished clothes, even large containers of silk dyes, their German names and instructions still readable.

For a second Gunter could not believe his eyes; then he realised. In Germany it had been said, in 1914, that the war would be over by Christmas. Presumably the same feeling had been common in England. Leaving everything here made sense if his grandfather had expected to be back within a few months.

His excitement growing, he struggled to open the next door and sighed with satisfaction. Silk was notorious for the length of time that it could survive and this silk was still as his grandfather had bought it from the manufacturers. The fibre was woven "in the gum", just as it had been produced by the silk worm with the fine silk thread protected by a gummy layer of sericin. It was a harsh, unattractive brown colour, nothing like the silk cloth that the public knew, but once it had been degummed it would be suitable for printing.

He went out to the courtyard again. There, under the overhanging building which had probably once been a net loft, was the winch that was used to assist the washing of the silk, dragging it like a rope through hot soapy water that would remove the gum from the fibres.

Excitement built. He went back into the central hall of the main building and limped swiftly up the stairs, his heart thumping.

The whole of the upstairs was one long room, with extra windows knocked into the wall overlooking the sea to give more light. The windowed side of the room was occupied by a single long table, about three feet wide. He walked across, leaned on it, shook it, sat on it. It stayed rock solid. This, then, was the printing table, designed to withstand the hammering of three or four men simultaneously pounding the dye into the silk with small mallets.

Gunter lifted his arms exultantly. He had everything he needed to start the factory up again.

Except the workers.

"Sixpence, my handsome."

Catherine jumped. She had been so overwhelmed at being inside an art gallery that she had not seen the man behind the wooden desk.

"I – I'm sorry. I don't have—" She stopped. To be so close and still he denied the right to enter – she felt as if the gates of paradise had been barred against her at the very last moment.

What had she got to lose? "Please, can't you let me in anyway. I am" – she stumbled over saying the word – "I am an artist." It came out in a rush and she hoped that the man could not see that she had her fingers crossed behind her back.

"Can't let you in without you pays." He was implacable. "If I was to let in all they what said they was artists no one would ever pay round here, would they?"

Catherine had been turning away, disappointed, but this gave her the opening she wanted and she swung back again. "I suppose there are a lot of artists around here?"

"A brem lot," the man agreed. "And a brem lot of old women who think that they can paint when all they do is waste good paints. Terrible, it is, the way women can fool themselves 'bout what they do."

Catherine felt that this was directed at her and felt herself grow red – but she had to know the answer. "I know that you have had lots of famous artists here in the past but I wasn't sure . . . Are – are Mr Lamorna Birch and Mr Augustus Farley still here?" Mr Birch was slightly known to Miss Rose and Mr Farley had always been her favourite artist.

"Aye, they're still here – and Stanhope Forbes. Farley is even living in the village still." He made it sound as if this reflected glory on him personally. "What d'you want to know about them for, I'd like to know?"

"I—" She took a deep breath, summoning all her courage. "I'd like to meet them. Do you – can you tell me their addresses?"

He rose, his brows lowered. "You women are all the same, chasing after a man like any lightskirt, just because he's famous." He caught the appalled look on Catherine's face and softened slightly. "You take my advice, maid. You forget all this about art and famous painters. You go home to yer ma and marry a good man and forget all this rubbish. 'Tes all right for men, if they have talent, to be a painter, but women—" He snorted. "Art indeed!"

Catherine's face flamed. That he should think she was that sort of person! She moved swiftly away, hurrying down the steps, as ashamed as if she had been the sort of woman he obviously thought her, his last remark still rankling.

Just because she was a woman it didn't mean that she had no talent. If only, Catherine thought, she knew what Miss Rose's friend had thought of the painting she had taken him. If there was a chance that Catherine might one day be good enough to sell her paintings, she would defy her father, continue painting in the hope that one day she would be able to make enough money to pay for her college training. But she had to know.

If she really wasn't as good as Miss Rose thought then she would give up the whole idea, try to be the sort of daughter her father wanted, but if she was good . . .

Her father had forbidden her to leave an address so that Miss Rose could contact her when she returned from London. He was determined to cut her off from her past as firmly as he was denying her the future she had expected, Catherine thought bitterly. But if she wrote to Miss Rose and asked for the letter to be sent to Penzance Post Office until she collected it, he would never know that she had written.

She began to run. Father and Robbie would be back soon and she wanted to get the letter written before they arrived.

Then another thought brought her up short, her heart beating.

Miss Rose might not return from London for weeks but Catherine had discovered that Augustus Farley still lived in Newlyn itself.

Why didn't she take her paintings and show them to him?

Five

"You will stay in, won't you?"

"Where are y-y-you going?" Robbie eyed his sister suspiciously. "F-F-Father told us both to s-stay in."

"Oh, just out around the town."

She always was an awful liar, Robbie decided. You just had to look at the expression on her face to know when she wasn't telling the truth. And she had some secret she wasn't telling him.

Robbie knew that, whatever his teachers thought, he wasn't stupid. True, he was terribly clumsy and when he tried to read or write the letters just twisted themselves into incomprehensible shapes, but in some ways he knew that he was cleverer than Catherine. He didn't always believe what he was told, whereas she would swallow any story. Just look at how she believed those stories about Father.

"Why can't I c-come with you, then?" he demanded, more to see her reaction than in the expectation of getting a proper answer.

"Because you can't." She looked flustered. "I won't be long, honestly."

He lay on the narrow bed, watching through the half-open door. He could hear sounds of preparation through the thin wall that divided them: rustlings, thumps, not at all the sounds of a young woman merely pinning on her hat before going out. Sure enough, when she bustled swiftly past the door to his room five minutes later, even the dark hall couldn't hide the fact that she was wearing her best hat and skirt and carrying a large, flat parcel.

Robbie waited until he heard the front door close then slipped off the bed and grabbed his cap. She was up to something – and he was determined to find out what it was.

Newlyn was bustling. It was high tide and the harbour jostled with boats. The fish market was in full cry. Men haggled incomprehensibly over huge silver fish or threw wicker baskets laden with smaller fish around as though they weighed nothing. Around the harbour the rails were packed with gossiping women and pipe-smoking old men, their seamed faces brown from the sun and wind.

The village was a nightmare of crooked streets and small alleys that led into the dead end of a small court. Catherine asked passers-by again and again for directions to the house of Mr Farley, the artist.

Some shook their heads. One old man puffed on his evil-smelling pipe and advised her, in broad Cornish, to "stay away from that there devil". Women looked shocked.

Catherine ignored it all. Artists had a reputation, she knew. She was sure that one of the reasons her father was so against her painting was because of the stories. But that was rubbish. Miss Rose was a dear. She was the daughter of an artist and no one could be more respectable than she was.

Finally Catherine caught sight of a young woman whose bright complexion and bold eyes suggested that she would not be so strait-laced.

She eyed Catherine appraisingly. "Looking for 'im, are 'ee? Well, I reckon you might be lucky at that." She grinned. "Back to the bridge over the stream then up the hill and turn left. 'Tes the big house at the top." As Catherine thanked her and started to retrace her steps she shouted out, "And don't let that there bitch of a wife put you off."

Catherine found herself blushing at the coarseness. No respectable woman would ever refer to another woman as a bitch, but she did hope that she would not meet the lady concerned. Now that she was almost there, her nervousness grew. Should she start by saying how much she liked his paintings? Or should she start straight in. "Mr Farley, I want to be an artist. Please will you look at my work?"

The door loomed over her, the brass furnishings glittering against the bright blue paintwork. Now that the moment had come she felt sick with fright and her hand shook as she raised the knocker. Supposing he answered the door himself? Supposing she just stood there like an idiot and lost her chance of getting the great man to look at her paintings?

For a second she was tempted to let the knocker down silently and slink away, but what would become of her then? It would be impossible for her to get a job as an assistant teacher in a strange place and her father would insist that she work in the fields or as a servant, tied for ever to the sort of life Mother had been determined that she should not have.

With sudden decision Catherine let the knocker drop with a bang. Footsteps approached and she took a deep breath, wiping her sweating hands down the side of her Sunday-best serge skirt.

The maid who opened the door was elderly but looked kind and Catherine felt her confidence growing. "Please" – she tried to sound calmer than she felt – "I would like to see Mr Farley if that is possible."

"Well, miss, I don't know." The older woman sounded doubtful. "I'll go and ask 'un, if you like."

Catherine breathed a sigh of relief. "If you please."

Then a voice spoke from behind her. "What does this young person want, Martha?"

Catherine spun around. Behind her stood a tall, slender lady in a smart summer hat with a small terrier on a lead and Catherine realised with a sinking heart that it could only be Mrs Farley.

Robbie realised that she was going to show someone her paintings – paintings Father thought he had destroyed. Robbie grinned in appreciation. He had never suspected her of being so crafty.

He had no trouble following her until she set off into the back streets of Newlyn. She obviously didn't know where she was going, stopping people to ask and often backtracking so that he had to dodge hastily down a side alley before she caught him.

The streets twisted, with so many side turnings and courts that it was some time before he realised that he had lost her. Robbie was standing still, trying to work out where he had gone wrong when there was a sudden shout from behind him. "There's that Jerry spy. Let's scrag 'un."

He cast a swift glance over his shoulder at the gang of boys peering up at him from the bottom of the street then began to run. With whoops and catcalls they joined the hunt, their feet pounding. They could run faster than him, Robbie knew. Sometimes it seemed as if every boy in the world could run faster than him.

His only hope was Catherine, but she was nowhere to be seen. He called her name once but his voice was drowned by the hallooing of his hunters and he did not have time or breath to shout again.

His boots skidding on the rough cobbles, Robbie chose streets and alleys at random, dodging around corners, trying to lose himself in the warren of alleys. But this was home territory to the boys. He could hear their shouts getting closer as they hounded him. At first, the cries were all behind him, then, just as his strength was running out, he heard other answering cries from in front.

They had penned him in.

He skidded to a halt, his chest heaving. His hunters were still out of sight but from the sound of their voices he could tell that they would be on him at any second.

Panic-stricken, he glanced up and down the narrow alley. There was no other way out. They had him trapped, without even a grown-up around to intervene if the boys went too far.

The shouts were louder, closer. In desperation Robbie put his hand on a dilapidated door beside him and pushed. To his amazement it swung open.

Just one glance over his shoulder then he was through, pushing the door shut behind him. He fumbled in the darkness of the room beyond, feeling for some way of barricading the door. The ringed handle of a large key sticking out of the lock was so welcome that he could have shouted in triumph as he turned it, locking himself in, away from his tormentors.

Robbie leaned thankfully back against the door, panting. He was safe.

Then a man's voice spoke from out of the darkness – "What do you want, little boy?" – and Robbie's horrified ears heard the sound of a German accent.

"Well, young woman?" Mrs Farley's voice was tart. "May I ask what you are doing here?"

"I-I—" Under the woman's cool gaze Catherine found herself stammering like Robbie and pulled herself together with an effort. "I want to see Mr Farley."

The delicate eyebrows rose under the low brim of the hat. "And may I ask why you want to see my husband?" There was a slight emphasis on the last two words that added to Catherine's embarrassment.

"Well, I . . ." She cursed herself. This was no way to impress anyone. With an effort she raised her head and looked the woman straight in the eye. "I wanted to show him my paintings."

Mrs Farley glanced at the portfolio Catherine was hugging to her chest. "Indeed. And what gives you the idea that you are an artist?"

The question startled Catherine. It was something she had never asked herself. She had always liked drawing, she had always been the best in her class at copying flowers in nature study, her mother had always told her how good she was. And Miss Rose, whose father had painted, had admired her work, taught her what she knew for nothing. How could she not be an artist?

Mrs Farley clicked her fingers impatiently. "Don't just stand there like a *dummy*, girl. I suppose you have your work there. Show it to me."

Catherine stared. "Show it to you?" Somehow, this seemed more daunting than showing her work to the unknown Augustus Farley.

"Show it to me," Mrs Farley insisted, with a lilt that almost made her sound as if she was imitating Catherine's own startled words. "Good Lord, girl! I *am* an artist in my own right. Or didn't you even know that?"

Catherine hadn't known. She had admired Augustus Farley's paintings, had imagined herself being taken on as his pupil, fantasised about his amazed response to her work, but she had never, until the woman in the street had mentioned it, thought that he might have a wife.

But it was rapidly becoming obvious that the only way to see the artist was to get past this woman. Hastily, she struggled with the ties on her portfolio, her fingers made awkward by nervousness. "I – of course you can see them." She moved to pick up the top one, paused. "They're – they're only water-colours."

"Only water-colours! I shouldn't let my friend Walter Langley hear you say that. He does all his best work in water-colours." She clicked her fingers. "Come on, girl, I haven't got all day."

"No, of course not." Catherine took the top painting and held it out, her heart thumping so much that she felt sick. "This picture is—"

The portfolio was twitched from her grasp. "Good Lord, girl, you shouldn't need to tell people about a picture. If a picture is any good it will speak for itself."

She flicked swiftly through the paintings and drawings while Catherine waited with bated breath, her eyes on the woman's face, hardly daring to breathe until the woman gave her verdict.

All the stories his father had told him about Germans crowded into Robbie's mind: their cruelty, their vicious behaviour . . . Automatically, he reached for the key, ready to bolt outside to safety – but there was a shout from outside. The boys were there. He heard the door rattle as one of them tried it, then: "'Tes locked, I tell 'ee. Like always. He idn't in there."

Robbie turned again, terror adding to his breathlessness. His eyes were growing accustomed to the dim light and he could see a tall figure looming over him. He cringed as he saw a hand reach for him, then his shoulder was caught in a strong grip and he was pulled through the far door and out into the next room.

It was lighter in here, small windows letting in the June sunshine. After all the stories he had heard he would not have been surprised if the German had had long eye-teeth, ready to eat babies with, but to Robbie's disappointment he seemed quite ordinary.

"Well, little boy. Did you break in to steal?" A hand moved, gestured at the empty room, the cobwebs that adorned the ceiling and fluttered black in the sunshine. "As you can see, there is nothing here."

The horror at being accused of being a thief was so enormous that Robbie began indignantly, "I-I-I-I—" He stopped, the struggle to get the words out temporarily overwhelming him.

The German smiled slightly. "Take a deep breath, and think of what it is that you wish to say. Then say it slowly."

The advice, so similar to what Mother and Catherine had told him a thousand times, brought him up short. "Y-you know about st-stammering?"

The smile broadened. "Of course. Children in Germany also stammer."

"They do?" Robbie was enthralled. It suddenly made the German more human. He had never even thought that there

51

were children in Germany. He had always imagined the country peopled with vicious soldiers. "Wh-what happens to them?"

The smile grew broader. "Usually, they grow out of it. You, too, probably, will grow so that you do not stammer any more."

He had always been the only person he knew who had a bad stammer and no one had told him this before. He felt as if a great weight had been taken off his shoulders. Never mind if he had to wait until he was as old as Catherine, or even – unbelievable age – until he was twenty-one: if his stammer disappeared, he would be able to talk as he wanted, speak when he wanted to, say what he chose. It was a liberating thought.

He moved forward, enthralled. "Did you stammer when you were little?"

"I do not think so. But always, my mother, she says to me, 'Slow down. Do not talk too fast. You will get your tongue into a twist'."

Robbie laughed. "I get told that too." He looked around the empty room. Now that he was less frightened his curiosity was growing. "Wh-what is this place? Do you live here? Is it a h-house?"

"Whatever it is, it is mine," said Gunter firmly. "You should be telling to me the reason that you are here."

"It wasn't because I was going to steal anything," Robbie said hotly. "But there were these boys and they were chasing me and so . . ."

"And why," the German asked, "were they chasing? Had you done something bad to them?"

"No, honestly. But I am a stranger and they said—" He stopped. Tact had never been his strong point but he could see that it would not be polite to say that the boys had thought that he, too, was a German. "I'm just a stranger here," he finished lamely.

"And the Cornish people, they are afraid of strangers." The man sighed. "I, too, have discovered that, though where it is my case, they have perhaps more reason." He clapped Robbie on the shoulder. "It is said in my country that the English drink tea all the time, and as I am thinking of living in your country, I, too, am drinking tea. Would you like some?"

"Yes, please." Robbie followed him into yet another room. A fire burned cheerfully in the grate and there was a table and chairs and, rolled on the floor, a nest of blankets. His eyes grew rounder. "You're living here?"

Gunter swung a blackened kettle on a hook until it was over the fire. "It is all I have, but it is my own so no one can stop me."

"How do you own a place in Cornwall if you're German?" Robbie demanded. "Why are you going to live here? Why don't you go home to Germany?"

Gunter raised an eyebrow. "I own this place because, before the war, my grandparents came to this country and they started a factory here. Now they are dead and it is mine. As to your other questions—" He paused.

"Yes?"

Again a smile lit up the man's blue eyes. "Little boy, I know two things. One is that you are the sort of person who will ask of me questions until I go mad and blow bubbles at the mouth like a cross bull."

The incorrect idiom made Robbie laugh. He sat himself comfortably on the chair opposite the man. "And the other thing?"

The man reached out and ruffled his hair. "The other thing is that, when you are happy you do not stammer your words any more," he said.

Robbie's eyes grew round. "I never noticed that before," he said wonderingly. He sat and thought about what the man had said.

"You see, the thing is," he confided, "I don't think that I am happy very often."

To Catherine it seemed as if the woman's scrutiny of her paintings would never end. She pulled one painting after the other from the portfolio, scrutinising it first at arm's length and then close up.

Her hands clasped so tightly together that her knuckles were white, Catherine prayed silently. Please let her say they are good. Please let me meet her husband.

Finally, Mrs Farley thrust the last picture back into the portfolio. There was a long moment of silence.

Catherine could bear it no longer. "Please." It was no more than a whisper. "Please. What do you think of them?"

"Your paintings?" She raised her fine eyebrows. "Daubs, all of them. Just daubs."

And she thrust the untied portfolio back into Catherine's arms and vanished inside the house.

Six

D aubs!
       Her legs shaking, a pulse hammering in her head,
Catherine walked unsteadily back down the steep hill from
Farley's house, her untied portfolio clutched under one arm.

Daubs! All her favourite paintings dismissed like that, as if
they were not worth a second look.

She walked on, dry-eyed, too shocked and disappointed to
weep. Her whole life – ruined. For the second time in less than
a fortnight all her plans for the future had been swept away.
In her disappointment she staggered slightly, unaware of the
sights and sounds around her, lost in her disappointment, her
heart-shattering misery.

The afternoon sun was high now, and even the Cornish hedges,
thick with gorse, could not provide any relief from the heat. The
rays beat down on her head like hammer blows, despite the
protection of her best hat which she had adjusted so carefully
before setting out.

Daubs! Her head was throbbing. Catherine felt as if all the
hurt and anguish of the last two weeks was swirling round in
her head, threatening to burst out.

She couldn't bear it any more. With a sudden movement she
ripped the hat from her head, desperate to get some comfort from
the raging headache that was threatening to make her sick. The
long hat-pins which held it on dragged at her hair, caught in the
hairpins that held up her heavy tresses and ripped them out too.

With a gentle sigh the whole of her carefully constructed hairdo
came undone. The intricate coils slithered and dropped, hanging
to her hips in a chestnut cloak.

"Brem good hair you got here, maid. Want to sell 'un, do 'ee?"

The words broke through her misery, making her jump around,
her hair swinging out around her like a matador's cape. "What?"

A rag-and-bone man smiled at her from his laden cart drawn by a small lop-eared donkey. Suddenly aware that she was standing in the middle of a public thoroughfare with her hair loose about her like some modern day Mary Magdalene, Catherine reached up to gather together the loose tresses and her portfolio slipped from under her arm.

It tumbled, the untied ribbons falling open, the papers scattering wildly. "Oh, *no.*" It was the final straw. They might be daubs but they were all she had left. Ignoring her hair, she bent to pick them up. But this close to the sea there was always a breeze and the papers fluttered away from her, brushing against the mossy stones of the hedge, catching against the lush greenery.

"No!" She knelt on the ground in her best skirt, trying to catch as many as she could, careless of her hair hanging down to sweep the dusty ground. Painting was her life. She could not lose all this work. It was all she had, possibly all she ever would have. Without Miss Rose, without the facilities of a school, would she ever be able to draw or paint again? No – Father would not allow her to waste time on such things. She scrabbled frantically, reaching for the flapping sheets.

Suddenly she froze.

"Brem handsome hair."

She had forgotten the stranger but he was beside her now, leaning over her. His hand, rough and dirty, smoothed down her hair in a long, lascivious stroke, all the way from her head to her hips. "Some wonderful." His voice was hoarse and low.

A fear she did not understand gripped her. "Go away." She leaped to her feet, heart pounding. "Leave me alone."

The man was old and seamed; black pores pitted his skin. He stood beside her, one work-thickened grimy hand still reaching out, stroking her hair. "I'll buy 'un off you." He voice rasped as if he found it difficult to get his breath. "I'll give you good money for hair like that. The best price you could hope for."

Catherine looked frantically around but they were alone apart from the donkey.

He's a rag-and-bone man, her common sense told her. He is just touting for business. But the fixed look in his eyes as he stared at her hair, the hoarseness of his voice, frightened her.

"Please." She moved away but he followed her.

"Let me buy 'un off you."

"No." Her voice was high and frightened. "It's not for sale. Leave me alone." She backed further off. At her feet her paintings fluttered like dying moths. Her life. Her whole life.

Instinct told her to run, but how could she leave her paintings? Daubs! The words came back to her. Daubs!

He followed her. "The best price. I'll pay you the best price. For a maid's hair like yours, even just a lock of it." He reached out again with his filthy hand.

"No." If only she was not alone with him. She looked frantically up and down the road, fighting with the temptation to scream, but the road was deserted.

"Please." He was panting now, winding her hair around his filthy fingers as it were the finest silk, lifting it to touch his face, kissing it.

She could stand it no longer. She didn't understand what was driving him but it frightened her. She stepped away from him, away from her precious paintings. They lay on the ground around her, fluttering like lost souls, calling to her.

For a second she paused. How could she leave them? Then he moved towards her again. One thick boot ground on to a delicate water-colour painting of a flower, ripping through paper and paint alike, ruining it. One filthy clawed hand reached out and stroked her hair again, passing down the full curve of her spine, lifting her hair to caress his face.

"No!" It was too much. With a shrill cry she whirled around and ran, leaving her paintings scattered at his feet.

Daubs, just daubs. But now the tears ran freely down her face as she raced down the street, her hair flying around her, clinging to her wet cheeks, wrapping itself across her nostrils, filling her mouth. *Daubs, just daubs.*

The end of her dreams.

"I have a name for you."

Random had arranged for Captain Walton to meet him at his club. Now he sat forward, quickly enough to aggravate the lurking pain that had been bothering him all day. "Just one?" His single eye gleamed. "I was afraid . . ."

"That there would be too many?" The captain shook his head. "The British Army honours its brave men, sir, as we both know. Every effort is made to recover the bodies of those who died. It takes time but we are still working at it. Men who had been buried in haste are reinterred with proper ceremony, and, now that there is peace, other bodies are found. Many are still missing, of course, but I was able to find only one man who met all your criteria."

"And his name?" Random signalled to the club servant. "Two more brandies, quickly." He leaned forward again. "Come on, man. His name."

The captain hesitated. "You realise, of course, that the chances are that this man died an honourable death in battle. Just because he meets the criteria you gave me and we have no body doesn't mean that the man is a deserter. You are only working on a supposition."

"Good God, man!" Random erupted. "D'you think I'm going to go round there and tell some poor family that their son is a deserter? I'm not a fool, you know. I realise that there is little hope of being able to find the man who did this to me." One lean brown hand rose to touch the black silk patch he wore over his ruined eye. "But I have to do what I can. I am not" – his clenched fist hammered on his good knee – "going to let this man get away with it if there is any chance that I can find him and return him to justice."

"That's it, sir. Justice." The captain's hand still grasped the envelope tightly. "The army and the police are both more capable of doing this than you are." He raised worried eyes to Random's ravaged face. "Why don't you tell them what you have told me? They can investigate this more easily than you can. They have the right, the authority to do so. Let me give this name to them. There's no need for you to get involved at all."

"I want to get involved for the very reason you have just given me, Captain. Precisely because this man may be innocent. If it's done through official channels, word will spread. Good Lord, these local policemen know everything. Do you think that word won't get around if official enquiries start to be made about some dead soldier?"

The club servant appeared at his side and he took the proffered brandy with a brief word of thanks. When the man had left he leaned forward again. "I can do this discreetly, Captain. No one need ever know why I am asking about him. If he is innocent, there is no harm done."

"But how will you know, sir? The family won't tell you. They may not know themselves that he is still alive."

"He would need to be hidden away. If he is the man I saw, he is only about forty years old and he deserted eighteen months before the armistice." He sipped his drink. "At the time, all men who were half-way capable of fighting were in the army, except for those in reserved occupations and even they were mostly older men. If he had suddenly appeared, someone would have wondered, begun to ask questions. He could only have got away with it if someone hid him – and that would mean his wife or his family. If he is alive, they will know."

He reached out his hand. "The name, Captain." His voice rang with an air of command and men across the room turned to look at him, but he did not notice them. All his attention was concentrated on the young officer before him and the envelope he held in his hand.

Walton sighed and handed it over, then stood and saluted. "I have done my best to dissuade you, sir. I just hope—"

Random also rose. "You will not be implicated in any way, Captain. You have my word."

Walton bowed, saluted and turned on his heel.

Random waited until he had left the room then limped to the window. It was dark outside now, or as dark as it ever got in London. People were strolling, laughing, just as they had before the war, just as he and Jenny used to do, only now the women looked strange, almost like little girls dressed up, their skirts shorter than before the war, their hair short.

For a moment he sighed for the young women as he remembered them, voluptuous in their tight-fitting clothes, their bodies swayed into an "S" shape by their corsets, their mountainous, high-piled hair surmounted by enormous hats. In Scotland, he could still see the remains of the styles he had enjoyed so much, though, after four years of war, the clothes were plainer, the skirts shorter. He sincerely hoped this style of dressing women like five-year-olds was a passing phase that didn't catch on in the rest of the country.

He tapped the envelope against his other hand. He knew he was procrastinating. It was one thing to decide to find the man who had crippled him, but this was different. There were real families out there who might be hurt by his actions;

possibly a man, frightened, guilty, only just now trying to live his life again.

Did he really want to spend the last few months of his life spreading misery like this? Should he just rip the envelope up, forget the whole thing, live his last days in comfort?

Another couple passed on the other side of the road, older, still dressed in the pre-war styles. For a second the woman looked so like Jenny that his heart contracted and he turned his head away blindly.

Then he thrust his finger under the flap and ripped it open impatiently, feasting his eyes on the name and address the young officer had given him.

Richard Walter Harrison.

Random took a deep breath. He was committed.

Where was Robbie?

Catherine stood uncertainly on the step of the boarding-house. Concern for him was the only thing that could have brought her out of her misery.

Daubs! The word still cut at her. Against the misery of that, even her father's announcement that she was to work in a fish-canning factory had no power to hurt her. Daubs. *Daubs*.

She dragged her mind away from the echo of the word and tried to concentrate. It was dark now and Robbie, who had promised he would stay in, had disappeared.

But why should he have gone out? Robbie wasn't a coward but long experience had taught him that he was not able to talk or fight his way out of trouble with other children and, after yesterday's experience, she had expected him to go out only when she was around to look after him.

Of course. She took a deep breath. He would have followed her. Curiosity alone would have driven him and he would have relied on her presence to get him out of trouble if he called. For a second her cheeks bloomed as she recalled the scene with Mrs Farley. She did not want that terrible denunciation – "Daubs!" – to have been heard by anyone else.

But if he had been near he would have seen the horrible rag-and-bone man and would certainly have intervened on her behalf. If he had followed her, she had lost him by then.

The most likely place was Newlyn. Until then the road had been straight and obvious. Only in the back streets of Newlyn had she twisted and jinked. Relieved to have a place to start looking, she set out determinedly to walk the mile to the village.

"I will see you to your house." Gunter rose. "The boys will not attack you if I am with you."

Robbie rose slowly. He liked Gunter, welcomed the thought of his protection, but what if Father saw him? Robbie had heard too many diatribes against the Germans to believe that Father would welcome his companion, even if he had helped to rescue Robbie.

"What about you?" he asked. "Won't people attack you if they see you out?"

Gunter threw back his head and laughed. "Attack me? No. They send the police after me to read my papers but they are all in order and so it is no more than a little trouble to me. And as for other people" – he grinned, baring his white teeth – "I am a big bad German who eats little children. They are all afraid of me."

Robbie smiled back less certainly. Certainly Gunter looked tall and strong enough to scare off most people but Robbie didn't want his kindness repaid by Walter's anger. Besides, he was planning to see Gunter again and Walter would certainly forbid that.

"I-I-I can go home b-b-b-by myself," he insisted.

If he had noticed the sudden tell-tale return of the stammer Gunter didn't mention it. "Of course. That is understood. But I have been in this house all day, brushing floors and cooking food for us both. I want the clean air before I go to sleep and to walk with you is a good reason to get it." He ruffled Robbie's red hair. "Don't worry, little one. I shall not force myself on to your family."

So it was that the two of them were walking along the Promenade, happily discussing life, when they met Catherine.

Seven

"**R**obbie! Thank God!"

Catherine clutched him to her, ignoring the stammering protests. So much had gone wrong today that she had scarcely hoped to find him at all; to see him safe was more than she could believe.

Impulsively, she held out her hand to the tall, fair-haired man beside him. "Did you look after him for me? Thank you very much. It was kind of you."

The faint click of the heels, the slight bow over her hand, gave her some warning. She stood stiff with disbelief as he murmured, "It has been a pleasure, Fräulein. I have been happy to keep him with me."

A German! She could only stare at him, her mouth open with shock. Mother had always insisted that the Germans were just ordinary people like themselves but in the last two years she had not been allowed to say such things in Father's hearing. Instead, Catherine had been forced to listen to her father's anti-German ravings. Now she found herself responding automatically, dragging her hand from his as if it were contaminated.

Immediately she regretted her action – it didn't matter whether he was a German or an Englishman, the important thing was that he had been kind to Robbie – but it was too late.

For a brief second she caught a glimpse of hurt in the blue eyes that stared down at her; then the German straightened and turned to look at Robbie. "Now that you are safe I shall leave you alone. I have been happy to meet you." He reached out and gave the boy's hair a swift ruffle, then turned on his heel and strode quickly away.

Robbie pulled himself from Catherine's grasp. "Gunter, wait. P-p-please, Gunter, don't go."

The man never faltered, walking swiftly away, and within

seconds the slightly halting sound of his footsteps was masked by the rattle of gravel pulled back and forth by the waves on the beach below.

Robbie turned on Catherine. "Why d-d-did you do that? He was n-n-n-nice to me. I want to go and see him again."

"Robbie, you can't." Catherine was appalled. "What would Father say? You know how he hates Germans. It might bring back his neurasthenia, start up all those nightmares he used to have."

"Y-you're stupid," Robbie said crossly. "You're like all girls, you're really s-s-silly."

"What do you mean?"

But he would not answer, turning away and stalking off so that she had to hurry after him.

"Father is really cross with you already. He said you're not to have any supper."

"I've eaten it anyway." He did not turn to look at her. "Gunter gave me lots and lots of s-supper. *And* he's a better cook than you are."

She felt even more guilty. Robbie had so few people that he was happy with and if this man had been kind to him . . .

But a German! Her heart quailed at the thought of the explosions there would be if Father found out. She had to put a stop to this somehow.

"We know nothing about his man," she began.

"*I* know about him," Robbie retorted. "He's going to make women's dresses."

"He's *what?*" She couldn't believe it. From the brief glimpse of him he had seemed too masculine for such a trade. "In *Cornwall?*"

And that was another thing. Cornwall. Dorset had been backwards enough and after four years of war nobody was wearing smart clothes, but in Cornwall people were still wearing the clothes that their grandparents could have worn. She had attracted disapproving glances even though her skirts ended modestly just above the ankle. The only smart woman she had seen since they had arrived was Mrs Farley.

She dragged her mind from the thought, her heart still aching as she remembered the woman's denunciation. Daubs! And now Catherine did not even have those "daubs" any more: they were scattered in the wind.

63

Or were they? She stopped dead in the middle of the street. She was half-way to Newlyn anyway. They might still be there – and they might be able to be saved.

She looked down the Promenade. Robbie was almost home, now, running fast. She turned and walked back towards Newlyn.

If she could see her paintings again she might be able to judge for herself whether Mrs Farley had been right or not.

Gunter walked away, the sharp, uneven clip of his heels deliberately emphasised to hide the voices behind him.

Inside, anger burned. From what Robbie had told him he had deduced that the boy had had an unhappy life; a mother who, until her death, had been wrapped up in her ill husband, a father who was cold and self-absorbed. Only the sister had seemed kind and, listening to Robbie's artless chatter, Gunter had gained a favourable impression of Catherine – except for her artistic leanings.

Matilde had been the same: young, impressionable, mistaking a liking for pretty things for talent and an uncontrollable temper for artistic temperament. He felt shame as he remembered the way she had hunted him down, weaving her spell around him, asking for help and advice about her paintings when all the time she was only after him; him and the factory to which he had been heir. Had she used the same spells to entrap Friedrich?

And now this other girl, with her high-piled hair and green eyes, so like Matilde. Like her, too, in her instant prejudice.

The thought of Matilde made him burn inside. He cursed her – and he cursed the girl who had resurrected the painful memories. It was still not late, a fine summer's evening, and he knew that he would not be able to sleep with this churning anger inside him.

Although the main streets in Penzance were lit by gaslights they had not reached as far as Newlyn yet and, apart from the area around the harbour with its public houses catering for the many fishermen who lived there, the village was quiet.

He did not want to see people. In particular he did not want to see that look in their eyes when they realised that he was a German. The way that girl had looked at him – the warmth and friendliness in her eyes turning to ice, as if he were a monster, when all he had done was make sure her brother reached home safely . . . It had felt as if she had slapped him in the face.

He walked aimlessly up the steep hill, anxious to keep away from people, ignoring the ache in his leg.

He had just decided that it was time to turn for home when he heard the scream.

She was almost half-way up the steep hill that led to the Farleys' house when she heard a soft clip-clop behind her and turned.

The rag-and-bone man was just behind her.

Catherine's heart jolted painfully then settled into a racing roar. She moved back against the high Cornish hedge, hoping that he would not recognise her in the darkness. Her hair was neatly up again now but she could still feel his rough hands caressing it, feel the flakes of skin on his fingers catching and dragging at the silky strands.

The slow clip of the donkey's feet came nearer. She held her breath, willing them to carry on past her, but they slowed and stopped.

A Cornish voice which she thought she would hear in her nightmares for ever after asked hoarsely out of the darkness, "Anything I can do for 'ee, my dear?"

Catherine swallowed. "N-nothing."

She hoped that he would not recognise her voice from this afternoon but he immediately said, "Why, 'tes my little maid with the lovely hair. Changed your mind, 'ave 'ee?"

"No." Her voice was high with fright. "Go away. Leave me alone."

"Well, now." The cart creaked as he swung himself down from it. "I don't know as how I should leave a nice little maid like you to wander around all alone in the dark. I reckon as how I should come and see you safe home."

"No." The thought of being alone with the man was terrifying. "I don't need you. Go away."

"I think I should come and look after you."

"No." She backed against the hedge, breathless with fright. "If you come any closer, I'll scream."

"I don't know as how there'll be anyone to hear you all the way up here." He was almost on her now and the smell of his unwashed body made her want to gag.

She reached out, pushing him away with all her strength, recoiling at the greasy feel of his clothes, but he was too strong for her. He pressed nearer. "Want a tussle, do 'ee, my little maid? Well, I'm game."

His breath was hot and stinking on her face. Back against the hedge, hands braced against his chest, she turned her face from his approach and screamed.

It rang through the quiet night, echoing off the stones in the hedge, but the rag-and-bone man only laughed, pressing nearer.

There was no one to hear, Catherine thought, her heart sinking. She was alone, alone with this filthy brute of a man.

"Leave her alone." The voice, coming suddenly out of the darkness, made them both jump.

The rag-and-bone man released her, swiftly stepping back. "No problem. Only a bit of slap and tickle." He started to move towards the donkey, standing patiently in the shafts of the cart.

Catherine gave a cry of relief and ran towards the man standing silently in the darkness, his fair hair a light blur under the starry sky. "Please. Please will you stay with me? Until this person—"

"Here, maid." The rag-and-bone man had stopped, one hand on the reins, and was staring at her rescuer with shock in his face. "Here, maid." His voice was suddenly urgent. "You don't want to stay with him. Don't you know what he is? He's one of they Huns. You can't trust they. They go around raping nuns and eating babies and things, they do. You'll be better off with me. I won't hurt 'ee, I promise."

"Please." Catherine ignored the man and reached out to the German. I'm Robbie's sister. I met you just now." For a second her heart quailed. She knew he had been upset by her instinctive shrinking from him earlier, but he had a kind heart; he had shown that by looking after Robbie. Surely he would not leave her here with the peddler?

"If you wish me to remain with you I shall certainly do so." His voice was cold but he moved to interpose his body between the man and herself. "This lady does not wish you to remain. She wishes you to leave. Now."

The last word was like the crack of a whip. To Catherine's surprise the rag-and-bone man obeyed instantly. "Yes, sir. If you say so, sir." The evil-smelling cart creaked as he climbed on to the tail of it and for a second she was afraid that his weight, added to the steepness of the hill, would lift the tiny donkey off

66

its feet but it threw itself forward against the harness and the cart slowly began to move off up the hill.

Catherine turned to him, her knees trembling. "Thank you. Thank you so much. I was so afraid."

Gunter was staring after the cart. "He would probably not have hurt you. He is, I think, a known person in this place."

"No, not hurt perhaps," she said doubtfully, "but . . ." She remembered again the feel of his hand stroking the full length of her loose hair from head to hips and shuddered.

He was instantly concerned. "I shall accompany you home? You are cold?"

"No, I'm fine, but—" The thought of having him walk by her side was strangely comforting. But she did not want to go home yet. She could not be more than a few hundred yards from where she had dropped her paintings. "If you could just come a little further up the hill with me? I – dropped something this afternoon. Then – well, he will have gone by then and I shall be all right."

He bowed his strange foreign little bow. "But of course." He turned to accompany her up the hill and she heard again the halt in his step which seemed more noticeable now than when she had met him with Robbie. "Have you hurt your leg?"

There was a long pause then he said, "A wound from the war."

Catherine felt herself blushing in the darkness. Of course! How could she have been so gauche? This was the second time she had acted thoughtlessly towards him, as if she had been a child and not an educated young lady. Her father's constant refrain came to mind. "You're not a young lady now, you're a working-class girl." Was it true? Had she already slipped from the standards her mother had tried to inculcate into her, into the sort of person her father thought she should be, one who would be happy doing a menial job for a living? No, she vowed, she would *not* slip back into that sort of life; she would maintain her standards. Somehow.

She took a deep breath and turned to her companion. "I am sorry," she said simply. "I am sorry about the way I reacted when we met and for being tactless just now. I—" She floundered, trying to think of an explanation for her behaviour without mentioning her father. "I appreciate what you did for Robbie and for rescuing me now. Really, I want to assure you . . ."

Her voice trailed away but he seemed to understand. "You are not really a German hater? But I understand that already since you chose to stay with me rather than the man with the cart."

"Him!" Catherine shuddered again. "If you knew . . ." They had rounded a corner and even in the dark she recognised the place where she had dropped her paintings.

There was nothing there.

The relief that Robbie felt at finding Father had gone out when he returned was short-lived. He was back in less than ten minutes, angry as always, demanding to know where he had been, who he had talked to.

"N-no one," Robbie insisted. "I j-just walked." He knew from the Dorset days that his father hated him to have any friends and, while he had more sense than to mention Gunter to his father, he was determined to see him again, whatever Catherine said. Gunter was the first person he had known who seemed happy to talk to him.

Even going to bed without supper was no real punishment after the tea he had shared with Gunter. Robbie gave a pleased sigh and reached into his bedside cupboard for the Military Medal that Uncle Robert had won in the war. Father hated him to have it but Robbie took it whenever he could, comforted by the thought that Uncle Robert, his namesake, had been brave and perhaps, one day, he too could be a soldier and win medals.

It wasn't there.

For a few seconds he rummaged, disbelieving, before he began to notice other things that should have been there but weren't: the penknife with different blades that Mother had given him for Christmas, a silver-framed picture of her family when her brothers were his age.

Fury rushed through him. He leapt off the bed, his stockinged feet thudding on to the bare floor boards, and jerked at the door of the wardrobe. It opened with a protesting screech. His best coat, worn only to church, had disappeared too.

That loss wasn't important but it confirmed his suspicions. He marched, feet stamping, to his father's room and threw open the door.

"S-s-s-someone's stolen my th-th-things," he announced.

Walter looked up from the bed where he was lying. "I've told you before never to come in without knocking. And you're supposed to be in bed."

Robbie ignored him, his indignation too strong to bother about such trivialities. "S-s-s-someone's stolen all my important things," he repeated.

Walter rose from the bed. "Rubbish."

"It's t-t-true. Th-th—"

"I've got the medal. I've told you before not to take it. And as for the rest – I've sold them." Walter stretched. "Didn't Katy tell you that I'd got a job on a farm? There's a house thrown in but we have to furnish it. I sold all the things we don't need to get money for the furniture."

Robbie's eyes widened. "You sold m-m-my kn-kn-kn—" He was so upset the words just wouldn't come. To sell his knife, his last present from his dead mother, was an unimaginable betrayal. He stared at his father, mingled hate and disillusion in his eyes.

Walter loomed over him, his head seeming almost to touch the ceiling. "Stop stammering, you little runt. And don't look at me like that. I'm your da and I make the decisions around here. I've only sold what we don't need. I'm a working man now, and as a working man's son you don't need that fancy coat your ma wasted her money on, or a silver picture frame. And if I find you with Robert's medal again I'll whip you, understand?" His voice hardened. "You're no more than an overgrown baby. You'll never be the man your uncle Robert was."

This complaint was old hat to Robbie but another, dreadful thought suddenly struck him. He hurtled out of Walter's room, slamming the door behind him, his feet thudding as he flung open Catherine's door.

He dragged open the wardrobe, stared at the virtually empty rails. The smart coat that she had worn this afternoon was gone, and her best hat. He scrabbled under the bed and pulled out the trunk where she kept the treasures she thought he didn't know about. The silver napkin ring that had been their mother's had gone, and her small supply of novels and—

Robbie sat back on his heels and breathed an awed, "Golly!"

Walter had even sold Catherine's paints and brushes.

Eight

"I cannot help you."

The old man was as thin and desiccated as a dried twig, holding himself with the kind of unnatural uprightness that suggested arthritis in the spine. Just looking at him made Random aware that in the months since his own injuries he had lost some of the stance of a professional soldier.

"Surely you have some idea of where your daughter is living?" he suggested.

"I have no daughter." The old man's hands shook on the walking stick he was holding in front of him. "I lost her the day she married that – person." Random had a suspicion that a coarser epithet had trembled for a moment on the bloodless lips.

"Perhaps another member of your family . . ." he suggested delicately. He could not leave the trail here. Harrison's wife – widow? – had left the address the captain had given him at about the time Random himself had been attacked. About the time her husband had been presumed dead. A grieving widow trying to make a new start? Or a woman trying to shield her husband from a capital charge?

This decaying manor house was the only address he had been able to pry from her one-time neighbours. That Miss Tranter of Coombeside had married beneath her and was living in a workman's cottage had probably been the talk of most of the county. Her disappearance, with her children, was of little importance beside that fact.

Now he had to deal with this old man, who was trying to keep up appearances because, Random guessed, there was nothing else to live for. The house was Georgian but it was decaying rapidly, the gardens unkempt, the paint peeling. It was a house that should have rung with the sound of children playing cricket on the lawn, running up the stairs, but it was silent.

70

Now Mr Tranter raised his head painfully, pride evident in every twisted sinew. "I have no family. Now."

Now. The word was a death knell to hope. Random asked quietly, "The war?"

"All three." He blinked and Random could not tell whether it was the watery eyes of old age or the tears of lost hope that he blinked away. "There is no one left to answer your question. I had four children. Four. And they are all lost to me."

What could he say? Random rose to his feet. "I'm sorry. I hope that my meeting has not revived old hurts."

"Old pride, rather. Except where *she* is concerned." The voice was bitter. Was it just the fact that the only daughter had married beneath her, Random wondered, or was it that she had married at all? Had she been groomed as a prop for her parents in their old age, deprived of her own life to look after them? Had it been that prospect that had driven her into the arms of a man she should never have met?

The old man rose unsteadily with him, then limped over and picked up a photograph. Three young men laughed in the sunlight, their bodies straight and true. Tranter sighed.

"The best." He stood, if anything, even straighter as he said it. "We gave the best." He glanced at Random's stick, the black patch that covered his ruined eye. "And you too?"

"The war," Random confirmed briefly. In essence that was true.

The old man sighed again. "The best. But it was worth it. This country – it will get back to what it was. It will be great again, a land fit for heroes as they said."

Would it? wondered Random as he shook hands and left. Or had all the heroes been lost already in the mud and the trenches? Was it only the wrecks like him or the rotters like the man who had attacked him who would inherit the bare bones of a land deprived of all its best? A whole generation, gone. What country could lose a generation and survive unscathed?

His quest, too, was over. The woman had vanished from sight. Widow or deserter's wife, she was beyond his reach. Remembering the old man and his coldness Random was half thankful that he did not have to risk bringing more pain to her.

"Sir."

The whisper came from behind a low bush. Walking round, he

71

saw an elderly lady. The indication that she had been gardening, suggested by the trug basket and secateurs in her hands, was contradicted by her lack of a hat, her breathlessness.

He came round to her, pulling off his own hat. "Mrs Tranter?"

She nodded, glancing warily back at the house as she pulled him further into the screen of bushes. "You want my daughter?"

Hope sprang again. "You know where she is?"

She shook her head, one tear running down the withered cheek, slow as despair. "She's dead."

He sighed. "You mean that she was cut off from the family when she married Richard Harrison."

She stared at him. "Not Richard, it was—" She stopped, her faded eyes staring at him as she must have stared at her beaux when she was a young girl. "Silly me. Of course his name *was* Richard – Richard and Robert, two brothers – but when he came to work here we already had a gardener called Richard so he was always called Walter, his second name, and it stuck. Everyone always thought of him as Walter after that."

Random breathed deeply. It all helped. To ask after a Richard Harrison when he was known as Walter would have been fatal.

The word reminded him of her original comment. "You said your daughter was dead," he prompted her.

She nodded. "Dead. I had a letter from Catherine, my grand-daughter, only a week ago." Another tear trickled slowly down. "My only granddaughter." A glance at the house, once lovely, now rotting and decrepit. "*He* doesn't know. He doesn't know that I ever saw Elizabeth – but I did. Even though he forbade me."

"And you know where your granddaughter is now?"

She shook her head. "Not now." A sigh. "Those poor children. I" – she glanced at him – "if you find them—"

"Yes?"

"While *he's* alive . . ." Again the glance at the house. A domestic tyrant, Random decided, and wondered whether the boys had wanted to join up or if they were glad to get away from the old man.

Mrs Tranter cleared her throat. "When he's gone – I'll do what I can for them then. And in my will, of course. I have a little money of my own. Not much, but – you'll tell them that, won't you? Let them know that they are not forgotten."

The request embarrassed him. How could he get the children's father arrested, imprisoned, possibly shot, and then pose as a bringer of good news? But on the other hand, it gave him an excuse to find the family in a way which would mean that if Harrison was not the man he sought there would be no embarrassment involved.

"I will tell them. But if you had a letter . . . there must have been an address?"

"No address. I think perhaps she was afraid that we might think she was asking for help. The envelope was postmarked Dorchester but that will not help you. They are no longer there. She said that they were moving on."

"Moving on? Where?"

The old woman sighed. "She didn't say."

"Your grandchildren. How old are they?"

"Catherine is seventeen, I think – almost a young lady now – and her brother would be younger, eleven or twelve I should think."

The girl at least was old enough to work if necessary, perhaps marry now that men were being released from the army, though there would not be enough husbands to go round.

The thought reminded Random of himself and Jenny. Abruptly, he asked, "If I find them, do you want me to write with their address?"

"No, dear, not while—" Again the glance at the house. "But tell them, won't you. Let them know that I haven't forgotten them." She squeezed his hand. "It was so kind of the dear child to write."

So kind. He thought of the words as he limped down the drive. She had the social grace to write to her grandmother to tell her of the mother's death but omitted to tell her where they were planning to move. Possibly she was a proud girl, kind but unwilling to be seen to be asking for help. Or perhaps . . .

Perhaps she had been trained like that. A man who had deserted would have to cut his links with everyone who might have known him in the past. Random's good eye gleamed. More and more it looked as if Harrison was the man he was after. And he was hunting him down.

Of course, Dorchester was a big place, but there would be neighbours. The children would have gone to school, the mother would have a death certificate.

73

His stick hammered into the dry earth with a new ferocity as he limped down the lane. He was coming. He would find Richard Walter Harrison yet.

"All my paints and brushes. Everything."

Catherine sank on to the bed, her face white. She felt sick with disappointment and frustration. But what did it really matter? If she had no talent, as Mrs Farley had said, if her paintings were no better than daubs, then there was no point in keeping the brushes anyway.

"It wasn't m-m-my fault." Robbie leaned against her, peering nervously into her face. "He did-did it while we were out."

"I know, sweetheart." She held his eleven-year-old body against hers for comfort. Her whole future, gone, just like that. She was seventeen and she was condemned for ever to the sort of life her mother had so wanted her to avoid.

She turned and hammered her fist into the thin pillow with all her force, time and again, venting all her anger and frustration.

Today had been a dreadful day. Mrs Farley, the loss of her paintings, the strange rag-and-bone man, the loss of her painting equipment, the news about the fish-canning factory . . .

She knew why Father had done it. He wanted to turn her into a working girl; he wanted her to stop dreaming of bettering herself, of teaching or painting or wearing nice clothes. He had found himself the job on the farm and he had found work for her too, work that would drag her down to his level. Her heart twisted at the thought.

She lay back on the bed, staring up at the ceiling with unseeing eyes. All her life she had been brought up to obey her parents without question; now she was at a crossroads.

If she obeyed her father, all hope of the future her mother had planned for her was over. She would be condemned to a life of drudgery, and Robbie – she turned to look at him as he sat, pale-faced, beside her – what would happen to him?

She had to find a way out – for both their sakes.

Nine

"Can I help you, sir?"

The man's smile was open and enthusiastic but Gunter knew that this would change as soon as he himself spoke. He was growing accustomed to the way friendliness changed to suspicion as soon as people heard his German accent.

"I wish to hire some workers." It would have been amusing to see the change in the man's face if it didn't happen every time he spoke. But then, he had known what he was letting himself in for when he decided to make his future in England. The looks he would get in Germany, from people who knew about Matilde, would be far more difficult to handle.

"You're – er, you are – not English?" Suspicion and amazement chased each other across the man's face as he attempted to hang on to the welcoming smile with which a possible employer should be greeted.

Gunter sighed. "I am a German," he stated flatly. "I was a prisoner of war in your country. I have inherited a small manufactory in this area which has been closed during the war and now I wish to work it. My papers are in order."

"A manu – a *factory*?" The man looked amazed – as well he might. Except for the mine chimneys that stitched the skyline to the hills, Cornwall was a rural haven. It was difficult to imagine that anything could be manufactured here.

"It is very small," Gunter explained. "Almost a workshop only. It will print silk."

"And the workforce that used to run this factory?"

Gunter shrugged. "Much was done by my grandparents. Of the others – who knows? I would welcome them back if any could be found, but I think that perhaps they are all dead or old."

"Well . . ." Gunter could tell by the look on the man's face that he did not hold out much hope. "We're not much into printing silk

75

and suchlike down here. Farming and fishing are more our line, though if you want a shop-girl—"

"I do not want a shop-girl," Gunter said patiently. "I will sell my cloth to other people to sell in shops. I require a dyer, a block carver, men who can print, boys who will assist them."

The man rubbed his chin. "See, there's no call for that sort of skill down here."

"But it must be possible," Gunter said passionately. "My grandparents – they found these skills only five years ago. Why, now, is it so impossible?"

"Well, see" – the young man looked embarrassed – "it was the war."

Gunter believed in facing trouble head-on. "You mean that because I am a German no one will work with me?"

"I reckon you've just about got that right," the young man agreed.

Catherine paused outside the peeling door of the building, her heart pounding.

Normally, she would have worn her best clothes, just to give herself some confidence, but she no longer had that option. Instead she had brushed and brushed her long hair until it shone, then coiled it high in an intricate knot. Mother had always said it was her best feature.

Could she persuade Gunter to offer her a job? He had been kind to her last night, but only in the way that an older man would be kind to a frightened schoolgirl. When she remembered the way she had clung to him, trembling, just because of the rag-and-bone man, she felt her face flame with embarrassment. But he was the only person she knew who might possibly employ her and anything was better than going to work in a fish-canning factory.

She swallowed the lump in her throat and rapped loudly on the door, then pushed it open.

"Hello?" There was no response but from somewhere up above light flooded down a steep, narrow staircase.

Intrigued, she began to climb and gasped as she reached the floor above. It consisted of a single long room. The windows lining the opposite wall had all been enlarged, so that the summer sun flooded the room with golden light, lying in broad bands across the long table that filled all one side of the room.

The brightness dazzled her eyes and it was several seconds before she could make out the dark figure, slumped in a chair at the far end with his head in his hands. He looked so unhappy and alone that she was embarrassed at intruding on him.

"I – I'm sorry." Catherine hesitated at the top of the stairs. "I did call out, but . . ."

Gunter raised his head, then swiftly rose to his feet with the meticulous politeness that she remembered from last night. "It is I who should apologise. I did not listen you."

"Hear me," she corrected, smiling.

"I did not hear you," he repeated, but there was no answering smile on his face. "I hope that all was well when you reached home last night."

The question almost made her laugh. Well? When her painting equipment and her best clothes had all been sold and she had been told that her future was to be in a fish cannery? She dared not answer the question in case she burst out with a childish list of complaints, so instead she replied tentatively, "I hope I have not come at an awkward time."

He sighed. "The time is as good as any. I was just" – he waved a hand around the sunlit room – "looking at the ruin of my dreams."

He too! "But why?" she burst out impulsively, then, blushing scarlet, "I – I'm sorry. I didn't mean to be inquisitive."

"It is of no importance. It is that I am unable to get people to work for me, so—" He shrugged. "I must find something else to do, go somewhere else."

"Back to Germany?"

"No!" It came out explosively, making her jump. "Never shall I go back to Germany. This is my homeland, now, this and no other." He stabbed the table emphatically with his forefinger.

Catherine leaned forward, her heart thumping. "But there's me!" she exclaimed. "I will work for you. If – if you wouldn't object," she ended shyly.

He looked, his eyes blue under lowered brows. "You? But what can you do?"

His voice was cold and she felt herself quail. "Well, I could . . ." Her mind raced. "I can paint," she said.

He snorted, half amused, half exasperated. "I too can paint. It is what I have been trained in. That and in printing. I do not need another painter."

"What do you need then?" She fought to keep the disappointment out of her voice. "Perhaps there is something I could do."

He leaned towards her. "Can you carve wood blocks so that the colours of the patterns can be laid exactly, one over the other, where they should be? Can you use a heavy hammer, hour after hour, to get the printed blocks exactly right? Can you mix dyes or bleach the raw silk cloth? Because that is what I need. People who will do that. And I have no one."

Her heart sank. She did not know how to do any of the things he had mentioned. "Is – is it very difficult to learn how to do these things?"

He turned away with a sigh. "Most I could teach people if they are willing but others . . ." He leaned heavily on the long table, looking out of the bright windows at the tumbling roofs, falling away below him to the sunlit sea. "A carver of wood blocks is an essential. It is a skill which my grandfather had and which I, alas, do not, though I can design the blocks easily enough. And the wooden block is the centre of all that I am planning. All!"

"If I found you a carver," Catherine said nervously, "if I did that, would you give me a job? I can learn and I work hard."

He turned round, and she could no longer see his face, just his silhouette, black against the window. His broad shoulders seemed to block out the light from the centre panes.

"Why?" he demanded. "Why should you want to come here to work?"

Catherine's mouth opened. For a second she was tempted to say that she was fascinated by the craft of silk printing, that she wanted to be involved with something artistic, but when the words came out they were nothing but the brutal truth.

"It's that or work in a fish factory."

Even admitting that someone thought it was the type of work she should do made her face flame. When Father had told her last night that he had the job for her she had been speechless with anger and disappointment. All her education, all the efforts her mother had made to ensure that she was brought up like a lady – and she had come to this. A fish factory.

"A fish factory?" She thought that for a moment she caught a quiver of laughter in his voice. "You do not look like a girl who would do such work."

"I should hope not," she replied indignantly.

He moved forward, away from the window. "Very well. If you can get me a carver of sufficient skill then I will give you a job."

She was breathless with delight. "Thank you. Oh, thank you."

Gunter opened his mouth to warn her of the difficulties but she was already gone, clattering down the echoing wooden stairs like a child.

And that was all she was, he decided, remembering the way she had clung to him last evening when he had rescued her from the rag-and-bone man. A lovely child who had still to make the elusive step across to womanhood. How different from Matilde.

It was difficult to imagine Matilde as a child. She had been the sort of person who had been born a woman, practising her seductions in the cradle. Despite his best intentions, her image was suddenly before him, her dark hair a scented cloud, her voluptuous figure an open invitation to pleasure.

Pleasure, yes; but not only for him. Set against that betrayal, the bankruptcy of his father's factory and his death were pinpricks; Matilde's death only a relief.

He could not go back.

He could not go back to face the knowing glances, the winks, the subdued laughter behind his back. When he had found out he had sought death. Nearly found it too. Even when the Englishman had held the gun to his head he had rejoiced that the pain in his heart, so much worse than the pain in his wounded leg, would soon be over.

Only the intervention of the officer had condemned him to this life. Well, he would live it if he had to, but he would live it where he chose. In England he saw fear and hatred in the faces of the people he met, but even that was far better than seeing derision and amusement.

He stood, running his hand over the long table. It had been specially made, he knew, to take the full width of a roll of silk and was unusually strong and stable so that it would not move under the constant hammering it received as the printers beat on the blocks with wooden hammers to drive the colours deep into the material.

Each colour was printed with a separate carved block of plywood and had to be positioned accurately or the pattern would not register correctly. In its heyday, he knew, there would have been four or five men, moving slowly down the long table, each accompanied by a boy with a trolley who painted a pad with a mixture of dye and gum arabic from which the printer would colour his block. The room would have resounded to the dull thuds as they drove the pattern deep into the silk.

But he would never see that. Grandfather had come over before the war, taking his English-born wife back to her roots to die. He had sensed, too, that the anti-Semitism that underlay so much of German life was growing and he wanted a refuge where he could be happy.

He had been happy, Gunter knew. For a short year. He had built this tiny factory, minute in comparison with the German factory that his son-in-law owned; he had produced his first patterned silks.

Then, in a few short months, the idyll had come to an end. Grandmother had died, the war had broken out and although Grandfather had not been interned, out of respect for his age and grief, he had been forced to leave the area. Coastal waters, where German submarines might patrol within easy reach of a signal from the shore, were barred to all aliens.

Now he too was dead. Only Gunter was left. And of the two factories that should have been his inheritance, the one in Germany was sold to a competitor to recover the debts and he could not find anyone to work this one for him, tiny though it was.

He strode about the long room, his shadow limping black on the wooden floor. It was the carver who was the important person. He could design blocks himself, he could teach people the other work, but a carver . . .

He knew what he wanted. Not the formal flowers of yesterday, pretty but old-fashioned. He wanted to design for the future; bold, bright fabrics that captured the romantic spirit of this county. He had grown up hearing the legends of King Arthur on his grandmother's knee, had dreamed of Launcelot and Guinevere. Now that he had seen the county with its towering cliffs and moors yellow with gorse, he had not been disappointed. He wanted to trumpet its beauty to the world, capture it in the very clothes that people wore.

80

And no one would work for him.

For a second he remembered the girl, her slim body poised for flight even as she blurted out her ridiculous request, her slender neck and delicate features overwhelmed by the mass of chestnut hair. She would be a beauty one day, he decided – when she had found her true self. As yet she was only a child, with a child's faith that anything was possible. Get people to work for him, indeed!

For the first time that day a smile of genuine amusement lit up Gunter's face, then he sighed and limped his way over to the stairs. He had spent all his time recently preparing the building to print silks – time which was probably wasted. If he couldn't get the factory working again, he knew that he would have to move away. Perhaps he could go to Paris. He had enjoyed Paris before the war and in a big city like that, he knew that he would meet with less prejudice than in small villages.

Today, he decided, looking out at the brilliant sun and the silver-edged ripples on the calm sea, today he would devote himself to pleasure.

Throwing bread and sausages into a small bag, he locked up the door and left.

Ten

" **A** nd don't come back!"
As Catherine stumbled down the stairs the door slammed behind her, shaking dust from the rafters on to her hat.

That was the third time. She dusted herself down, admitting ruefully that she had been altogether too sanguine about her ability to find a man who could carve the blocks for Gunter. It had seemed so easy. Carpenters worked with wood, didn't they? And there must be one at least who enjoyed carving rather than the more mundane side of carpentry. It had never occurred to her that self-employed men would consider it to be an insult to be asked to work for someone else, or that, in large firms, the manager would not take kindly to someone trying to poach his trained staff.

She had never got as far as broaching the delicate subject of working for a German; long before she could have brought the subject up she was being shown the door – with various degrees of force.

She sighed, easing her foot out of its shoe. She had walked a long way today, her feet were aching and there was not a sign that she would ever find a carpenter who would carve Gunter's blocks.

But she had to find someone, she told herself. If she could get work with him then at least she would be with someone who was artistic, who was doing something creative. She had been impressed by the easy way he had said that he could design blocks – as if such a skill was of no great moment.

There must be other carpenters around, she knew, but the thought of facing the kind of reception she had already had three times today made her hesitate. Even if she found someone, would he be willing to work for a German? When she remembered her father's outpourings on the subject she doubted it.

She had to find someone. The thought of spending her youth working in a fish-canning factory sickened her.

Wearily, she dragged her shoe back on to her aching foot and set off towards the next carpenter's shop.

"You could have th-thought about me!" Robbie complained. "Father was out all day and I didn't dare leave here. Not without s-someone else."

"I'm sorry, love. But I had to see Gunter. He" – her voice became husky – "he offered me a job – if I can find someone who can carve the blocks he needs to print the material." Her eyes shone. "He's an artist too, you know. He says he can design printing blocks – just like that."

"So why's he employing you?" Robbie demanded. "You can't do anything except p-paint and teach a bit."

"I can do all sorts of things," she protested. "Anyway, perhaps" – her voice dropped – "perhaps he'll teach me to design blocks. Or, at any rate, let me borrow his paints and things." She leaned back on the bed, gazing up at the cracked ceiling. "He's probably a *real* artist."

Robbie stared at her disgustedly. "You're lying," he stated flatly.

Catherine sat up, her face flaming. "I am not! I never lie."

"Y-yes you do. You lie all the time to yourself."

"To myself?" Catherine stared at him. "Don't be stupid. How can a person lie to themselves?"

"Y-you do," Robbie insisted. He kicked moodily at the end of the bed. "Y-you think just because I can't read and write properly and keep stammering that I'm stupid, but I'm *not*! I'm cleverer than you are even if I c-can't paint. And I can tell when you lie to yourself."

"But I don't!" she almost wailed.

"Y-you lie," he insisted. "You lie about Father, and now you're lying about Gunter. And I saw him first," he added with total illogicality.

Anger flooded through her. How dare he deny her right to Gunter? She was the one who had gone to him for a job, she was the one who had been entrusted to find a carver for him.

She swung her feet off the bed, ignoring their throbbing as she forced them back into her shoes. "I'm not going to stay around to listen to this." Grabbing her hat she skewered it to her piled-up hair with long hat-pins. "I'm going to find a carver if it kills me."

She marched down the stairs, ignoring his shout of, "Let me come too!" She swept past Mrs Penrose, the landlady, without a word and the woman's muttered, "Hoity-toity," was lost in the slamming of the door.

She stormed past the legless soldier selling wooden toys on the corner without a glance, even though she usually had a polite smile for him, and set off down the hill as fast as she could walk.

She had no intention of visiting any more carpenters today. Her feet were too sore and her feelings too battered by the rebuffs she had already suffered but she was too angry to stay any longer in the same house as Robbie. How dare he say she lied to herself? What could he mean by it? It was stupid, not worth thinking about.

And the subjects – Father, Gunter – how could she lie to herself about these things? Robbie was stupid. Everyone knew that. Despite all the help she and Mother had given him, he still wrote half his letters back to front and he spelled as badly as a six-year-old. He was stupid and he was wrong and—

She heard the noise behind her – boyish shouts and cries, a man's voice raised in warning and anger – and her heart thumped.

Robbie. He must have followed her out of the house.

Holding her hat on with one hand she turned and raced back up the street, unaware now of her throbbing feet.

It was all her fault. She knew that the boys were picking on him. She should not have left him alone all morning. She should not have run out of the house and left him.

The mêlée was larger this time. She recognised some of the boys she had chased off once before and realised that somewhere in the centre was Robbie. She caught the occasional glimpse of his startling red hair through the press of taller figures. She gritted her teeth. How dare they pick on someone smaller and younger than themselves? With a furious cry she hurled herself into the fray.

There was so much shouting and pushing going on that she found herself battered and swept back again, on to the outskirts. But Robbie was in there somewhere and it was all her fault. She set her teeth and, pulling a hat-pin from her hat, she lowered her head and bored her way into the centre of things, her progress marked by sharper cries from some of the fighters as she used the pin to help clear the way.

The men all seemed to be around the outside of the fight; the centre was all boys – a heaving mass of arms and legs. Catherine saw some black hair and made a grab at it. As far as she was concerned the fight was Robbie and herself versus the rest.

A flailing arm caught her and knocked her back into a boy behind. She levered herself off him with her elbows, ignoring the shout of pain, and threw herself back into the action, her pin at the ready.

There was a cry of pain which made her smile grimly, then she was suddenly plucked into the air by a strong arm. For a second she dangled helplessly, then she was dropped, sprawling on hands and knees against the foot of the chair from which the old soldier sold his wares.

The shock rocked the man back and his tray of wooden animals went flying. Catherine suddenly found herself caught in a shower of small, hard objects. For a second she could only lie still, catching her breath, preparing for the fray again, but already the noise was dying down. The shouts had dropped to scolding, the cries to embarrassed mumblings. Turning her head slightly she could see that the battle had come to an end as suddenly as it seemed to have started.

She glanced further up. Robbie was there. Unhurt, thank heavens, though a strong-looking man was holding him and another boy apart, one in each hand, and giving them both a good talking-to. That was unfair, Catherine knew. Robbie would never have started it.

She was about to push herself to her feet and tell the man that it was not his fault when she saw another body she recognised. Horrified, she twisted further.

Standing at the edge of the crowd was Gunter, taller than the more thickset Cornish men around him, his fair hair a beacon in the golden light. Hastily she ducked her head, praying that he hadn't seen her. To be caught rowing in the street like an urchin – he would despise her for ever as an ill-mannered child and she could not bear that.

The crowd was thinning rapidly. Soon she would have no

protection from his bright blue eyes. Trying to keep one eye
on the German, Catherine began to crawl further around the
chair on which the legless soldier was seated – and something
hard and knobbly splintered under her hand.

"Oh!" A new embarrassment overcame her. "I'm so sorry." Her
face flamed. Not only had she acted like a child and a hoyden but
she had just destroyed the man's wares on the sale of which he
depended.

She raised embarrassed eyes – and met laughing green ones
twinkling down at her. "Don't you worry about that, my beauty."
The rich Cornish voice trembled with laughter. "I don't reckon I
seen such a good fight since Chalky White had a bust-up with
Nipper over whose turn it was to boil the tea."

She cast another look over her shoulder but the crowd had
dispersed, taking Gunter with it. She breathed a sigh of relief
and rose to her feet, pushing her hat-pin back into position with
shaking hands. "Those boys attacked my brother." She felt she
had to justify herself.

"Young varmints. And it idn't the first time, either. I saw 'em
the other day. Give him a bloody nose they did. I shouted but
there idn't much as how I can do."

"No. Of course not." Catherine was horrified lest he should
think she was criticising him. "Only, I was afraid . . ."

He laughed again. "Don't you worry about the little lad. Game
as a fighting cock, he is. And it won't last. Did the same when I
was a lad. Any stranger, you see what he's made of – after that
you're all friends, happy as puppies in a nest."

"But meanwhile he can't go outside with out being picked on."
Catherine glanced down at the small wooden cow she had found
under her hand. One of the legs was cracked across and a horn
was missing. "I'm so sorry." She bent, scrabbling around under
the chair to retrieve the other animals she had knocked to the
ground.

There was a whole farmyard of them: cows, pigs, chickens
and horses, even, amazingly, an elephant. Each seemed to have
a character of its own. The bull pawed the ground, head lowered,
about to charge; the pig had a smug look on its face, as if it had
just been fed very well and the goat, head on one side, seemed
to be considering what mischief to get up to next.

She smiled at it as she handed it back, amused by its sheer

vitality. "These are wonderful. I'm so sorry that I broke the cow."

"And I told 'ee not to worry, maid. They cost me nothing but a bit of whittling and I do enjoy that as much as anything these days."

She had been about to turn away but this brought her round again, her heart thumping with excitement. "You – you made these yourself?" She looked again at the beautifully carved animals he was arranging on his tray.

"No one else, maid. There's not a lot a man like me can do with his time, after Jerry shot my legs clean away from under me."

The words died on Catherine's lips. The Germans had ruined this man's life and health. How could she ask him if he would work for a German? But if she didn't . . .

She swallowed hard. "I – I suppose, I mean, you must hate them now. After what they did to you."

He shrugged, intent on arranging the animals on the tray around his neck. "Well, I don't know as how I holds it against them specially. I were doing the same to them, weren't I? And a brem good shot I were until I copped it. Besides, I don't reckon they're any different to what we are."

His green eyes stared far away, into another time, another country, when he was a young man with two legs and a future. "One Christmas – it were the first Christmas of the war – we was in the trench and we heard a shout from the enemy lines. Just about a hundred yards apart we were then. 'Hey, Johnny.' That was what they called us, see, like we called them Jerry," he explained to Catherine.

"And?"

"Well, they wanted some Christmas presents, didn't they? Things to send home to the kids. So we come out and did a swap."

Her eyes were round with astonishment. "You gave them your guns?"

He snorted. "You're brem soft, maid. What would be the point in that? Use them to kill you with the next day, they would. Besides, the officers would have come down on us like a ton of bricks if we'd done that. You could be shot for getting rid of your rifle in the face of the enemy."

He grinned at her, his green eyes alight. "What we swapped

87

was bits of uniform, stuff people at home had knitted and sent out, knives, stuff like that." His grin broadened. "I swapped a knife for a helmet. Two days later I was on sentry-go and saw this bloke crawling towards us through the mud. Just about to shoot 'un, I were, when I recognised my friend Jerry."

"What did you do?"

"Well, he whispered that there were a surprise visit by some big-wig general and he'd get into trouble if he didn't have his helmet, so I give it back to him." He laughed. "Couldn't get the poor blighter into trouble, could I? To tell you the truth, I thought it were a con, that he'd just thought up a story to get his helmet back, but I thought he deserved something for crawling through to us like that so I gave it him. And you know what?

"The very next day there was a shout out of the darkness – 'Catch, Johnny' – and that helmet come flying out of the darkness like some gert ball. Laugh? I nearly wet myself. Begging your pardon, miss."

Catherine was enthralled. She had never heard stories like this before. On a very few occasions her father would mention the Germans but he spoke only of their cruelty and viciousness, never stories like this. "So you *don't* hate them?"

"Gerry? Well, not specially. That there German were more trustworthy than some of the men I fought alongside of. Steal the teeth out of your mouth, some of them would." He glanced up at her. "You any special reason for asking, maid? Because it seems to me that you're brem concerned about what I think of they people."

She crossed her fingers behind her back, her heart thumping so hard that she thought it would choke her. "It's just that – I know a German man who might have a job for you."

"No."

Catherine gaped at her father. "But – why not? I'd rather work there than in a fish-canning factory." She had smelled the place as she passed it in Newlyn; the smell had been repulsive, even from the street.

"You don't know nothing about it." Already her father's accent was indistinguishable to her ears from the accent she heard every day in the street. "It could be all be a sham. The man might be a crook. He'll use you for a few days or weeks and then, when you want pay, he'll be off and you won't see a penny of your earnings."

"He is genuine," Catherine insisted. "His grandfather had the factory before him and—"

"I don't care if his great-grandad had it. You don't know nothing about him."

"He is genuine," Catherine repeated.

Walter stared at her, his eyes suspicious. "You seem brem set on working with him. Sweet on him, are you?"

Catherine's face flamed. "No. Of course not."

"Well." She could see that he didn't trust her. His cheek was twitching again, something that had almost stopped this last week. "I aren't going to let you get involved with no fly-by-night. Nor I aren't going to let you be seduced by some man who'll leave you in the lurch."

As Catherine opened her mouth to protest that Gunter wasn't like that he added, "I'd better come and see him for myself, I reckon."

"What?" She had never thought of that. Her mind raced. Once Father knew that Gunter was German she would never be allowed to work with him. "That's not necessary." She tried to sound more confident. "I assure you—"

"Yes, well, I'm not certain how much your assurances are worth. I mean to say—" Walter leaned back in his chair and stared at her – "you've had a brem silly upbringing until now. If I had my way you'd have been in service since you were fourteen, but your ma wouldn't have anything to do with that. This is your first job and, as your da, I reckon I should go along and see what sort of place you're going to be working in."

She made one last attempt. "You haven't been to the fish factory to check, have you?"

"My friend Nabbo's girl works there so I reckon I know all I need to know about that place." Walter sat up straighter. "So come on, maid, what's it going to be? The fish factory or this new place?"

Catherine knew when she was beaten. She stared at her hands, the fingers entwined in an anguished knot.

"The fish factory," she whispered.

Eleven

"I think I have found you a carver."

Gunter Steiner jumped at the sudden voice from the doorway. Catherine had the ability to move as silently as a shadow.

"A carver?" His heart leapt.

"You may not think him suitable," Catherine warned. She moved further into the room. Now that she was no longer a silhouette against the light Gunter could see that she was paler than he remembered. There were dark shadows under her eyes and a small frown that indicated that she probably had a headache.

The contrast between the tired, subdued woman in front of him and the boisterous girl he had caught a glimpse of yesterday, fighting like a tigress to save Robbie, caught at his heart. He climbed to his feet. "Are you well? Forgive me, but . . ."

She shrugged. "I am all right." Even her voice was different from yesterday. She sounded defeated. But why, when she had achieved what she had set out to do? He had been so cynically certain that she had been like Matilde, only using a different scheme to hunt him down. He could not understand why; he had no money now, no inheritance, but – he was an outsider. Some women liked outsiders – or losers; they liked to rescue people. Remembering the way she had set upon Robbie's attackers yesterday he wondered if this was the reason.

Gunter turned away again. "What is the problem with the carver?" He might be no good – no one knew better than Gunter how much skill was involved in carving the wooden blocks for printing material, one for each colour of the dye, which had to line up exactly with the other blocks if the colours were to register correctly. Or she might not have told the man that he would be working for a German.

Catherine gulped. At times like this, wearing her drab school-girl skirt and with her old-fashioned hairstyle, he found it hard to see any resemblance to Matilde in her.

"He hasn't got any legs." The words came out so quickly that he had to replay them in his head to make sense of them.

"No legs?" He raised his brows. "Is he then—"

"He's an ex-soldier." Then, earnestly, "I did tell him about you – that you were a German, I mean – and he doesn't mind. The only thing is" – again the gulp – "you have to go to Penzance to see him as he can't come here." She glanced around the building. "He won't be able to go upstairs, I am afraid."

"I shall have to see him first, see what his work is like, before I agree to anything."

Catherine nodded, turned away. "You will find him at the bottom of the street where we are living."

He had expected her to claim her job here but she said nothing. She pushed open the door, was stepping through . . .

He had not made the offer in any seriousness. He had never thought that she would be able to find him a carver. He wanted nothing to do with young women – any young women – and if she had asked about the job he would have tried to put her off, but – just going like this . . .

He found himself hurrying after her, ignoring the sharp pain in his leg at the extra strain. "If he is suitable, do you wish to work with me?"

She turned again, standing in the doorway against the bright light outside, so that he could not see her face, and when she spoke her voice was the cold, controlled voice that he always associated with upper-class English women.

"No thank you, Herr Steiner. I have had another offer in the meantime which I shall take up."

Then she turned and was gone.

Blöde Kuh! An epithet he had never used for any woman except Matilde exploded from him. To turn him down like that! With never a "thank you" or a proper explanation. For a second he felt so angry at the cavalier dismissal of his offer that he was tempted to ignore her suggestion of the carver; then reason reasserted itself.

He had always prided himself on his common sense – and he needed a carver. Besides, he was pleased that he did not have to

offer her the job. He found her child-woman mixture of behaviour
oddly attractive, so different from Matilde's sophistication. It was
better that he had nothing more to do with her.

Really it was.

Robbie saw Gunter talking to the legless soldier and skidded to
a halt. "Wh-what are you doing here?"

Gunter smiled at him, the friendly smile that made him feel
wanted and safe. "I have asked Mr Pentyr to come to work with
me. And he has agreed – and his daughter, too, will come. That
means that I am having the core of my factory."

"That means you'll stay here." Robbie's face lit up. "Can I come
and help, Gunter? I won't get in the way, I p-promise."

Mr Pentyr snorted. "I seen you around, young 'un. The day
you don't get in the way'll be the day they screw down your
coffin lid, I reckon."

"Aw!"

Robbie's mouth opened in a wail but Mr Pentyr stopped him
with a gesture. His eyes were focussed on something behind
Robbie's shoulder. It gave Robbie a second's warning before
Walter's voice broke in sharply. "Robbie! Who're you talking to?"

Robbie jumped as if he had been kicked unexpectedly in the
behind. He was stammering his excuses even before he had turned
round. "N-n-no one, Father. J-j-j-just the man who sells toys."

"You've no time for that." Walter was looking furious. "You
can come with us. We're going to get furniture for the new
house."

Robbie was suddenly aware of Catherine standing beside
Walter. Her face was white and drawn, as it had been ever
since she found her paints had been sold, but now she looked
terrified as well, her eyes fixed desperately on Gunter.

Walter glanced at Robbie, at Gunter, at Catherine, and Robbie
saw his face harden. "And who's this other person you're
talking to?"

If he ever found out that Gunter was a German . . .

Robbie saw Catherine open her mouth and broke in quickly.
She was hopeless at lying, hopeless at knowing when other people
were lying too. "D-d-don't know, Father. He was j-j-j-j—"

Nerves made his stammer worse than ever but he had done what he set out to do. "Oh, shut up and come on," Walter said crossly. Taking Catherine's arm he set off towards the town centre, and Robbie, pausing only to make a warning face at Gunter, hurried after them.

Inwardly, he was feeling happy. Gunter was going to start up the factory and that meant that he would stay in Newlyn.

Robbie had a friend at last.

Random wiped the sweat from his face.

The pain was worse today, worse than it had even been before. He could feel time running out on him. Six months, the doctor had said, but for how many of those would he be able to continue his search?

The woman he was talking to eyed him solicitously. "Would you like to come in and sit down, sir? You look – tired."

"It's just the heat." He stuffed the handkerchief back in his pocket, adjusted his weight on his silver-topped stick. "So you cannot help me find Catherine Harrison?"

"I think Miss Rose was the only one who might have known where they were going. Catherine was very friendly with her." She paused. "We were very sad when Catherine left so suddenly, without saying goodbye. She was a lovely girl – and so talented."

"I have already tried Miss Rose. She seems to be away."

The teacher shrugged. "I can't help you there, I'm afraid."

He had to move forward. Time was so short, so horribly short. "Catherine and her brother went with their father, I believe?"

She looked puzzled. "I don't think so. He was never mentioned. I had assumed he was dead." She glanced at his eye patch, looked away again. "So many tragedies in the war – it's no good dwelling on them. That is what we decided. If the children wish to talk, of course, we do our best but" – a smile – "Catherine was nicely brought up. She would not dream of talking about her personal problems in public."

"So – no father." Was he on the wrong track after all? Another spasm of pain hit him and he felt the sweat break out on his forehead again.

She looked puzzled, then laughed suddenly. "There was an uncle, I believe. I remember Doctor Thompson saying that he met him unexpectedly the day Mrs Harrison had her accident.

He said it gave him a surprise but, after all, so many men are coming back from the army now. It is natural for them to look up their families after all this time."

But Mrs Harrison's brothers were dead – and Walter Harrison's only brother had also been killed in the war.

Even through the pain, Random could feel the sudden exhilaration. He was on the right track. He shifted his weight on his stick and fumbled for his card.

"Here is my card. If you could ask Miss Rose to write to me when she returns . . ."

She gazed wide-eyed at his full title, complete with all his war honours. "Of course, Mr Random. I shall be delighted."

As he limped away Random smiled grimly. She would be inventing a romantic tale, he knew. Within a day it would be all round the village. An Honourable had been looking for Catherine Harrison. He could guess at the stories they would come up with. She might be his daughter, his heir, his love. He didn't care.

They would invent a happy story and that would mean that he would definitely get a letter when Miss Rose returned.

He winced at a sharper-than-ever stab of pain.

He hoped she would come back soon.

Twelve

As always when she left the fish-canning factory, Catherine was struck by the light.

Even after more than a month in Cornwall she still could not believe how lucid the air was. The views and the air here almost made up for all the horrors of her working life; the grinding boredom of the work, the constant smell of fish, the Cornish girls with whom she had nothing in common and whose accents were almost incomprehensible. If it hadn't been for the improvement in Robbie over the last few weeks she did not know how she could have borne it.

Today, there was a magic in the light which transformed Newlyn harbour from its normal workaday self into something dreamlike. For once, she did not hurry home to the constant work that awaited her there but leaned on the rails alongside the blue-jerseyed fishermen, staring at the ripples that shattered the boats' reflections into a wild mosaic.

If only she could paint like that, capturing on the stillness of dull canvas the constant movement of water under a clear sky. She concentrated on the colours. At first glance the ripples seemed like silver but that was wrong. They were actually grey with a hint of the colour of the sky. She watched as the images fragmented and reformed, as the reflection of a swooping gull was kaleidoscoped into a hundred pieces of scintillating white.

Across the harbour she could see a small group of people sitting around easels, all concentrating. She knew who they were. Stanhope Forbes was the founder of the Newlyn school of painting and even now he attracted artists from all over England who came to learn at his classes. They were all ages, some of them young women no older than she was.

Catherine stifled a feeling of envy. She could never be a part of that life now. She was caught in the everlasting exhausting tedium of the working woman: at the factory all day; cooking and cleaning, fetching water and filling lamps all evening. All her education – wasted; all her hopes for the future, gone. She would labour like this, for little money and no respect, from now until the day she died.

Besides, her paintings were daubs. She sighed heavily. There were times when she wondered if the criticism was correct; if, perhaps, her paintings did have some merit. Miss Rose had thought so. Miss Rose had taken one to her artist friend.

Catherine rubbed her throbbing temples. She had still received no letter from Miss Rose though she had twice walked into Penzance to ask, ignoring the knowing smiles of the clerks who probably thought she had a secret lover. Catherine could think of only one reason why she hadn't written.

The artist's opinion had been similar to Mrs Farley's. Her work was too bad for comment.

Her heart heavy, Catherine dragged her eyes away from the fortunate group and set off unwillingly on her next errand. Gunter's factory.

If only she could have worked there. Robbie spent every moment he could in the place, lying to Father that he was spending his school holidays on the beach or the moors, quite alone. Even Father, who seemed happier when Robbie wasn't around, was beginning to get suspicious.

Catherine knew that if Robbie did not get home tonight before their father returned from the farm there would be trouble, and there was no chance that he would leave early of his own accord.

After a month she could no longer smell the stench of fish that clung to her clothes and body but she knew that she must move in a noxious cloud. To appear before Gunter looking like this, her hands torn and cut, dry and red from cold water and dead fish, with the smell of what she did each day branding her as a working woman of the lowest sort – her whole soul revolted at the thought.

But she had to collect Robbie. He was looking better than he had looked for years, his formerly pale face now pink and smiling as a child's should be. Even his stammer was better – as long as Father wasn't around. Catherine knew that she couldn't let him slip back again, as he surely would if

Father found out that he was spending his time with a German.

She squared her shoulders and set off on the short walk to the factory. From the outside it looked even worse than when she had first seen it. The paint was still peeling from the doors, but now there were anti-German slogans scored into the wood as well. It wasn't only her father who still hated Germans, Catherine thought sadly as she pushed open the door and stepped into a different world.

All the shutters had been thrown back and light flooded in from the yard outside. There were voices everywhere. Robbie had told her that Gunter had found workers and she could see that it was true. Most of the men were obviously old soldiers. In an area like the far west of Cornwall where most jobs involved farming, fishing or mining, a man with only one limb was unlikely to find work and would have to eke out a living selling matches. Here, in an enclosed environment, he could easily handle the work.

"Can I help you, my handsome?" A high-coloured woman came in, wiping her hands on the apron that covered her full body.

"I'm looking for Robbie."

The woman gestured with her head. "Up in the print room, helping out as a wiper."

Aware that the overwhelming aroma of fish must be filling the room, Catherine climbed swiftly. Here, in the bright sunlight, three men worked on the long table that stretched down the length of the room in front of the windows. Now its wood was covered with a long calico cloth and pinned to it was a length of heavy silk, dyed pale green.

Even as she looked one of the men carefully positioned a block of wood on to the silk then hammered it with a mallet. It was lifted carefully and he turned to recolour the block from a pad on the trolley beside him before turning back to the silk again. Immediately, the young man behind him spread more dye on to the pad with a brush and Catherine realised with a shock that the serious young man was none other than her brother.

Seeing him here she could appreciate how much he had changed in the last few weeks, growing and filling out. In him now she could see the young man he would one day become rather than the child he had once been. Pride filled her. How Mother would have loved to see him like this: steady, concentrated. Then he glanced up and saw her and his face split into the urchin grin she knew so well. He hadn't completely changed.

She moved over to him, her footsteps muffled by the constant thud of the mallets on the wooden blocks. "I've come to take you away, Robbie. You must be home before Father tonight."

"But I'm working."

His seriousness made her lips twitch but she had to insist. "He's been fussing about you being out so much, Robbie. You don't want him to start trying to find out where you spend your time." Her voice was calm but inside she was nervous. She wanted to get Robbie out of here as swiftly as possible. She did not want Gunter to see her looking like this, her clothes and hair stinking of fish.

"Well." Robbie paused to apply more dye to the pad from which the printer replenished his block. "If I can get someone to take over."

"Have a break, lad." The printer stretched, then, seeing Catherine's fascinated glance at the silk, offered, "Want to see how it's done?"

She knew she should go but she couldn't resist it. "Please." She moved over to the table. The printer Robbie was servicing was producing the finishing touches to the pattern. To his left, the material was fully printed, the entire surface covered with a pattern of greens and blues on a pale green background. As her eye became accustomed she could see that it was a picture of a stormy sea, not drawn as an artist would have represented it but capturing the basic elements: a surge of waves, a boat heeling over, dolphins half hidden – all stylised but somehow alive.

To the printer's right was the material still awaiting his block's completion of the pattern. Here the material looked duller, lacking the finer details which his block impressed on the material. Fascinated, she moved down the table.

The first printer was working on the plain dyed silk, carefully positioning the block, but with just one colour printed the pattern was meaningless.

With her artist's eye she could see that even a slight misalignment would spoil the pattern. "How do you know where to put the block?"

He grinned, showing her the bottom of his block. From each

corner a small pin stuck out a fraction of an inch from the raised part of the block which was covered with felt to hold the dye. "They mark the silk, see, but 'tis covered by the pattern. The other printers set their block so they exactly match the marks I've set in."

He had only one eye. Did it help, she wondered? She was about to ask when she heard Robbie shout, "Gunter!"

"No, Robbie." She didn't want him to see her looking like this, her hands rough and red, her hair and clothes stinking of fish, but already she could hear footsteps on the stairs. She swallowed, angry with herself for being so worried about meeting him. What did it matter what he thought of her, anyway?

He appeared at the top of the stairs, his fair hair gleaming in the evening sunlight that filled the room, then stopped abruptly. Catherine was suddenly aware that she had stopped breathing. She forced herself to move, hoping that the shame she felt at appearing like this did not show in her face.

"I've come to take Robbie back. My father is getting concerned about him being out so much."

"I would not wish that Robbie should anger his father in anything." He smiled at the boy. "You go home with your sister now. I can take your place as a wiper."

Before he spoke Catherine's only wish had been to get away from the small printing works as soon as possible, taking the smell of fish with her; now she felt annoyed that Gunter should seem to be dismissing her without a glance after the heartache it had taken her to even enter the place.

Moving boldly to the table she said loudly, "I like the pattern."

"You, perhaps, but there is no one else who does." He sounded gloomy but moved to stand beside her, staring down at the completed pattern.

"No one? But it's so – fresh."

"Yes," he said soberly. "To you, with your young eyes, it is fresh. But to the shopkeepers I have shown it to the pattern is strange. 'Why not stripes?' they say, 'Why not flowers?' As if we in the last century are. Huh."

The deterioration in his English made Catherine realise how upset he must be. It was an achievement to have got the factory working at all, handicapped as he was in the aftermath of a

99

dreadful war by his German nationality, but to produce the silk and not be able to sell it . . .

It felt disloyal to her own countrymen but she made herself say it. "Could it be – is it because you are a German?"

He hammered one fist into the palm of his hand. "Foolish I am! I never thought." Then he stared at her. "You think – even in a commercial matter—"

"I don't know," she said wearily. There was so much hatred around, yet he was doing a good job here, employing men who had been fighting against him until recently and who were considered unemployable by their fellow citizens.

The unfairness of it angered her. "How many shops have you been to?"

"Only three. After that I felt . . ."

She nodded. Gunter must have felt the way she did when Mrs Farley described her paintings as daubs. But—She looked at the silk again. It was a *good* pattern, she could see that. She could imagine the way it would look as the soft material moved and draped. It was unjust that all Gunter's hard work should be wasted. And if he could not sell the silk, what would happen to the men he employed? To Robbie?

It felt like presumption, but she had to make the offer. "May I try to sell it? I—" She glanced at him, at the blue eyes which could seem so remote at times. "I am English, at least. That may help. And if I clean myself up" – she blushed – "get rid of the smell—"

"Smell?" He stared at her.

Her face grew hotter but she made herself meet his eyes. "You must be aware, Herr Steiner," she said formally, "that I have been recently employed in a fish-canning factory."

"I knew from Robbie, but" – again the smile that could turn her knees to water and a deprecating lift of the shoulders – "I suffered from the influenza last year and since then I smell nothing."

"You don't?" Ridiculously, happiness flooded through her. The worst thing of all was imagining how he must have been standing beside her, trying not to gag at the smell of her clothes. "Then let me try to sell your silk. I am only young, but . . ."

"But you may have better luck than I." He held out his hand. "We will be in a partnership, young lady."

His fingers burned her. She saw the smile in his eyes and

realised that he knew exactly how she was feeling. He probably saw her as no more than a child, she decided, scarcely older that Robbie, but she would show him. She would sell that silk if she had to stand in Market Jew Street draped in the stuff.

Miss Rose looked at the card Random offered her and bobbed a swift curtsy. "It is an honour to meet you."

"Please." He was a soldier. He hated the whole system of deference as practised by civilians and had only used the card with his title on because it was the surest way he knew of ensuring he was notified of Miss Rose's return. Every Englishman loves a lord, he thought, his lip curling in derision.

"I'm sure I have no idea why you should want to see me." Miss Rose peered at him through thick spectacles. He had expected her, perhaps because of her name, to be small and prim but she was tall and angular, with no beauty, but a certain intelligence.

"I am trying to trace an ex-pupil of yours, Catherine Harrison. Her grandmother wants me to give her a message." He was grateful that he had such a convenient excuse.

Miss Rose obviously knew the family's background. "Her grandmother!" Behind her thick glasses her eyes grew even larger. "It would be so good if she could help the poor child." She glanced around the small sitting-room into which she had shown Random. "She just went away, you know, without telling me where. I was hurt, really hurt. I had thought that Catherine liked me. I would have thought that she would turn to me after her mother died; I thought I was her friend."

In her voice Random could hear the bitterness of frustrated motherhood. Poor Miss Rose. One of the class that was brought up to be a wife and mother but without the looks or, he suspected, looking around at the furniture, the money to catch a husband. And the girl she had set her heart on had deserted her.

"So you don't know where she went?" He paused as a stab of pain ran through him. They were getting worse now, and more frequent. When he shaved he could see the greyness of death under the pallor of his skin. How long before he would have to give up this hunt? Miss Rose had taken so long to write to him that he had almost given up hope.

"I found a letter when I returned from London." The thin, ugly face broke into a sweet smile that illuminated the room and almost took his breath away. "She is in Penzance. Though why she didn't tell me – why she should want to go away at all . . ."

"She gave no explanation in her letter?"

"None. Though, of course, as an artist I can see why she would want to go to Penzance."

"But – is Penzance a place for artists?" He would have thought London would be better. Didn't artists live in Soho or Bayswater or somewhere and drink in low dives with anarchists?

Miss Rose's eyes grew larger still. "The Newlyn school of artists, my dear sir, and the St Ives school. Stanhope Forbes. Lamorna Birch. Augustus Farley. Norman Garstin. A. J. Munnings. George Grantham. Laura Knight." She reeled the names off without stopping for breath and with an almost religious awe in her voice.

The names meant nothing to Random, who doubted if he could recognise any painting other than the *Stag at Bay*. "They – they're well known, are they?"

"My dear sir!" Words failed her and she stared at him with pursed lips, her ugly face disapproving. "They comprise possibly the most important movement in modern art today. And it was a movement that Catherine was especially interested in as she was such a wonderful landscape artist. Farley was always her favourite but she admired them all."

This was what he wanted to know. "So you have her address?" Please, dear God, please.

"Not her actual address. She said that they were not settled yet and asked me to send the letter poste restante to Penzance Post Office." She shook her head. "All this is so unlike dear Catherine. Normally she is the most well-organised and considerate person. It sounds almost as if she is at the beck and call of another person but, as far as I know, she has no other relatives except for her grandparents, and you are here on their behalf."

At last. The information he wanted. Random leaned back in the chair and closed his eyes in relief. *Walter Harrison, I am on your trail. At last.*

He became aware that Miss Rose was still talking. "The poor child must be so worried. She would have expected to hear within a week and it has been over a month now."

He leaned forward. "A month since she wrote to you from Cornwall?" Would they still be there?

"She asked for some comments about her painting." She smiled at him. "I took one of her paintings to a friend of mine for an expert opinion. When you nurture an artist it is sometimes difficult to decide quite how good they are." She laughed coyly. "I am afraid, Mr Random, that I fancied a little dissipation after all the troubles of the war – though you, of course" – she glanced apologetically at the eye patch that covered his ruined eye – "will know more of that than I."

Would she never get on? Now that he had the information, he wanted to leave immediately. Time was short, so short. "Was the opinion good?"

"Better than I could have hoped." She clasped her strong, bony hands together. "She is young, of course, and has had no training but what I could give her. She needs proper training: Paris, perhaps, if she could afford it. 'A possible new major talent' my friend said. I wrote immediately, of course, but I directed the letter to her old address and it must have missed her. It wasn't until I arrived here that I discovered she had left."

"You have written to her now?" He had to go. He could be in Cornwall tomorrow. While his voice made polite responses to her his mind was planning ahead.

"I wrote three days ago. I posted it at the same time as I wrote to you."

His heart leapt painfully. "Did you tell her I was looking for her?" If Harrison had found out they would be away from the area by now and he would have lost the trail.

She hesitated, glancing at him, "I'm afraid I didn't." She looked embarrassed. "I didn't know anything about you, you see. And one hears so many strange things. If I had found you not – respectable—"

Random forced a smile. "I hope I have convinced you of my respectability."

They had been given no warning that he was looking for them. He had them – as long as they hadn't moved on already. But he was a month behind them; the trail was growing cold. As if to remind him of how short time was another spasm of pain shot through him before sinking back to a steady ache.

He could not stay any longer. Time was even more important now. He was still weary from his long journey from Scotland but he dared not rest. He had to get to Cornwall.

He still didn't have an address but he knew the area they

were in. Surely he could find the man. Walter Harrison was a Yorkshireman. He would stick out like a sore thumb in Cornwall.

Random felt his confidence grow. He would find his quarry. He knew he would.

Thirteen

"Are you sure that I look all right?"

For the twentieth time that afternoon Catherine wished that Father had not sold her best clothes. Dressed in a good coat and her best hat with flowers around the brim she would have felt far more confident about entering the smart shops that lined the Terrace, the raised section that ran down one side of Market Jew Street, the main shopping street in Penzance.

"You look very well," Gunter said shortly, shifting the roll of printed silk from one arm to the other. "Besides, it is not you that they should be looking at but the silk."

That, Catherine thought crossly, was typical of a man. As if she wasn't representing him in some way. Still, she had done the best she could. She had collected extra buckets of water yesterday, carrying them bumping against her legs from the pump down the lane to the cottage, then heated the water and washed herself and her hair until she was certain that no lingering trace of fish remained. With her better skirt on and with gloves covering the ruins of her hands, she looked, if not like a young lady, then at least respectable.

Probably it was a good thing she couldn't wear her best hat, she decided, as an errant breeze caught at her. With its wide brim it would have been difficult to manage in the tricky breeze and a strong tug might have pulled all her newly washed hair down around her shoulders.

She paused at the top of Market Jew Street. By the domed Market House, used as a meat market, the statue of Sir Humphrey Davy stared impressively down the street. Catherine swallowed nervously. Now that the moment had come she did not want to have to enter any of the shops, their crowded windows filled with dresses and corsets.

"Which shops have you already been in?" Her voice sounded thin and young in her own ears.

105

Gunter indicated the shop to her left. "I started at the top and visited the first three."

That meant that she would have to start in the very smartest shop of all. Catherine could feel her knees shaking but she dared not linger. Father had mentioned that he intended coming into town today. He believed she had gone to work as usual. If he saw her here with Gunter . . . She felt sick at the very thought.

"Very well." She opened her arms and received the heavy roll from him. "I'll start there." Without any further hesitation she marked towards the shop and through its door.

"Yes, madam?"

The lady in the black dress looked down her small, round nose at Catherine, indicating, as well as she could without the advantage of an aquiline nose, that Catherine was lowering the tone of the shop.

Catherine did not care. At seventeen she was still young enough to relish her recent transition from "miss" to "madam" and the word gave her courage. "I want to see the manager," she said boldly.

"The manager?" Thick eyebrows rose. "I am afraid that our manager does not condescend to see just anybody."

The strange thing was, Catherine decided, that if she had been in a similar situation trying to sell her paintings she would have shrivelled into a small ball under the woman's gaze. Now, she merely said defiantly, "I am not just anybody. I have here the very best of modern printed silk which a shop like yours will be eager to sell."

"You are a – *salesperson*?" The woman made it sound as if it were an insult.

"Like you," Catherine agreed amiably.

"In *our* shop!" The woman seemed almost apoplectic.

Catherine knew that she would never be able to afford to shop in here herself so she had nothing to lose. "Waiting to see your manager," she reminded the woman politely.

The woman drew herself up to her full height and Catherine noticed that she was still several inches shorter than herself. "Mr Tremayne," the woman announced, "does not see *representatives.*"

"Then I will see the person who does." Catherine sat down in one of the spindly chairs arranged by the mahogany and brass counter for the refreshment of favoured customers and balanced the roll of silk across her knees. It almost completely blocked the front of the counter.

There was a ting from the brass door bell as a customer entered the shop. The woman gave the newcomer a frantic look, stared at Catherine, and made up her mind. "I will be with you directly, madam," she called to the new customer, then, coldly, to Catherine, "Come this way, miss."

Gathering her awkward bundle in her arms, Catherine followed her through the door into the dark recess at the back of the shop.

"They didn't want it either."

Catherine wiped a weary hand across her face. She had been sure that the only reason Gunter had been turned down was because he was a German, but she had not made a sale either.

He said nothing, standing straight and silent beside her, the roll of silk which he had taken from her held in his arms. His face held the cold, closed-in look which had so frightened her when she had first seen it, though now she recognised it for what it was: an attempt to hide his emotions.

Catherine could guess what emotion he was trying to hide. It must be heartbreaking to work so hard, to produce material, only to fail to sell it. She wondered how long he could continue before his money ran out, before all the men who worked for him would lose their jobs.

"It might be me," she admitted. "I – I don't look very much like the sort of person who would sell high quality silk." She glanced down at herself. Despite all her efforts nothing could disguise the fact that she was only seventeen, that her clothes were the sensible, drab clothes of a schoolgirl, not quite as long as those of an adult. She would have been promoted to that honour when she had gone to college . . . She jerked her thoughts away.

"I have told you already that there is nothing wrong with the way you look," Gunter began, then stopped abruptly. A large woman pushed her magnificently corseted bust between them, separating them, while Catherine fought to hide the sudden burst of pleasure she felt at even so temperate a compliment.

As they came together again in the woman's wake, Catherine said comfortingly, "I think that part of the trouble is that the buyers can't see how the silk can be used. They all say, 'Why not stripes?' or 'Flower prints sell well.' And they said the silk was too heavy for blouses."

"Blouses! It is for dresses that the silk is made. Not for blouses," Gunter erupted.

"I – I don't think that people down here wear that sort of dress." Catherine eyed the bustling crowds around her. Almost to a woman they wore the long dark skirts that their mothers or grandmothers might have worn in Victorian times. She had even seen one elderly lady wearing a strange head-dress of white cotton, elaborately goffered, the sort of which Catherine thought had died out fifty years ago.

"Then they should. Are they still living in the last century?" Gunter began, then stopped as Catherine gasped. "What is the matter?"

"My father." She could see him standing at the top of the Terrace. Had he seen her? If he met Gunter . . . Her heart thudded at the thought of how he would react, how rude he would be. Father would certainly stop Robbie going to the factory if he ever found out and Catherine had rejoiced in the improvement in Robbie since they had arrived in Cornwall. It had been the one bright spot in the aching darkness of her life.

Now she acted quickly. "Go away," she hissed. "My father mustn't see you."

Gunter's worried face cleared. "Ah, I understand now. Robbie has told me—"

Catherine cast a swift glance over her shoulder. Father was coming, marching down the Terrace with long strides. "Just go." She would have pushed Gunter away but she did not want to make it appear that there was any connection between the two of them. "Hurry."

"But I am not afraid—"

Walter was almost upon them. "I am." She snapped the words. "Go now. For my sake. With no goodbyes."

For a second he hesitated while she tried not to scream with impatience, then with a swift bow he was gone, striding swiftly down the street. Catherine closed her eyes briefly in relief but she could not relax yet. Although Walter seemed to have recovered from his neurasthenia he still had the nervous habit she had become so accustomed to in Dorset of interrogating them whenever they came home about who they had spoken to and what they had done. Robbie always lied these days but Catherine was incurably honest – she knew she was a poor liar. Now, however, it had to be done, for Robbie's sake.

She leaned on the railing for a second, outwardly admiring the busy road scene, golden in the strangely clear evening light, while her mind was busy planning. Even so, she jumped nervously when Walter tapped her on the shoulder. "Who was that man I saw you with?"

She shrugged. "A stranger. He asked about shops for women." Try as she might she could never lie as convincingly as Robbie.

Walter frowned at her, his dark brows almost shading his eyes. "Have you got a follower, miss?"

A follower! As if she were some fourteen-year-old kitchen maid. Catherine raised her chin, her green eyes hostile. "I would never have a 'follower', as you call it. And it is possible to speak to a man without having any ulterior motive."

Her genuine disdain carried the conviction her earlier words had not and he turned away. "No need to snap like that. I was only looking after your interests. It's just that . . ." He paused uncertainly, something he seldom did. "You say the man was a stranger?"

"He was not Cornish, at any rate." Catherine knew that when you were a poor liar it was best to tell the truth whenever possible.

"He looked familiar somehow." Walter stood silently, lost in thought, then shook himself as if he were a dog, throwing off the strange mood. "I'm going to see my friends in the Star." He pointed at the old inn across the road, then turned back, suspicion in his eyes. "What are you doing here, anyway? Why aren't you at work?"

Catherine swallowed. She had played truant today, spending the morning with Gunter learning the technicalities of silk printing so that she could answer questions from buyers. "The fish factory closed early and I wanted some . . ." Her imagination faltered as it always did when she had to lie. Luckily, his mind made up what she could not.

"Feminine gewgaws, I suppose. Well, miss" – he waved a finger in her face – "don't you go wasting any money on those damn paints and things. I won't have it. And don't go talking to people. You keep yourself to yourself, do you hear?"

"I hear." She paused. "I am going home soon, anyway."

As he moved away she sagged with relief. There was no sign of Gunter, but she dared not go to look for him.

Why does Father worry so much about us speaking to people? Catherine wondered as she turned to go. Did he really think that she was such a catch that she needed him to fight off her suitors? As if anyone would ever marry her, with her thin body, especially now, stuck as she was between two worlds. Even if she was buxom and well rounded she would have trouble attracting a suitor. She was too well spoken and educated to appeal to the workmen with whom she would otherwise have mixed – and what educated man would marry a girl who worked in a fish factory?

It was unfair of him to expect her not to speak to people when he had new friends that he mixed with. Suddenly, Catherine was angry. She had been on the verge of having so much and had lost it all because of her father, while he seemed to have made himself a new life, a life far better than the one he had had in Dorset. Yet he expected her to work all day and then come home and cook and clean for himself and Robbie while he went out and enjoyed himself.

The anger was like a force rushing through her. She could feel it fizzing through her veins, pounding in her head.

It was unfair – and if there was one thing she hated in life it was unfairness. She would fight on Robbie's behalf against unfairness, and even for Gunter, so why didn't she fight for herself?

Abruptly, she turned around. She would go to the post office to see if Miss Rose had written. Even if the artist to whom Miss Rose had shown her work agreed with Mrs Farley it would not matter. She had accepted her lack of talent now; she was ready to move on.

She had given in to her father long enough. She was a woman now. She had a right to make her own decisions.

It was early but there were already a few of Walter's friends clustered around the bar.

He took a deep breath and strolled over to Nabbo. "You!" It was the strange Cornish greeting which for weeks he had had trouble acknowledging before he had finally realised that no response was required.

Nabbo glanced up from his pint. "Let you off the treadmill, have they?" He grinned at Walter, moving over so that he could take the seat at the end of the bar. Walter hid the smile. Already he was the acknowledged leader of the little group that met in here on Friday evenings. He always pretended not to recognise the small signs of deference that they showed him but inwardly he felt his soul expand with pleasure.

After two years of hell; two years of trembling whenever anyone walked past the isolated cottage, of looking out of the window only after dark, in case anyone should see him, it was wonderful to be able to share the company of men again.

The terror had subsided. Walter knew that with every week that passed he was safer. None of the men now thought of him as a stranger. He had a job, a family, friends. He could satisfy any casual enquirer about himself – and with the memories of the war receding fast, who would make anything more than a casual enquiry?

But that man with Catherine – his face had seemed somehow familiar.

Walter ordered a beer and tried to forget the face. He had been here a month now; there must be a lot of men whose faces he had caught a glimpse of. But Catherine had said the man was a stranger. A shiver went down his spine.

A stranger with a familiar face.

That could only mean danger.

The letter burned in Catherine's hand as the Penzance crowds streamed past her, talking of cattle prices and scandal, of hats and chickens.

The final decision against which there was no appeal. She almost wished that she had not gone to the post office after all, had not disobeyed her father and written to Miss Rose. She could have continued hoping that Mrs Farley was wrong, that she did have talent, but once she opened this letter . . .

Coward, she told herself. She stuck a finger under the flap and ripped it violently open. She must know the truth. The truth was always better, wasn't it? And Miss Rose was her friend; she

111

would never lie to Catherine, however much she knew the truth might hurt.

Evening was drawing in and the light was fading. Catherine stood motionless in the middle of the pavement, unaware of the bodies that barged into her as they tried to pass. The elegant script blurred before her eyes.

"My dearest Catherine, I must apologise for not contacting you before but . . ."

"Get out of the way, girl." A fat farmer with a red face and gaiters pushed her sharply aside but Catherine did not notice. Her eyes were glued to the paper. "Nathaniel is very impressed by your work. He has shown the painting I sent him to his agent . . ." Catherine realised that she had stopped breathing. His agent! "And he would be interested in other paintings of yours. In the mean time I enclose a letter from him to . . ."

Catherine turned the page and the enclosed letter fell to the ground. She scrabbled for it among the hurrying feet, not noticing the kicks and buffets she received.

She straightened, gazing at the page in rapture, the words blurring before her eyes. Augustus Farley! He had written her an introduction to Augustus Farley! Another impatient pedestrian sent her stumbling against the granite wall of the post office and she clutched at it gratefully as a bulwark against the reeling of this wonderful, wonderful world.

Augustus Farley! She tore her eyes away from the scrawled envelope and back to Miss Rose's letter. "Take your paintings with you when you visit him with the letter so that he can see for himself what your work is like."

Take her paintings! Her mouth opened in a disappointed "O". But she didn't have any paintings! Her mind went back to the ones Father had made her burn, to the others, so carefully preserved and hidden away at the bottom of the trunk. All gone! She had nothing to show him, nothing.

A fat woman stood on her toes but she scarcely noticed. The pain in her foot was so much less than the pain in her mind.

This was the chance that she had worked for all her life and she could not take advantage of it. She had no pictures, nothing!

She had been offered a chance of heaven – and she couldn't take it.

*　　*　　*

112

Robbie crept through the garden, an eye open for possible gardeners or dogs.

He worked hard at the factory every day, doing any and every job that Gunter entrusted to him, but today neither Gunter nor Catherine were around and his eleven-year-old sense of adventure had prodded him into action.

It was too early for there to be any blackberries but surely, up that tree, there were the first signs of apples?

Robbie glanced around the garden. It was big and, like so many these days, splendidly overgrown except for the lawn and a small patch near the kitchen where someone was fighting a valiant battle against weeds and slugs. The tree was surrounded by long grass and Robbie was sure that, even if there were people indoors, he could worm his way undercover like an Indian and get to the tree.

He jammed his cap more securely over his bright curls and set off. There were slugs in the grass, which he didn't mind much, and stinging nettles which he did, but it only took a few minutes before he had reached the tree and was shinning up it, scraping his bare legs and covering his shorts with green.

There were apples. He grinned delightedly. They were small but he did not care. He grabbed those he could reach, stuffing them into the pockets of his shorts. He cast a swift glance at the house but there was no movement from it. He reached out, stretching for one extra large apple that was almost out of reach, and—

"You, there. Boy!"

The shout from behind him startled him and he lost his grip. There was a moment of heart-wrenching fear as he felt himself slip then, bang, bump, he ricocheted off two lower branches and landed with a jolt on a pocketful of hard apples.

"Ow!"

"I'll 'ow' you, you young heathen. What did you think you were doing, eh? Stealing my apples like this." A hard finger and thumb caught him by the ear and dragged him upright.

"N-not stealing, sir. Just s-s-scrumping a bit." Stealing sounded awfully bad. Stealing sounded as if the police might be called. Robbie's heart sank at the thought of what his father would do to him if the police came round.

"Scrumping is stealing." Held almost off his feet by the grip on his ear, Robbie could only see his captor out of the corner of one eye but he got an impression of implacable decision. "You're coming along with me, young man."

The man was tall and angry. He pulled Robbie along so that his feet only just reached the floor as he stumbled alongside ear first, into the house. He dragged him into a large room, shut the door.

"Well?" he demanded, releasing Robbie's ear and settling himself behind a large desk.

Robbie felt as if his ear would never be the same again but he dared not rub it in front of this angry man. Instead, he poked at the patterned carpet with his heavy boots. "It was only a f-f-few app-les," he insisted sulkily.

"Let me see them." The man held out his hand and Robbie dug into his pockets, holding out his finds. Now that he looked at them coldly they were very small and very green and – he could feel the bruises on his hips ripening already – very hard.

The man leaned across his desk to look at them and seemed to share his opinion. "Hardly worth going to prison for, are they?"

Prison! Robbie gulped. "No, sir." He could feel himself shaking. It was almost a relief that Mother had died. She would never have forgiven him for letting the family down like this. Never.

The man looked at him. He was balding under his hat but his eyebrows were thick and bushy. "No. I don't think they are worth going to prison for either."

It took a few seconds for the words to sink in. "Y-you're not going to call the p-p-police?" Strangely, Robbie found that he was shaking harder at this news, not less.

"I think not. But it doesn't mean that you're not going to be punished, young man."

Any punishment would be as nothing compared to being arrested by the police. Besides, big though the man was, Robbie doubted if he would hit harder than Father. There was almost enjoyment in the way Father took off his belt at Robbie's slightest misdemeanour. Robbie raised his eyes to the man's face. "No, sir."

"No, indeed. And I believe in making the punishment fit the crime, so . . ." He paused, and Robbie wriggled awkwardly under his gaze. "So, young man, you will stand there until you have eaten all the apples that you have picked off my tree. Do you understand?"

For a moment Robbie thought that it was a joke and he stared at the man open-mouthed. Then he glanced down again at the apples and he began to wonder. They were so very green and very small.

"I am waiting." The man was unsmiling. "You will not go until every last apple that you picked has been eaten." He pushed one across the desk towards Robbie. "Start with that one."

Robbie took it in his hand. He looked again at the face in front of him but there was no mercy there. Slowly, unwillingly, he bit into the apple.

It was so hard that he thought his teeth would break and so sour that his mouth twisted up inside. Left to himself he would have spat it out at once but when he caught the man's eye he shook his head. "Eat. Unless you would prefer that I call the police."

He ate. Every mouthful was a purgatory in itself and he had a horrible feeling that eating the apples wasn't going to be the end of it. These apples were going to continue the punishment for the next day at least. He thought of the spider-ridden privy at the end of their unkempt garden and shuddered.

"Eat."

He ate. Apple after apple. He hated every mouthful. He would never eat another apple again as long as he lived, he vowed, as he bit and chewed in a mouth which was screwed up by the bitterness of the fruit. He would certainly never steal another apple.

One to go. One apple. The biggest. The one he had just reached for when the man had shouted at him. He looked at it. He looked at the man. His stomach churned.

"I think that's enough." The man reached forward and shied the apple into the waste-paper basket. It landed with a dead clunk at odds with its small size and Robbie breathed a sigh of relief.

"Thank you, sir. I – I'm very sorry. I p-p-promise I'll never steal your apples again."

"No, I don't think you will." He leaned back in his chair and to Robbie's astonishment began to laugh. His shoulders shook as he guffawed loudly. "I don't think you'll ever eat another apple as long as you live."

Despite the growing discomfort in his stomach Robbie could only stare at him helplessly.

The man was lying back in his big chair, tears of laughter rolling down his cheeks. He was mad, Robbie decided, completely crazy. He raised his eyes to heaven in exasperation at the peculiarities of grown-ups, trying to distract himself from his stomach by staring at the pictures which crowded on every wall.

Through the griping pain which was beginning to double him up he wondered, vaguely, why one of them seemed somehow familiar.

Fourteen

G unter hefted the roll of silk in his arms. It was heavy, but not as heavy as his heart.

Catherine had been right. The buyers he spoke to all seemed incapable of imagining the silk made up into the type of clothes he had intended it for. That was not a surprise, he admitted, looking at the women around him. Few of them had any style and the ones that did were older and invariably dressed in the styles of their youth.

Couldn't they see that times were changing? It was 1919 not 1910. He could feel the way things were going. New fashions didn't happen by chance, they evolved. Fashions had changed during the war because conditions had altered. There had been no money, no material, no time. Women had adopted a new role as workers and the fashions had reflected it. Skirts had grown shorter to enable them to work in factories, delivering the post, acting as policewomen – all types of work which they would not have considered before the outbreak of the war. The full skirts of the Edwardian era had narrowed because of the cost and the fact that factories were too busy turning out uniforms to make material for women. The materials they did produce were dull coloured because with so many people in mourning it was unseemly to flaunt bright colours, and besides, dull, dark colours were more harder-wearing, required less looking after – a vital consideration for women deprived of their maids.

Things would change now. Women had the vote in Britain – provided they were over thirty. They would not give up the freedoms they had experienced during the war. Indeed, they would have the time and money to enjoy them – and their clothes would reflect that.

He knew how they would look. Skirts would get shorter, colours would get brighter, clothes would become easier to look after, more fun. He had seen a few of the clothes he recognised as the forerunners of the future when he had passed through London on his way here. It had been obvious that the women wearing those clothes had been the rich few, but they were leading the way. And with his materials he could allow other women to dress in the same style. If only the managers of the shops would realise it.

But perhaps Catherine had shown him a way. He was a dress designer, after all. His ultimate ambition was to own a factory making clothes, like the one his family had owned in Hamburg – before Matilde had brought about his downfall and put him in a position where even keeping this small printing works open was almost beyond him.

He felt his face grow tight as he fought to let nothing of what he was feeling appear on it. It had been a useful accomplishment during the war, when terror was all around. Then a straight face and a steady hand had won him a reputation for fearlessness which he did not deserve. Even the medals had come as a result not of courage but of a reckless disregard for life, when he had realised the extent of his wife's betrayal.

Women. He shifted the heavy roll from one arm to the other. But you could not include Catherine in that, he told himself. She was no more than a child – the same age as Matilde had been when they had met, but a hundred years younger in experience. It was almost laughable, the way she worried about her appearance and whether it would affect the sale of his silk when, in reality, all she looked like was a well-brought-up schoolgirl.

He stopped. A well-brought-up schoolgirl. Wasn't that the type of person he had envisaged wearing his clothes? Not the mothers and aunts but the young women, recently released from the schoolroom, slender and alive. The older generation would always be wedded to the ideal of their youth, the women with their big bosoms and wide hips, curved into an "S" shape by their boned corsets and balanced by their big hats, but the younger girls – they would want the look they had become used to during the war, brighter, younger even. If he could dress Catherine like that . . .

He couldn't, of course. It wasn't done for a man to provide clothes for any woman who wasn't his wife – or mistress – and he had no intention of making Catherine either of those. Anyway, at twenty-seven he was too old for her, as well as lame, poor, an alien. Once he had been an attractive proposition as a husband but not now.

He couldn't even ask her father if he could let her wear his clothes as an advertisement. Robbie was surprisingly reticent about his father, turning the conversation around whenever Gunter approached the subject, but he had let enough drop for Gunter to know that he would never agree to either of his children becoming involved with a German.

Perhaps one of the other women he employed could do it? Their fathers invariably worked for him too. Gunter reviewed them in his mind's eye. Pleasant girls, all of them, and hard-working, struggling with the heavy wet silk when it was washed in the hot soapy water and when it was steamed to set the colours, with a willingness that amazed him, but they did not have Catherine's look of class. Without exception they were buxom, red-faced and busty, far better suited to the fuller skirts and old-fashioned blouses that they already wore than they would be to the design he could see growing in his mind.

He looked at the roll in his arms. This silk would be ideal for her, the cool greens and blues offsetting her clear skin and green eyes and the chestnut glint in her hair.

Suddenly he could not wait. She would never wear it, of course – there was no way that he could ask her to – but it would be an experiment. It would show whether the silk he had produced would adapt to the sort of clothes he had envisaged for it, and it would also give him a dress which could be shown to buyers so that they could see how it worked in a real garment.

It would also show Catherine that he had accepted her comments about the buyers being unable to imagine the material made up – but he banished that thought from his mind.

What Catherine thought of him was of no consequence. He was not going to get hurt by another woman.

Especially one scarcely out of the schoolroom.

The noise in the Star Inn was loud and Walter knew that he was making a lot of it.

It was the first time for two years that he had drunk more than a couple of pints; the first time he had felt confident enough to relax in the company of his new friends.

They had accepted him now, he knew. Now they told him of the tricks they played on the Customs men, of equipment liberated from the navy, of rabbits and even chickens stolen from local farmers.

He was their leader, too. Walter could feel himself smile at the realisation. Before the war it had always been Robert, great, laughing Robert, who was the leader. Walter had been second in command, second – but never first. Even in the army Robert had been the one who was offered promotion, never Walter, but Robert had always turned it down. "I'll stay with my brother," he had said, laughing. That was how Walter always remembered him, laughing. Until the machine gun had torn away half his face.

The thought disturbed him. He shifted uneasily on his seat, leaning forward, and noticed how the movement galvanised his companions. They, too, moved, shuffled, leaned forward, unconsciously copying his movements.

No doubt about it, he was the leader now. He grinned, happy in himself, his fingers turning over the coins in his pocket, when his fingers found one that felt unusual.

If he had been sober he would not have done it but, relaxed and careless, he pulled it out of his pocket.

His brother Robert's Military Medal shone silver in the subdued light of the bar.

He remembered now. Robbie was fascinated by the medals won by his namesake and was forever disobeying him by taking them to look at. Last evening, when Walter had found him playing with them yet again, he had cuffed him around the ear and . . . His memory was a blank after that but he must have slipped it unthinkingly into his pocket to keep it away from the boy.

Walter moved to thrust the medal back into his pocket but he was too late. Already Nabbo had reached for it.

"Here, what's that?" Then, amazed, "A Military Medal! You never told us you'd won a Military Medal!"

For a second denial quivered on his lips. He had no intention of claiming Robert's achievements as his own – but wouldn't he lose face if they realised that his brother had won the medal and he had not? And he would have to explain in detail how Robert had won it whereas, if it was his, he could feign modesty, close the subject as quickly as possible, *take the medal back before anyone noticed the name of the regiment.*

He reached out swiftly and grabbed at the silver disc. "I never meant to bring it. My boy was playing with it and I took it from him and forgot."

He thrust it hurriedly into his trouser pocket. Looking around, he could see that his apparent modesty had done him no harm with the other men. They were looking at him with renewed respect in their eyes.

Nabbo said, "But a Military Medal! You have to be recommended by a commanding officer for that!" He leaned forward, curiosity burning in his face. "Go on, tell us. What did 'ee do?"

Walter took a deep pull of his beer. "I don't want to talk about it." He turned his face from them, as if trying to hide his embarrassment.

"A Military Medal!" Nabbo couldn't get over it. "That's not one of they Pip, Squeak and Wilfreds," he added, referring to the common names of the 1914 Star, the British War Medal and the Victory Medal, awarded to all who had served for the relevant periods of the war.

"Leave 'un, Nabbo." William-John Tredissick, the man who had been the group's leader before the advent of Walter, elbowed him roughly in the ribs.

"What? Oh!" Realisation came slowly; Nabbo wasn't one of the brightest, Walter knew. Then, as if to try to make amends, he announced, "I got something to show 'ee, too." He began to rummage in the depths of his pocket.

"Another medal?" William-John jeered. "What would they give 'un to you for? Putting your feet in your mouth?"

"No, look." In his open hand the heavily chased gold watch gleamed with the lustre of pure gold.

Walter's medal was forgotten. Open-mouthed, the men stared at the watch. "How did 'ee get that, boy?" William-John asked, awestruck. "Steal 'un, did 'ee?"

Nabbo look at it fondly. "It belonged to my grandad. Went mining in South Africa, he did, and made a mint afore he come home. Course, 'tes all gone now; all except this." He clicked the catch and the watch sprang open to show the ornate face and the inscription inside the cover. "There's more inside."

He began to fiddle with the back of the watch but William-John

121

Tredissick put a hand over his. "Put 'un away, Nabbo. You don't know who's looking. You don't want 'un stolen, not something like that."

"What? Oh – no."

There was a silence as Nabbo thrust the watch back into the hidden recesses of his trousers, until William-John said to Walter, "I saw that red-haired lad of yours up Paul Hill this afternoon. Not often you see him out, is it?"

Walter hadn't even realised that anyone knew Robbie was his son but of course, in a place like this, a stranger stood out. He felt a cold shiver run up his spine. He had settled in so easily here he had forgotten that he would be a source of interest to the others, that he and his family would be watched and commented on.

Perhaps he shouldn't have made himself so much at home? Perhaps he should have stayed in at night, kept himself to himself? But even as he thought it, common sense asserted itself. He would still have been watched had he done that, perhaps more so. Now he was in a stronger position. These men were his friends now, his allies. If anyone came looking for him . . . but they wouldn't. The war was over, deserters forgiven. Councils were even including their names among the lists of dead on the new war memorials that were springing up all over.

He took a sip of his drink. "Could be my son," he admitted. "He's always off by himself. He's a little runt with a stammer that would drive a man mad if he listened to it for long, so he doesn't get on with other boys. He spends a lot of time by himself."

"Not what I'd heard," Nabbo said. "I heard he was spending all his time with that there German what's set up in Newlyn."

"He does, too," another man broke in. "My Sally-Ann knows Penny Pentyr what works there with her da and she says he's there all the time with his nose into everything. Bright little lad, she says. Knows more about what goes on than anyone except the Hun."

At any other time Walter would have been pleased to hear something good said about his runt of a son; now he ignored it. One word was echoing deafeningly in his head. "German? What German?"

"You must have seen him." Nabbo had become so used to Walter that he seemed to forget that Walter did not know everybody in the district as he did. "Quiet chap. Keeps to himself. Tall, fair-haired. Penny Pentyr says he's making up silk cloth for women's clothes. Though I must say," he added fairly, "he don't look the type for that sort of womanish nonsense."

A tall, fair-haired German. Walter found that he couldn't breathe. The man he had seen with Catherine had been tall and fair-haired. He had been carrying a roll of what could have been silk.

And his face had seemed familiar.

With a sickening lurch all the pieces fell into place. He was back in the trenches again. He could smell the cordite and the blood, decomposing flesh and rats. In his hand a gun; in his heart, murder. Before him, white-faced, injured, defiant, the German who had killed his brother.

The same man he had seen talking to Catherine on the Terrace.

Fear gripped him. He had to do something. He had to do something quickly.

Walter realised that he was still staring at Nabbo with his mouth open but even as he looked away, trying to feign normality, an answer came to him.

Catherine knew she could not sleep, not with Miss Rose's news whirling round in her head.

After the misery of the last month, after the way she had woken each day with Mrs Farley's condemnation of her painting echoing in her ears, to know that someone thought she had talent should have made her ecstatic; instead, her heart bled for her lost opportunities.

A letter of introduction to Augustus Farley and she had nothing to show him. Looking at her red and cracked hands, Catherine doubted if she would be able to paint now, even if she had access to brushes and paints. There was no point in going to see him without any examples of her skill. Her heart ached as she remembered the oil paintings Walter had burned in Dorset and the water-colours scattered to the winds here in Cornwall.

She was too upset to sleep but there was plenty of work to do. She started on the pile of ironing, working out her frustration on her father's shirts and the never-ending heap of Robbie's clothes. The stack of neat ironing grew steadily taller, the cottage filled with the smell of hot cotton, and still she ironed, trying to soothe her restless mind with the action of the instrument.

It was only when she heard the outside door open that she realised how late it was. She looked up, surprised, as Walter dropped his cap onto the hook by the door and came to stand over her, his arms folded across his chest.

"You bin lying to me, maid!" His voice was over-loud and excited and Catherine felt her heart sink. Drinking always made him unpredictable. He pointed a finger at her and she saw that his cheek was twitching again as it used to. "You and the boy – you think you can fool me, don't you? But you can't."

She tried to brazen it out. "I don't know what you mean."

"I got good mates, me handsome." Even when they were alone together now he kept up the Cornish accent now. "They tell me what's going on, see. They tell me the truth – even when you and that lying young heathen upstairs don't."

She could only think of one subject on which she had lied. Gunter. Somehow he had found out about Gunter. She felt her heart contract. "I – I still don't know what you're talking about."

"I'm talking about that bloody German I saw you with this afternoon, the one Robbie has been spending all his time with." He leaned towards her, his face contorted, his cheek twitching constantly. "You don't think about me, do you? You don't think about how I would feel, knowing my children are consorting with the enemy, that they spend their time sucking up to a bloody Hun!"

He took a deep breath. "Well, it won't happen again, miss. That I do know."

"Oh, but—" Catherine knew it was hopeless but she had to try for Robbie's sake. "He is not a bad man, Father. Just because he is a German—"

He interrupted her. "He *is* a bad man." He straightened, a smile lighting his eyes. "It may interest you to know that tonight he attacked a friend of mine on his way home and robbed him."

As she stared at him, silent with shock and disbelief, he added, "The bastard will be in prison by now. And I hope he dies there."

Fifteen

"Are you all right, sir? If you don't mind my saying so, you don't look very well." The breakfast waiter poured Random's tea with a professional flick of the wrist then left him to stare out of the window of the Queen's Hotel at the lazily swelling waves, silver-tipped in the early morning sun.

Not looking well. Random knew it. Six months, the doctor had told him. Had he been wrong, or trying to provide comfort by being optimistic? At the time, Random had half welcomed the news. He would be with his beloved Jenny again, he would leave behind the pain from his shattered eye and leg. Now the thought of dying too soon maddened him.

Walter Harrison was out there, he knew it. He was close – close to the man who had ruined his life, who had made him unable to comfort Jenny in her last days, unable to say goodbye to her, tell her how much he loved her.

Random's good eye glared. So much was left undone – and all because of this man. He could not die until he had seen the man punished.

But he was nowhere to be found. A week Random had searched, asking everyone, "Have you seen a stranger with a Yorkshire accent?" He had not dared to mention the name in case it got back to his quarry. Most of the Cornish, he soon realised, would not have recognised a Yorkshire accent anyway. He had been directed to Londoners and Welshmen, even to a Scotsman. Most were fishermen. He sighed.

He had to find Walter Harrison.

"More toast, sir?"

The waiter again. Random shook his head. His appetite had almost completely gone now. He ate only because he needed the strength for his hunt. As the waiter turned away Random asked, suddenly, "If I wanted to find a stranger around here,

125

where would I look? Where are there collections of men who
are not Cornish?"

"Grockles, you mean?" Random had never heard the term
before. "Well, sir, a lot of the fishermen are furriners."

"Not a fisherman." He had checked them as thoroughly as
he could.

"Well, sir, there's all those artists, sir. They all come from
up-country and they have lots of friends visiting, not to mention
ladies who they teach to paint."

Artists. Random had dismissed Miss Rose's information about
Catherine; Walter was the one he was interested in. Now he
thought again. If he couldn't find the father perhaps he could
trace the family through the daughter.

He slipped the waiter a tip. "That's very helpful. Thank you."

"Thank *you*, sir." The fingers clutched at the note as if the
man couldn't believe his eyes. "Thank you very much."

"You don't want to go and see him, miss." The police sergeant
leaned his fat stomach against the high counter and stared down
at Catherine disapprovingly. "He's a Hun, he is, and a thief
to boot."

"He is a friend of mine." Catherine gripped her bag tightly.
"Please let me speak to him."

She swallowed nervously. The whole atmosphere of the building was intimidating. The wooden bench along the wall, polished
by the trousers of thousands of visitors, the high wooden counter
marking the barrier between the public and authority. Even the
sergeant himself made her feel nervous, recalling threats made
by her exasperated mother. *"I'll get the police to lock you up if
you don't behave."*

The sergeant looked more disapproving than ever. "What are
you doing having a German as a friend, miss? Aren't fine Cornish
lads good enough for you? You should be ashamed of yourself.
Comforting the enemy, that's what you're doing. Not to mention
consorting with criminals. I'm ashamed of a nicely spoken young
lady like you even knowing a person like that."

Such blatant prejudice in a man in authority horrified Catherine
and she opened her mouth to protest, then closed it again.
She could see by the mulish look in his eye that he was
not the type to appreciate intelligence in a woman and she

dared not annoy him if she were to have any chance of seeing Gunter.

She smiled at him from under her lashes while her fingers knotted themselves around her bag. "I have only been in the county a short while but I think that Cornishmen are the most upstanding men I have seen anywhere." She allowed her eyes to rest on his face, hoping that she hadn't overdone the flattery.

He preened, sticking his stomach out even further. "It has been said before, miss. Very fine men all the Cornish are, I reckon."

"Oh, so do I." Catherine smiled brightly. "I have been very impressed. And you are all so kind and chivalrous, too."

"Good of you to say so, miss."

Catherine's fingers loosened their grasp on her bag then tightened again as he demanded, "So, why do you want to see the Hun?"

"I—" Her mind raced. "He's – making me a frock and I want to know when I can have it. It's for best, you know."

"He's a *dressmaker*?" The disbelief in the sergeant's voice was patent.

"He owns a factory in Newlyn that prints silk materials." It would do no harm to boost Gunter's reputation. It might even help fight against the anti-German prejudice. "He studied in London and Paris before the war, and now he is employing many ex-servicemen whose injuries are too bad for them to return to their original occupations."

"That's not patriotic," the Sergeant grumbled. "Working for a Jerry like that."

"It's better than starving," she said crossly, then remembered her mission and raised her green eyes appealingly. "But you do see I have to find out about the frock. Please let me see him. Just for a little while."

He wavered. "You'll have to talk through the bars."

"I don't mind at all, but—" She hesitated. "It *is* about clothes. I mean, some of it is a little – intimate. You're not going to be listening to every word, I hope."

"Got to make sure you don't pass him any files in a cake, miss." He gave an avuncular smile. "But don't you worry, I won't listen in. Though I'm a married man myself and used to ladies' fol-rols if you know what I mean. I shall be at the end of the corridor if you need me – though the Hun is behind bars and can't get at you, so you needn't be frightened."

As she followed him down the narrow stairs Catherine felt her heart beating faster. She was half expecting a dungeon with rats but the cells were dry and clean.

Gunter was sitting with his head in his hands but he jumped up as he saw her approaching. "Catherine – Miss Harrison – I didn't expect—"

"I've come to see you about the dress you are making for me," she broke in quickly.

His jaw dropped. "But how . . . ?" Then he saw the frantic signal in her eyes and stopped. "Of course. I must apologise to you if I am causing you any delay."

The sergeant hesitated at her side. "Are you sure you are all right here, miss? You won't be frightened by yourself?"

"I shall not be frightened." She forced a smile. "I just need to find out about my frock."

She waited until his heavy step receded down the corridor then moved forward a pace. "Gunter, I am so sorry. This is my fault."

"Yours? But how?"

"Well, my father's." She dropped her eyes, embarrassed. "He found out about" – she hesitated – "about Robbie and I knowing you. He – he hates Germans and I think – I'm afraid he might have arranged this." She remembered again his late homecoming last night, his strange excitement.

"He hates us that much?" Gunter's voice rose in disbelief. "That does not make sense."

"You all right, miss?" The sergeant paced down the corridor towards them, alerted by Gunter's raised voice.

"There's no problem, thank you, Sergeant." Catherine swallowed her impatience, waiting until he had moved away again before she hissed, "What is it that you are supposed to have done?"

"A man was attacked on the way home to Newlyn. He said that his attacker looked like me and had a German accent. When the police came to the works they found the stolen watch in one of the storerooms."

"But can't you prove—"

"I can prove nothing! I was alone all evening. I—" He laughed bitterly. "I thought of your remark about making up a dress in the material to show people. I was working on such a dress when the police came. There is no one who can say I was innocent and, in this country, who would?"

"I would." Her vehemence surprised her. She moved forwards, catching at the bars that separated them. "I will look for proof. If you are innocent there must be some way to prove it."

She turned at the sound of feet plodding down the corridor.

"Don't get so close to the bars, miss. It isn't allowed and if he should turn nasty you could get hurt."

"Herr Steiner will not harm me," Catherine said coldly but she moved back anyway, fearful that the sergeant would cut the visit short.

When the sergeant had returned again to the end of the corridor Gunter said, "Even if it can be proved it will be too late. The printing works cannot continue without me and I will have no money soon. It is over. Everything is over."

"But the workers," Catherine protested. "Surely they can continue?"

He shrugged. "They know nothing. Only Robbie has knowledge to keep the works running for a week, two perhaps at the most. But he is a child – who would listen to him?"

She gazed at him, her surprisingly dark brows lowered in a frown. "There must be a way."

"No way. No future." He reached through the bars and touched her hand lightly, a faint smile quivering on his lips. "Forget me. I have caused you and your family nothing but trouble. You can do nothing for me. I shall" – he straightened, heels together, arms taut by his sides – "I shall face the future as a man. Without fear."

"No!" Careless of the sergeant in the background she moved forward again and seized the bars. "You must fight, don't you see? Fight this with everything you have!"

He stared at her, his eyes amused in his tired face. "You tell me that? You who have not fought your father once? You—"

A heavy hand landed on Catherine's shoulder, pulling her backwards. Startled, she glanced up at the sergeant's unsmiling face.

"That's enough of that, miss. You've spoken to the prisoner long enough and I can't have you hanging on the bars like that. You go now."

"But I—" His hand seized her arm, urging her back down the

echoing corridor. She turned, craning over her shoulder. "I'll do my best for you."

"Forget him," the sergeant advised as he escorted her up the stairs and into the brighter light of the police station. "He's no good, miss. They always said in the war that the only good German was a dead one and I reckon they had the right of it. And so will the jury, once they hear the evidence."

"Jury." She stopped dead, ignoring his pull on her arm. "But if they think like that he won't get a fair trial."

The sergeant stared at her. "This is England, miss. Of course he will have a fair trial," he asserted strongly. "And then they'll find him guilty as they should, the dirty Hun."

Unfair. Unfair. The words beat in her head as she walked back to Newlyn. She had always hated unfairness and now this. To find a man guilty just because he was a German was more than unfair, it was unjust.

Catherine was still angry as she pushed open the door to the canning factory. The smell rushed out to meet her, a smell of oil and gutted fish, and she wrinkled her nose in disgust as she did every day, reaching for her wraparound overall.

"Kind of you to condescend to appear for work at last." She glanced up at the supervisor's sarcastic words.

"I had to go—"

He gave her no chance to finish. "Slept late after your day off enjoying yourself, I suppose. Mixing with the nobs, were you? Too tired partying to get up in time?"

"I was not partying," she began angrily. "And yesterday I was—"

"You were with your young man." As she opened her mouth to deny it the supervisor rushed on, "Don't bother to deny it. I saw you with my own eyes, walking to and fro in Newlyn harbour, talking to him when you should have been here, working."

"But I was – he was—" Catherine came to an awkward halt. To explain that he had taken her there away from the constant noise and interruptions of the factory so that he could coach her in the technical terms she would need to know to sell his silk would only make matters worse.

The supervisor leaned forwards, pressing his face up against hers. "If there's one thing I don't need here, young lady, it's an unreliable worker. And you're one."

"But it was only—"

He pointed at the door, his face red with anger. "You're sacked. You and your posh little voice. You're out. And I tell you now it's the last time I employ any fancy-talking women like you again. Give me a proper Cornish maid what knows how to work properly, not some la-di-da woman what doesn't know how to get her hands dirty."

More unfairness. She was out of the building, walking slowly up the road, worrying about how she would tell her father before the thought struck her.

"You don't fight," Gunter had told her. It had never occurred to her that she should fight. Mother had always insisted that she should obey her parents, that she should do what she was told, act like a lady, not argue, but . . .

"You don't fight." Had her mother been right or should she fight? Where there was unfairness, where there was injustice – wasn't it her duty to fight as much as a man? In the last war women had, if not fought, at least assisted in the fighting. She had looked down on Gunter for not fighting, but wasn't she as culpable? More culpable, because, in prison as he was, Christian fortitude was probably his best way forward, while she . . .

Catherine stopped in the middle of the road. Jingles pulled by ponies passed her, there was a constant stream of people talking in their rich Cornish accents, in the harbour a fishing boat hauled up its brown sails, but she saw nothing of that.

"You don't fight." But she could fight, she realised suddenly. She could.

The thought shocked her like a bucket of cold water in the face and she found herself gasping for breath as the enormity of what she was proposing to do hit her. To turn her back on seventeen years of teaching, to forge her own way in life, to fight . . . it was terrifying and liberating at the same time. Her options spread ahead of her, limitless as the ocean. The decision as to which course she followed was hers alone.

Catherine took a deep, shuddering breath that filled her lungs to their very depths, then she turned and walked back the way she had come.

To the silk-printing factory.

Sixteen

There was no work being done.

As Catherine pushed open the door to the factory, the group of people gathered in the middle of the room paused briefly to stare at her then went back to their excited chatter.

For a second Catherine's heart sank. How could she do this? She didn't know these people, she knew nothing about the work they were supposed to be doing. Then the scene before her struck a chord in her memory. The people in front of her were all adults, but they reminded her of a disorderly class in school. And she knew how to deal with that.

She moved forward into the room and clapped her hands sharply together. Just like children they stopped talking, turning towards her again. While she had their attention she spoke quickly.

"Herr Steiner, as you know, has been arrested as a result of a misunderstanding." Mouths opened as if to contest this but she gave them no chance to speak. At school, as one of the oldest pupils, she had often been called on to help take classes of younger children, especially once it had become known that she was planning to become a teacher, and she had quickly learned that it was important to keep the initiative and not let the children take over.

She raised her voice, standing straight in her old clothes, still smelling of the fish factory. "I have been to see him this morning and it is his desire that you should continue with your work. He fully expects the misunderstanding to be cleared up very swiftly." She glanced around, holding everyone's eye for a brief second, hoping they could not see the fear under her calm exterior. "Are there any problems?" Please let there not be, she added to herself. She had scarcely set foot in this building. If anyone were to ask her anything . . .

Like children the workers moved away, the printers going up the stairs to the large room upstairs. Only Penny Pentyr came closer.

"There was this stuff left on the table this morning, miss, when I come in." She led Catherine to a small room off the courtyard which Gunter had been using as a living-room-cum-workshop. On the table a series of sketches and cut-out pieces of calico lay scattered, as they must have been when the police arrived. "I dunno nothing about any of this."

"I do," said Catherine briskly. "Herr Steiner mentioned it to me. He was working on a pattern for a dress to be made out of the silk he had printed so that it could be used as a sample to show the buyers." She glanced helplessly at the calico. She knew nothing about dressmaking. "I don't know whether he finished cutting out the pattern, though."

"Oh, he did, miss. I can tell that, being as how I was a lady's maid for a time."

"Then you could make up the dress?" Catherine's heart leaped. If that were done there was a chance that she might be able to sell the silk Gunter had printed.

"Well." Penny looked unsure. "'Tes usual, see, to make up a new pattern in ordinary material to make sure it do fit right before you cut it out of silk, in case there's a mistake."

"Then do that." If the woman knew what she was doing it was better to leave her to do it her way.

"Well, all right, miss. But it would help if I could have your measurements, too. Just to make sure."

"What?" Catherine stared at her. "But – this dress – it isn't for me?"

"Well, it looks like it, miss." Penny pushed the sketches that Gunter had made across to Catherine. Even though they were rough and had been drawn quickly, the quality of the draughtsmanship was immediately obvious to Catherine. It angered her that she had never realised that he was such a good artist. Then she took in the whole picture and gasped.

Rough though the drawings were, their lines corrected and re-corrected as Gunter had struggled to find the exact lines for the dress that he was designing, there could be no doubt about the model.

The slender body, the high mass of hair, even the roughly

indicated features were all hers. On one view Gunter had even sketched in her old hat, before scrubbing it out with angrily ineffectual strokes as if he had realised that it did not match the dress he was designing.

He had been thinking of her. Last night, while her father was plotting his downfall, Gunter had been planning this dress, using her as the model. Catherine bit her lip and let the papers fall to the table as the injustice of it all struck her again.

"So, if we can go somewhere where I can measure you, miss . . ."

Catherine blinked. Lost in her contemplation of the sketches, she had forgotten Penny for a moment. "That won't be necessary," she said firmly. "These are just drawings. He only needs a dress made up to show the buyers in Penzance."

"But it will be much better if they actually see it on," Penny argued. "Especially with silk. Silk only really comes alive when it's worn. And it looks as if the pattern he was cutting was meant to fit you too."

She held up a piece of calico that seemed to Catherine's ignorant eyes to bear no relation to any part of any garment ever worn. Certainly she could never have judged the size of the person for whom it was intended from it, but Penny seemed sure.

Catherine was about to tell her simply to make up the dress so that she, Catherine, could take it in to the shops when she stopped.

"Why don't you fight?" he had said. Well, wasn't this part of the fight? If there was a better chance of selling the silk because the buyers could see how it would look when it was being worn then surely she should take that chance. And it would solve the problem that, when she went to the shops, she did not look the part. With a silk dress on . . .

She took a deep breath. "Make it up," she said. "And as soon as possible. So that when Herr Steiner is released—"

"You think he will be released then?" Penny's voice was doubtful.

"He will be released very soon," Catherine stated. "And if we are to sell the silk before that happens we shall have to hurry."

She wished that she felt as confident as she sounded.

"Then it's steamed, see, to set the colours. But Gunter says he

134

likes that bruised look where the blocks have been hit, so he doesn't do much finishing to the cloth."

Robbie's excited voice rang in Catherine's head as they walked home that evening. Her arms and legs ached as if they were about to drop off. It wasn't because of physical exertion, she knew. Working in the canning factory had been far harder. It was the accumulation of tension, of always having to be ready to answer any question, even when she didn't know the answer, to make decisions when she had no idea what the considerations were.

And now Robbie was taking this chance to give her a crash course in silk printing. Catherine knew she should listen but it was all too much to take in. And there was her father – he would try to stop her working at the silk factory. How could she get out of this?

She had to clear Gunter's name. Once he was out of prison then he could take over the running of the factory again. Her intervention would only work for a few days, a week at the most. She had to clear Gunter's name – and fast.

"Robbie," she interrupted an excited explanation of the advantages of synthetic dyes over natural ones, "how could someone get into the factory at night?"

He paused. "You can't. Gunter always locks everything up. We've got acids and dyes can be poisonous, and the silk is valuable. He always makes sure everything is locked if he leaves the place empty."

Catherine rubbed her aching head. "But if he is there alone?"

He paused. "He *said* he always locks up as soon as we all leave. I've helped him sometimes."

"And you locked up tonight." She had been impressed by his thoroughness. "Did you notice anything strange?"

"There was a window broken but there often is. People don't like Gunter because he's a German. But there are bars on the window so it doesn't matter anyway." He looked at her curiously, his green eyes enormous under his carroty hair. "What are you thinking about?"

"I don't know." She hesitated. "Gunter didn't steal that watch, you know."

"Well, of course not!" The contempt in his tone was cutting. "He's against all kinds of dishonesty and fighting and everything like that."

135

"So how did the watch get into the factory?" she demanded. "Someone must have put it there." She could not bring herself to say that she suspected their father was involved. That would be too disloyal.

He was silent, pacing along beside her. She smiled down in sudden affection at the ginger curls and the skinny legs that stayed an unattractive pink between the bottom of his shorts and his thick woollen socks and heavy boots, no matter how much he was out in the sun. He was so staunch in his support of Gunter. She reached out and took his hand, grateful that she had an ally in him.

He dragged his fingers away instantly, glowering at her for being such a sissy. "I'll look tomorrow. I'm not going to have Gunter locked up for something he hasn't done."

"Nor me. Now, is there someone there who always knows all the gossip?"

He nodded. "Frank. The one who showed you how the printing was done. His brother is a postman and he always knows everything."

"Then, tomorrow, ask him what he knows about this robbery. Because there must be a way of proving that Gunter didn't do it. We've got to find out what it is – and fast."

Walter Harrison was waiting on Newlyn Quay for Nabbo as he finished unloading the fishing boat. "Recovered, 'ave 'ee, boy?"

Nabbo winced, touching his head gingerly. "Bloody Boche. He caught me a right one." He stared at Walter. "It's funny. I been thinking about last night. I can't remember seeing anyone before I was hit, or hearing anyone talking in German."

The very reason Walter had come to see him. "The blow scrambled your brains, that's why. As soon as you came round you told me he was a German and what he looked like."

Nabbo shook his head. "I can't remember nothing," he muttered. "One minute you was there with me and the next I was in the gutter with my head stove in. I can't remember nothing about it. It don't make sense."

"It's because of the blow," Walter consoled him. "I went for a piss and when I come back you were lying in the road with a bleeding head. You told me then about the man you'd seen."

Nabbo frowned. "I wish I could remember." He touched his bandaged head tenderly and repeated, "It don't make sense."

Walter forced down the sudden spurt of fear. Nabbo wasn't very clever. As long as Walter kept his head and stuck to his story he could convince him. "You were right, anyway, weren't you? The police found your watch in the German's factory."

The worried face cleared. "Yeah, right. I must have seen him, then, mustn't I?"

"'Course you did." Walter clapped him on the shoulder. "Anyone forgets things after a bang on the head."

"But – why weren't you around? You didn't come back with me to the house, Florrie said."

Again the spurt of fear. Nabbo had put his finger on the weak spot in Walter's story – his unexplained absence while he had broken into the silk factory to plant the watch. Walter felt his cheek start to twitch and he rubbed it hard, forcing an embarrassed grin. "Well, boy, 'tes like this. I've had a run-in or two with the police and I'm a bit lairy of them."

"Oh, well, who hasn't?" Nabbo passed easily over this apparent evidence of a criminal past. "But I just wondered, that's all."

"Nothing to wonder about," Walter insisted. "You saw the German who attacked you, the police got back your grandfer's watch and I didn't have to talk with them. So all's well. You just get an early night and forget all about it."

He watched, frowning, as Nabbo walked slowly away up Newlyn Slip. Nabbo wasn't clever but he had the sort of mind that would probe at a problem like a rotten tooth. As long as he didn't wonder any more about his attack last night . . .

"Here's your supper, Jerry."

The young policeman carried the covered tray carefully into the cell. Gunter sighed. He hated the way all the food he was given was swimming in gravy.

The policeman pulled the cover off the tray with a flourish. The potatoes and a couple of lumps of unidentifiable meat swam greyly in a thin brown sea. Gunter turned away, revolted.

"No need to turn your nose up at it," the constable said. "Plenty would like this, I reckon."

Gunter looked at him. He was tall and thin, with a prominent Adam's apple sticking out of his red neck over the top of his tunic, his face blotchy with pimples. He had seen many such in the war. "You can have it," he offered.

"Really?" The constable's face lit up. "But what about you?"

"I have no appetite." Gunter watched the lad sit down on the hard bunk and begin to tuck in hungrily. "When it is that I shall see a judge?"

"A magistrate, not a judge." He swallowed a chunk of potato whole. "Old Colonel Trahair's the chairman of the Bench and they're trying to get him. He'll be here this afternoon sometime."

"And then what?"

"Well, you won't get bail, if that's what you mean." Seeing Gunter's puzzled expression he explained, "You'll be kept locked up until the trial – unless you plead guilty."

"And if I do?"

He took another dripping mouthful. "You'll be locked up anyway."

For a moment Gunter was tempted. There was nothing for him here, no chance of escape. He might get a lighter sentence if he pleaded guilty; after all, what hope did he have of proving his innocence? He was a hated alien, with no money to employ a lawyer. No jury would ever find him innocent.

He opened his mouth – and heard a well-remembered voice ask, *Why don't you fight?*

He had sworn he would never fight again. He had never wanted to fight in the last war but he had done his duty, as he saw it, to his country even though he did not believe that the Kaiser was in the right. And after four years of hell he had come to believe in the depths of his heart that fighting was wrong, that fighting proved nothing – yet . . .

Why don't you fight?

Catherine didn't fight, he told himself fiercely. According to everything that Robbie had told him, she allowed herself to be bullied by her father without ever fighting back.

But she had fought for Robbie. The scene was instantly before him; Robbie's red head drowning in a sea of darker hair and, from the outside of the surrounding circle of watchers, battling her way through the combatants, Catherine, forgetful of her dignity, her reputation – everything, except Robbie's safety.

"You look very cheerful for a man what's likely to go down for a good stretch."

Gunter hadn't even realised he was smiling. The memory

138

had done him good, washed away the depression that had shackled him.

"That is because I am going to say to the magistrate and to the judge that I am innocent – and I shall be let free," he said, and burst out laughing at the policeman's astonished face.

"Harrison?" The three men shook their heads. "Never heard of any artist down here called Harrison."

"She will be young, almost a schoolgirl." Random had known that it was a long shot but still he tried. Time was so precious now. And he had been lucky to find the three artists together.

Only one of them matched Random's idea of an artist. Augustus Farley was dressed with almost theatrical flamboyance as if he were playing the part of an artist. Lamorna Birch, with his tweed plus fours and gold pince-nez, looked like a country landowner and George Grantham, his host, now pouring more whisky into the glasses set on a table in the summer-house, looked for all the world like a bank manager. But then, he reminded himself, they were all successful men. Miss Rose had mentioned all their names with the kind of awe that most people reserved for the king.

"If she's young it's amazing old Farley here hasn't heard of her," Birch said, digging his neighbour in the ribs. "Terrible man for the ladies, is Farley."

"Not if his wife finds out," Grantham smiled, handing the glasses around. "But you're right. It is strange. A new artist usually makes contact with someone. But you say that Stanhope Forbes hasn't heard of her either. He's practically cornered the market in young women down here and Farley picks up all the ones he misses. Birch and I never get a look-in. Not that we want to," he added swiftly, with a glance at the lawn where his wife and a nursemaid played with two small children in the evening sun.

"No one has mentioned seeing her work, either." Birch sipped his drink. "You'd think she was trying to hide. You usually need a stick to keep off talentless young artists trying to force their damned dreadful daubs at you."

Random sipped carefully at the drink. He had to keep a clear head. "I gather she is quite good. I met a Miss Rose in Dorset who seemed to think she had a great future."

139

"Saphira Rose!" Lamorna Birch leaned forward with a smile. "I knew her father well. If she says the girl is good—" He stopped suddenly as Grantham leaped to his feet. "Stung by a bee, old man?"

"Wait a moment. I've just thought . . ." He raced off across the grass to the house.

Farley shrugged. "That's what comes of trying to be a respectable artist. The brain can't take it. Sooner or later there's an explosion and then . . ."

Grantham was already on his way back, a picture clasped in his arms. He pulled his chair away from the table and set the picture on it, balancing it against the back. "There."

Random thought it looked pleasant enough; a scene of a river in the sunlight, with trees shadowing the racing water. The sort of a stream where you might find trout, he decided.

The reaction of the other two men was different. They rose and peered, moving close enough at one time so that their noses were inches from the painting then standing back, staring through half-closed eyes.

Birch was the first to comment. "That's got something, old man. That picture has definitely got something. But I don't recognise the style."

"Nor do I, but I wonder . . ." Grantham took a penknife and cut the paper that held on the back of the painting. The water-colour, when he removed it, was battered around the outside. "I put it in a deeper mount than usual to cover the damage and I wondered if—" He pointed. "There."

Intrigued now, Random rose to take a closer look. Right in one corner, where it had been covered by the mount, the lightly pencilled words "Catherine Harrison" leapt out at him.

"That's her." His heart leapt. "She's here. She must be. You've met her."

Grantham shook his head. "Sorry, old man. I've never seen her."

"But if we find out who sold you the painting we should be able to trace her," Farley objected. "No artist is such a fool as not to keep in touch with their buyers."

"That's the problem. I didn't buy it in a gallery," Grantham admitted.

140

"Where did you get it?" Random found it difficult to catch his breath.

Grantham looked embarrassed. "Actually," he admitted, "I bought it off a rag-and-bone man."

Seventeen

"Well, he got your measurements spot on, seems to me." Penny Pentyr pulled the thin cotton material a little tighter around Catherine's slender hips and pinned it into place.

Catherine felt a strange thrill at the thought that Gunter had noticed her figure to that extent but fought it down. He was a designer, after all. Perhaps he could equally as well have guessed at the size of Penny's opulent hips.

Penny was altering the toile, as she called it, in the small back room that Gunter had made into his bedroom-cum-living quarters. There was no looking-glass and Catherine had to judge how she looked by squinting down at herself. To hide the embarrassment she felt she said, critically, "It seems a bit lumpy around the hips." Actually, she decided, with a dress like this she would look as if she were larger than Penny.

"It's because it's cotton. When it's in silk it will be some different. You'll see." She began to pin up the hem.

"Not up there." Catherine was horrified. She hadn't worn skirts that short since before she was old enough to go to school. During the war, skirts had risen enough to uncover the ankles but this – she was almost showing her *knees!*

"That's where the picture Mr Steiner drew showed it." Penny sat back on her heels and grinned up at Catherine. "I reckon you'll be the talk of Penzance when you go out in this."

"I'll probably be arrested," Catherine said gloomily. She glanced again at the sketch. Penny was right. Previously she had just looked at the quality of the sketch, at the way Gunter had delineated her features with a few sure lines. But if she lowered her eyes she could see the shocking length of the dress – and the slim legs he had shown beneath the hem. Another wave of embarrassment flamed through her. How much notice of her had Gunter really been taking all this time when she had been forcing

142

herself to try to ignore him? She tried for composure. "Anyway, my stockings will look stupid with this."

"You'll have to get some of they new silk ones I seen in Penzance. Mind you, terrible expensive they are. Three and eleven the ones I saw."

"Three shillings and elevenpence!" Catherine's voice rose in disbelief. She had only earned twelve shillings a week in the fish factory. "No one pays that sort of money for stockings."

There was a crash from outside and she moved quickly to the door. "Robbie, what are you doing?"

"Looking round like you told me to." He piled up the empty tins of dye that he had knocked over then stopped, his green eyes enormous. "I can see your combinations, Katy." He could not have sounded more outraged if she had been naked.

Catherine's face flamed again. "I – this dress isn't right yet." She retreated around the door, leaving only her head outside. "Have you found anything?"

"Not yet. But I'm still looking."

"Well, try not to knock anything else over." She retired in good order and closed the door, to wail at Penny, "I can't go out like this. You heard what he said."

"'Tes because I'm using cotton and it do stick out. Silk will lie flat, you'll see." Penny began to help her struggle her way out of the dress. "I'll have this done by tonight, I reckon. Then you can wear 'un tomorrow and show they buyers what this silk we're printing really makes up like."

Catherine gulped. She could imagine what would happen if she walked out wearing that dress. She would probably cause a riot. The women down here weren't very fashionable. Most were still dressed in the tight white blouses and long, dark skirts that their mothers and grandmothers had worn. The only women she had seen wearing clothes that looked at all fashionable were the young ladies in Stanhope Forbes's painting parties and Mrs Farley.

As she pulled on her old skirt and blouse, still smelling faintly of fish, she wondered again at Mrs Farley. Why had she been so dismissive? If it hadn't been for her and that horrid rag-and-bone man she would still have some of her best paintings, but now . . .

She had tried to draw last night. Father was still out and Robbie had gone to bed. She had borrowed paper and pencils from Gunter's small store, hoping that he would understand. The result had been sheets of paper stuffed hastily into the range. She hadn't realised how quickly she would lose her ability to draw – and the cuts and calluses she had got as a result of working in the factory had stopped her even being able to hold the pencil correctly. She had no chance of being able to produce more paintings to show Augustus Farley now, even if she had the time.

With a quick smooth of her hair she set off to walk around the works. Everyone was at their jobs; the silk on the table upstairs was being printed. She paused, watching it as, slowly, the pale silk took on a new life as the patterns were hammered into the thin material. This was the same pattern as the roll of silk she had taken to Penzance and she wondered again at the skill that could design a pattern so that it matched up so perfectly that, even knowing where to look, she was unable to see where one repeat ended and the next began. Nor could she ever have split the whole pattern down into the three different colours and designed each block so that the resulting printed material looked as if it had been made from many colours.

If Gunter was so good at designing silk surely he knew what he was doing when he designed dresses, which, she knew, was his main area of expertise?

"Where's your young imp of a brother?" one of the men demanded. "I need some more dye and he's the only one apart from the boss who knows how to mix it."

Catherine finally hunted Robbie down in one of the storerooms at the back of the complex of buildings. He was hanging half out of the window and at the sound of her voice he swung round excitedly. "I've found it, Katy. I found what we were looking for."

She hated being called Katy. Her mother had always forbidden it but her father had used the name occasionally, complaining that Catherine was an unsuitable name for a working man's daughter and, since her death, he had used the name more and more frequently. Now Robbie was using it too, but at this moment she did not care. "What? Show me."

He stood aside. One pane of the window had been broken, just in the place where it was possible to reach in and open the catch. Smashed windows were a constant feature of the factory, she knew, as people took out their anti-German feelings on Gunter's property.

"No one could get in," Catherine objected, gazing at the bars that covered the window.

"Yes they could. Look." He leaned forwards and pushed at the centre bar. It came easily away. "It was screwed into the sill and the screw has r-rusted away." The return of his stammer showed how excited he was.

It seemed very insecure but then, Gunter's grandfather had been forced to leave in a hurry and had probably expected to be away only for a short time. Even as a child she had been aware that the war was expected to be over by Christmas. "How do you know that it didn't happen years ago?" she asked.

"'Cos I cleaned these windows when I first started to help Gunter. And they had shutters over them, then, as well." She could see them stacked against the walls.

"Is this the room where the watch was found?"

"Next door, but Gunter never bothers locking the doors into the courtyard when he's here all night."

So there was proof, at least, that someone could have broken into the building recently – but there was no sign of anything stolen. She was certain, in her own mind, that it had been done simply to plant the watch but she doubted that a court of law would be convinced, especially when the defendant was German.

"I'll go and tell Gunter at once." And she would buy those stockings, she decided. When she was sacked she had been given the money she had earned and, as Father did not yet know, he had not taken the ten shillings from her as he had done every week so far. He would discover tomorrow, of course, but by then it would be too late. She would have her stockings and the dress might even be ready. If she dared to wear it.

But the sergeant was not to be moved. "Not this time, miss. Things have changed. He's been remanded by a magistrate now and I can't let you see him."

"If he were a Cornishman you'd let me see him," she wheedled. "You wouldn't be that unkind."

"But he's one of they Huns." The sergeant spoke with triumph as if he had made a killing point in an argument. "They don't deserve to be treated like proper Cornishmen."

145

"But he must have rights," Catherine exclaimed.

He nodded. "We treats him as we should. He gets food and bedding, don't you worry. But we don't have to let him see no one except his lawyer, not now he's been remanded to the Quarter sessions, and that's what we're doing."

"But he hasn't got a lawyer," Catherine exclaimed. "I – I don't think he can afford one."

"Well, that's too bad that is." The sergeant sounded pleased at the news. "But that don't change the rules, miss." He leaned forward across the high counter and lowered his voice confidentially. "You're a nice young lady. You forget him, that's my advice. Plenty of nice Cornishmen around that will make you happier than any furriner could – even if he weren't a criminal."

Fury blazed through her. "He hasn't been found guilty yet," she snapped.

He shrugged. The look on his face said that it was a foregone conclusion – as it probably would be if everyone was as prejudiced as he was.

She stepped back, her head high. "He is innocent, you'll see. Unlike most of the precious *Cornishmen* you get in here." She swung round and stormed out, uncomfortably aware that she had sounded just as prejudiced as he had.

Only a lawyer could see him. But she knew that lawyers cost money – probably almost as much for an hour's work as she had earned in a week. Nevertheless, he would have to have one if he were to get a fair trial.

She bought her stockings in one of the shops on the Terrace where she had tried to sell the silk before. Part of her winced at the expense, but another, a new Catherine, whose existence she had not known of before, smoothed the pale material and gloried in its fragility. She had never owned anything like this before in her life. It had been part of her dream of the future, a future where she was a teacher, with her own house, with time to paint and, perhaps, the chance to sell some paintings. Then she had seen herself wearing expensive clothes.

She stopped. Hadn't Miss Rose written that one of her paintings might be sold? That would mean she would have some money somewhere. If she could use it to help Gunter . . .

If only she had not lost her other paintings. Her heart had been broken when Father had made her burn the oil paintings before

146

they left Dorset, but the water-colours were a still greater loss. If fate had been just a little kinder she would still have had them. There might have been a way to turn them into money which would help Gunter.

Meanwhile, her only course of action was to sell the silk. Even if it meant making a laughing-stock of herself and wearing a dress that looked as if it had been designed for a three-year-old, that was what she would do – as long as it helped Gunter. But she did not relish the prospect.

"I saw Nabbo today. Sick as a shag he looked." William-John Tredissick gazed into his pint of ale as if expecting to find money at the bottom.

"First time he's had a bad head that isn't caused by bad beer, I reckon."

A roar of laughter swept round the table at Walter's riposte. He had already noticed that the Cornish had scant sympathy for anyone else's ills. They lived a hard life and they expected everyone else to put up with troubles with the same sort of stoicism.

"Still, it's strange, idn't it?" William-John still stared into the depths of his glass. "Nabbo only got that there watch a few days ago and that night we were the only ones he showed it to. Strange that he should have been set on like that."

"Well." Walter dared not let this type of supposition go on. "These Huns – dreadful violent they are. I remember in the war . . ." He swiftly began to tell a horrific story he had once heard.

They listened appreciatively, but when it was over William-John still wouldn't look Walter in the eye. He had been the leader of the small group before Walter had arrived and usurped his place. Walter had secretly despised him for giving up so easily; now he wondered. Had the man been biding his time, waiting for his chance? Walter felt a cold shiver run up his spine.

He dared not allow anyone to become suspicious of him. For the first time he cursed himself for becoming part of this group. He should have stayed away after that first evening, when he had got the information he needed. But it had been so good to be with men again, to be accepted, to be able to swap jokes and laugh. What comfort did he have at home? Catherine was

147

obedient but he knew, in his heart of hearts, that she despised him. She still seemed to have no suspicion that he was a deserter but he could see that she believed that he had been exaggerating his neurasthenia while Elizabeth was alive.

And he would have thought that Robbie hated him, except that he doubted that the boy had the courage even for that. Even Elizabeth, towards the end, had loved him not like a husband but as another child. And now she was dead and . . . He drank quickly and turned his thoughts to counteracting the danger he could feel creeping up on him.

William-John suspected him of attacking Nabbo, he was sure, and William-John was the sort of man who would continue to think about the suspicion, like a man with a sore tooth, until he was satisfied one way or another. It would be better to take the initiative himself, state straight out what the charge was, get his defence in first.

"What you are saying is, did I take the watch? That's what you're saying, isn't it?" He climbed to his feet, letting his voice rise aggressively. He could see the other people looking at him but he could not worry about them now. William-John was the big danger. He had to be stopped.

William-John showed his mettle. He too rose, facing Walter calmly, though there was a tension in his stance that warned Walter that he might be in trouble if it came to a fight. "All I'm saying is, you left with Nabbo and he was attacked before he'd got to your turn-off, so where were you? Why didn't you help him?"

"No. What you're saying is, I attacked him. But think on this, captain. If I was the one, how come the watch was found in the Hun's house? Answer me that. And how come Nabbo said he'd seen the Hun and heard him talk, too, while he was being robbed?"

There was a mutter of agreement from the other men around the table and even from others in the room. Only William-John was not convinced.

"You haven't said where you was at the time." There was no submission in his face.

Walter laughed. "If you want to know that you should ask old Peg-leg behind the bar there. Reckon that last drink he served me was off or something. Went through me like water it did. I had to go and find a quiet place to relieve meself."

"And it was just then that Nabbo was attacked, was it?" Walter could see the heads of the people in the Star Inn moving between the two of them, waiting for the response.

"Well" – he put everything he knew into making his words sound reasonable and mildly condescending – "he wouldn't be likely to go attacking Nabbo while I was standing there watching, would he?"

There was a general laugh and a sudden relaxation of tension around the table, as if the audience had decided that he had won. Walter wasn't so sure. William-John was brighter than the rest. At the moment, Walter's best defence lay in the fact that no one knew he had a reason for wanting the German put away, but if anyone ever discovered that—

If anyone ever discovered that, Walter reminded himself, he'd be a dead man – but no one ever would. He'd kill to prevent that, if necessary.

As soon as she walked in through the door Catherine heard the new noise in the print works.

From above came the regular thud-thud as the printers used mallets to print the silk, from outside there was the squeak of the winch as a new roll of silk was dragged through hot, soapy water to remove the gum left by the silkworms when they spun the silk – and from Gunter's quarters came the soft thump and silky rattle of a treadle sewing machine being worked. Penny was making up the dress.

Half elated, half nervous, she hurried through. The dress was almost finished, a slight, shimmering rainbow which seemed to have far more colours than Catherine had seen printed into it. "You've done so well!"

"Not bad." Penny cut the last threads and held it up. It looked insubstantial and horrendously short. Catherine stared at it, worried. "Surely you've cut too much off?"

"Silk only needs a rolled hem. But I'll let 'un hang tonight and take it up tomorrow morning."

"Katy! Katy!" It was Robbie, his face excited. "Did you tell Gunter about the window? What did he say? Did you tell him it was me that found it?"

"I wasn't allowed to see him, love." She told him what had happened, becoming aware of more and more bodies crowding into the small room, their faces lengthening as they heard her story.

"A lawyer." Percy Pentyr shifted uneasily on his wheelchair. "They're brem expensive, say what you like."

"He has to have one," Catherine insisted. "There is so much hatred of Germans he won't have a hope of a fair trial without one." She paused, trying to lift their spirits. "Perhaps if I can sell some silk tomorrow . . ."

As one they all turned and stared at the dress Penny had hung up. It seemed so slight a prop on which to pin all their hopes, yet what else had they?

"What if you don't sell the silk?" Robbie asked on the walk home.

"I must. I will." Catherine dared not even think of failure. Whatever it cost her in dignity and respectability, tomorrow she would wear the dress and sell the material. She had to.

"But if you don't?" Robbie's face puckered. "I like Gunter. I don't see why he has to be in prison just because the Cornish hate Germans. It's unfair."

"I know, sweetheart." The memory of Miss Rose's letter came back to her. Perhaps Miss Rose could send on any money she might have got for Catherine's painting? It might not be much, but even a little might help. And the gallery had said they would take more paintings from her.

"Oh!" She stopped in the middle of the road. "If only I hadn't lost my paintings!"

"The ones Father made you burn, you mean?" Robbie asked.

"No. I – disobeyed him. I brought some others down in the trunk and then—"

"Then what? What did you do with them?"

"I – lost them." Even now she could not tell even him about the crushing criticism of Mrs Farley. *Daubs*! Her heart still thudded sickeningly at the memory even though she had since had Miss Rose's letter. And as for the rag-and-bone man – she dreamed of him sometimes, his hoarse voice, his filthy hands stroking her tresses from root to tip, sliding down her body, the torn fingernails and rough skin catching and pulling at her hair. She would wake, sitting up in bed, panting with fright, her heart pounding. A couple of times she had half glimpsed him and hurried away before he could see her, her hands cold and shaking.

"What do you mean, lost them?" Robbie was standing stock still in the middle of the road. In the soft evening light his ginger hair glowed with a golden sheen while behind him trees arched over a small stream that babbled and sang as it wended its way through the steep banks down to Newlyn. It was the sort of scene she would once have enjoyed trying to capture in paint. "How can you have lost them?"

"I took them to show to someone," she explained, "and the wind blew them out of my hands and on to the ground. They were all ruined. And—" She glanced at him but knew her secret was safe with Robbie. He would never speak to their father unless forced to.

"I disobeyed Father again and wrote to Miss Rose. She told me that she had sold one of my paintings and that she thought that she could sell others if she had them. And I've lost them all!" It came out as a wail. "I could have used the money to help Gunter! But it's too late."

He was motionless, with an arrested look on his face, a look she had never seen there before.

Catherine forced a laugh. "Come on, Robbie. It's sad but it's not the end of the world." Still he didn't move. "I'll make you pancakes for supper," she coaxed. No response.

She was getting worried now. "Robbie, what is it?"

He shook himself, like a dog out of water. "Don't worry about supper, Katy. I – I'm not hungry." He turned and began to run back towards Newlyn.

"Robbie!" she called after him. "Robbie, what's wrong? Where are you going?"

There was no answer.

Eighteen

R obbie hammered on the imposing front door, then, when no one came, gave it a kick for good measure.

He had never told Catherine about his misadventure with the apples. He had known that she would laugh and tell him off so it was easier to forget the whole thing – once the stomach pains had subsided. He had certainly never given a second thought about the picture that had looked so strangely familiar – until Catherine's announcement.

He lashed out again with his heavy boot – and the front door opened.

The maid was trim and smartly dressed. For some reason Robbie had imagined the man would open the door and his hot speech died on his lips. He stared at the girl, horrified.

"Oh – I-I wanted to see – I wa-anted to see the man with the moustache."

"Mr Grantham, you mean? Well, I am sure that *he* won't want to see a ragamuffin like you." Her snapping black eyes took in his torn shorts and unpolished boots. "He's very choosy about who he sees, is Mr Grantham."

Robbie recovered himself. "He must see me," he insisted. "H-he's got my s-sister's painting and she wants it back."

He took his chance and tried a quick dive under her arm but tripped over his trailing laces and she caught him. "You get out of here, you young heathen," she shrieked, then when he continued to struggle, hanging on grimly to a huge oak hall-stand to stop her hustling him through the door, "Mr Rogers. Mr Rogers. Come here and help me, please."

The hall was large and tiled and her voice and the noise of their scuffle seemed to Robbie's ears to be magnified a hundred times over. In the otherwise silent house he could hear hurrying feet and he struggled harder to get past the maid before reinforcements arrived though she was stronger than she looked, hanging on to him with grim determination while her shouts echoed through the house.

Mr Rogers, who appeared first, turned out, to Robbie's horror, to be a butler. He had never had to deal with a butler before. After him, far less frightening to Robbie's eyes, the man he thought of as the "apple man" appeared. Robbie had obviously disturbed him dressing for dinner because he was in his shirt-sleeves with traces of lather around his nose.

With a final, despairing effort before the butler reached him, Robbie kicked out at the parlour-maid's ankles and, taking advantage of her loosened grip, hurled himself at the feet of the apple man, throwing his arms around his knees so that the butler couldn't prise him away.

"I want my sister's painting." He raised his voice above the shouts of the two servants, determined to get his demands in while he had a chance. "You've g-got my sister's painting and she n-n-needs it back."

Rough hands grabbed at the back of his coat, angry voices bawled in his ear but he hung on grimly. "I want the painting. I want it now."

"SILENCE." It was a roar that would have satisfied a bull ape and the voices died instantly. Even Robbie felt that he could not go on shouting after such a cry. The apple man leaned down and spoke quietly. "I suggest that you let go my legs, young man, and stand up and tell me what it is you want in a quiet and sensible manner."

Robbie slowly rose to his feet, wrestling his shirt round until it stopped trying to strangle him. He had lost his cap in the mêlée but wasn't going to stop to look for it now. "Please, sir—"

"Good God." The man stared at him. "It's the apple boy. Come back for another apple, have you?" He started to laugh.

Robbie felt his face redden and his anger rose. He set his feet apart and stared up at the man under frowning brows. "I've come for my sister's painting you've got on your wall," Robbie announced belligerently. "You've no right to it. It's hers and she lost it and she wants it back."

"Your sister, eh?" Robbie had expected an immediate denial or, possibly, a demand that he leave. What he did not expect was for the man to fumble around in his pockets and produce a pipe, which he lit slowly, staring all the while at Robbie. "And how do you know it is your sister's work?"

What could he say? Because I've seen her paintings every day since I was a child and I would know them anywhere, immediately – as long as some bully isn't forcing me to eat green apples?

"She – she signs them in the corner." He gasped with relief as the memory came to him. "Her name's Catherine Harrison."

Still the man smoked, eyeing him interestedly. "I've never heard of her. Live round here, do you?"

"Yes, we—" Robbie stopped, staring at him. Mother had impressed upon him, almost as far back as he could remember, that he was not to talk about the family to strangers. He had made an exception for Gunter. Gunter wasn't a stranger, he was a friend – Robbie's best friend and, he rather suspected, Catherine's best friend too, although she always got cross if he asked her. But this man was definitely a stranger.

"That d-doesn't matter." He looked around the hall at the maid and butler listening in fascination. Definitely not a place to start blurting out where he lived. He stared at the man. "This is private business."

"You're right." Grantham glanced at the servants. "I'm sure you have work to do," he hinted, then, "Come into my study, young man."

Robbie followed him. He saw at a glance that the picture was still there, amongst the many that lined the walls, but his attention was concentrated on the man.

He settled himself comfortably behind the desk, still eyeing Robbie interestedly. "Your sister do a lot of painting, does she?"

Robbie remembered her anguish in the road as he had left her. "She used to – before Father sold all her brushes and—" He stopped suddenly. Another taboo broken. Of course, it couldn't possibly matter but . . .

"Does she still want to paint?"

Robbie nodded. "But" – he dragged the conversation back to what he thought was the important subject – "what she mostly wants is her picture back."

Mr Grantham smiled. "And is her eyesight as good as yours?"

Robbie stared. "Why'm I supposed to have good eyesight?" he demanded. He just wanted the picture. If the apple man gave it

154

to him he would leave immediately. He would let him keep the frame, Robbie decided magnanimously, because it belonged to him, though he did think that Katy's picture looked a lot better framed properly like that, rather than just pinned to the wall like they had been in Dorset.

"You have a look." He got up and reached down the picture from the wall, holding it in front of Robbie. "You recognise the signature?"

Robbie looked, looked again, then the reason came to him. "You've covered it up with the frame."

"Mount, actually. Why don't we take this picture to your sister and see if she can identify it?"

Strangers at the house were definitely forbidden. "No." Robbie was uncompromising. "I don't care if you have hidden her name, it is still hers and you've stolen it."

"Oh, not stolen." Mr Grantham looked amused. "I am a respectable person, young man – whatever you may think of my sense of humour," he added, ignoring Robbie's blank stare of incomprehension.

"But Katy didn't sell it to you." Robbie was certain of that.

"No, but it doesn't mean I didn't buy it."

All his suspicions rose, swamping him in doubt and fury. "I bet it does," he said hotly. He was tired, both mentally and physically. These last days Katy had been theoretically managing the works, accepted by the others because they thought, as he did, that she and Gunter were friends, but it had been he who had to tell her what to do, what to say. The responsibility was wearing. "No one else could have them to sell. They couldn't!"

"They could!" Mr Grantham snapped. "I got that picture off the old rag-and-bone man up at Kerris – and I paid good money for it. Here, wait a minute! Where are you—"

Robbie didn't wait any longer. He was out of the door in a second, swooping to pick up his cap as he skidded across the tiled hall. There was a moment of panic as he struggled with the door, hearing the apple man coming closer and closer, but the unfamiliar catch gave way at last and he was out in the open air and racing down the drive.

It was too far to run all the way but he still got to the village by sunset. The rag-and-bone man lived, he discovered, in a shack down by the moor. Rank grass and gorse bushes clogged the

155

uneven track to the front door. Around the house were piled bits of wood and metal that fascinated Robbie but which he knew from experience would be despised by all the grown-ups he knew.

For a second his determination to be a soldier wavered. He could be a rag-and-bone man and live in a house like this. Then he looked more closely. The roof of the shack was thatched with straw so old it had turned black. It was sagging dangerously under the weight of a small bush which clung precariously to the summit. The windows were thick with dirt and, from the corner of the house, a skinny donkey stared mournfully at him, ears flapping, as it chewed dispiritedly at some gorse, twitching its lips impatiently.

Perhaps he would be a soldier after all. He straightened his thin shoulders in what he imagined was a military stance and marched up to the sagging door. "Mr Rag-and-Bone man, are you there?"

No answer. "Mr Rag-and-Bone man!" He felt more nervous now. No one knew he was here; there was no one within calling distance. And rag-and-bone men were a bit like gypsies, weren't they? They might steal boys and sell them for . . . His overheated imagination supplied lurid answers. He was half sure that boys weren't allowed up chimneys any more but perhaps he would be press-ganged on to a ship and — He shivered, half terrified, half fascinated by the picture he had conjured up.

If the man was not here, he realised, then he might be able to find Catherine's paintings and leave before he came back. They were her pictures, after all. It wasn't as if he were stealing.

He pushed the door cautiously. In the fading light the room inside was dark and crowded with mysterious shapes. There were piles of paper, of clothes and boots. On one wall, looking horribly as if they belonged to shrunken heads, long hanks of hair hung from a shelf. He tiptoed in, wide eyes flickering round the single room, searching for any sign of the pictures he was after, and a hoarse voice spoke in his ear.

"I'm here."

He jumped, yelping, swinging round, his heart pounding.

Behind him, black against the lighter sky outside, a gross figure

156

loomed. Robbie's nose twitched at the smell of unwashed flesh, old clothes, an all-pervading mustiness.

Terror iced its way through his brain. Get out. He had to get out.

He ducked, heading for the doorway, but a hand, the gnarled fingers tipped with black nails, caught him and dragged him further into the evil-smelling hovel.

"You stealing from me, boy?" The voice grated and rasped horribly, hinting at the screaming of unthinkable curses.

"I-I-I was j-j-j-just looking for—"

"Something to steal," the grating voice finished for him.

"No!" The injustice gave him back some courage. "I – I was looking for my sister's paintings."

"I don't deal in paintings." The dreadful voice was accompanied by a breath so pungent that Robbie tried not to inhale. Terror still gripped him but he had to get those paintings: for Catherine's sake, for Gunter's.

"You do," he contradicted flatly, trying to ignore the frantic hammering in his chest. "You sold one of them to Mr – Mr" – the name came back after a search – "Mr Grantham."

There was a moment's silence. "Man with a moustache?" the voice grated.

He nodded. "And it's my sister's painting and she wants it back."

A long silence while Robbie tried to look brave and not breath too much. "Your sister." The dreadful voice grated. "Young woman, is she? Skinny? Long" – amazingly the hoarseness grew worse – "long chestnut hair she could sit on?"

He nodded. He could feel a new tension in the horrible man and it frightened him even more. "Th-that's her."

"I got her paintings here." The voice creaked. "Found 'em I did. I didn't steal them."

Relief washed over Robbie like a warm blanket. Even the smells seemed less noxious. "I'll take them to her." He was already imaging the scene. Soon, soon, Gunter would be out of prison, the works would be successful – and he, Robbie, would be the hero.

"I'll take them."

He held out his hand but the man shook his head. "You go and tell your sister—" he started to laugh, wheezing horribly "—you tell your pretty little sister that if she wants her pictures back she's got to come here for them herself, understand? I won't give them up to nobody else."

He leaned forward, pressing his face up against Robbie's so that the boy was almost sick at the stench of his breath. "And I certainly won't give 'em to her if she comes here with a little sneak-thief like you in tow. Understand?"

It was too much. Robbie's nerve broke. With a choking gasp he jerked away from the man's grasp and dived for the door, scuttling along the floor on all fours in an attempt to evade the filthy, grasping fingers. Then he was out – out in the cool evening air and running down the rutted track to the road as if his life depended upon it.

"Lovely hair you've got." Penny twisted and pinned the final locks into place. "I'd give anything to grow my hair like this." She sighed. "Mine is piled up on rats and it still don't look nothing."

Catherine forced a sympathetic smile. At least she never needed to use false hairpieces, commonly called rats, to pad her hair up, but at the moment she would have swapped a foot-length of hair for a few inches on the hem of the dress.

In the war, women had taken jobs usually done by men and skirts had risen to show their ankles. But it wasn't just her ankles she was exposing now, it was her calves as well – even, perhaps, her knees if the light material fluttered in the summer breeze.

"Are you sure this is right?" she asked for the sixth time that morning.

Penny pinned her hat firmly on to the piled-up mass of her hair. "That's the way Mr Steiner drew 'un and he should know." She stepped back to admire the final picture. "Anyway, 'tes a brem good thing it were you he designed that dress for and not me. Brem awful I should look, sticking out front, back and sides. There idn't a pleat there that would stay in place if I were to wear 'un."

"It makes me look like a little girl," Catherine wailed, suddenly losing her nerve. "It makes me look as if I haven't got any figure at all."

"Well, I dunno. Seems to me that it makes you look as if you've got something, though I dunno how." Penny opened the door. "You go and show the others. We've all worked hard for that there silk and what you got on is the crowning glory, so to speak."

"I feel as if I'm outside in my nightdress," Catherine muttered, moving unwillingly to the door. Actually, she would rather have been wearing her nightdress, which covered her completely from throat to feet. As she stepped into the courtyard a small breeze stirred and the material fluttered lightly. "And it's so bright!" she complained. "Much brighter than the material I saw them printing."

"That's 'cos it's been steamed. Sets the colours and makes them much brighter, Mr Steiner says. We've got three or four more rolls to do now, soon as we get the steamer set up." Penny picked up the wrapped roll of silk that Catherine was to take to Penzance to sell. "You just remember you're the bee's knees and you'll do very well." She looked again at the dress. "I must say, it do show off the material something lovely."

I wish it showed *me* off something lovely, Catherine thought, holding the heavy roll. But it had to be done. Gunter had designed the dress to show off the material and if she could sell just one roll it would be a help. If she could only get enough money to pay a lawyer to get him out of prison . . .

Penny opened the door into the street. "Good luck, my handsome."

Catherine swallowed and stepped out into the bright sunshine. Across the road a fisherman nearly dropped the oars he was carrying over his shoulder, staring at her with popping eyes. A motor charabanc clattered by and she felt the astonished eyes of the dust-coated passengers staring at her from behind their motoring veils. At this rate she would be lucky to get to Penzance without being arrested.

But she had to do it. For Gunter's sake.

Head high, trying to ignore the looks and comments of the people she passed, Catherine set out to walk the long mile into Penzance.

"Stop dreaming."

A hard hand caught Robbie round the ear, jerking him back into the present. He blinked at the printer, rubbing his face. "That hurt."

"Then concentrate." The printer pointed to the pad. "What would have happened if I'd used that? It's only half covered with dye. It only takes one misprint and the whole roll could be ruined."

"I know." Robbie applied himself to covering the pad correctly. Inside he was worried. He had to tell Catherine about the rag-and-bone man. He would have done so last night but Father had come back in a filthy temper and he had had no chance – and this morning she had been so worried about the dress that he had not dared to begin the subject. But she had to be told. Only she could get the paintings back, the man had said.

If only he could go with her. There was something about the man that made his flesh creep. He hated the idea of Catherine going alone. But if she sold the silk she wouldn't need to. She could pay for the lawyer from the money she got for the silk and then he wouldn't need to tell her about the man.

He saw again, in his imagination, the long hanks of hair pinned to the shelf, and he shuddered.

"They wouldn't buy it!" Catherine would have burst into tears of mortification if she wasn't so angry. "He called me a shameless hussy!"

She thumped the roll of silk down on to the table and threw herself into the chair. Penny and Robbie stared at her anxiously.

"So there's no money to get Gunter out?" Robbie said, in a small voice.

"I don't think there ever will be." Catherine was as exhausted as if she had been working hard all day, instead of just walking into Penzance. It had taken so much effort to ignore the startled looks, the comments from respectable women and the more embarrassing though almost incomprehensible comments from less respectable men. She had felt like an exhibit in a fair, except that they got paid and she had done all this for nothing.

"Did you visit all the shops?" Penny asked anxiously.

Catherine shook her head. "Only one in the end. But it took so long to talk the shop assistant into letting me see the buyer – and then the manager came in and acted as if I were some sort of – immoral woman!" She felt dirtied by the experience. Mother had brought her up to be respectable: she had been going to be a teacher and there was nothing more respectable than that. Her treatment this morning had shocked her to the core.

"Oh, well." Robbie, with the resilience of childhood, was already getting over his disappointment. "There are lots of shops in Penzance, Katy. You can go to the others on Monday."

She nodded, wondering if she would have the courage to wear the dress again – or even go outside properly dressed. Rumours of her appearance must have spread through the village like wildfire. But if she was to get Gunter out of prison it had to be done. He had to have a lawyer or she was certain that, with anti-German feeling still running high after the war, he would never get a fair trial.

"I had to come back to pay the wages." It was how she had justified her retreat all the way home, trying to hold the roll of silk so that it hid her legs from as many people as possible. "There's still enough in his money box to pay the wages this week."

"And then we can go." Penny grinned. Saturday was always a half-day. "I'm going to Penzance to see what people are saying about you. If I hear any comments about you not being respectable I shall give them what for – just you see!" She snorted. "'Tes just a new fashion, that's all."

Catherine would have felt happier if she had been sure of this. Was the dress she was wearing a new fashion – or just something completely ridiculous that Gunter had dreamt up to show off his silk? She had never paid any attention to fashions. She pulled on her comfortable old clothes with relief. Even if they did still smell of fish, at least they were respectable.

"Are you coming?" Robbie appeared, poised at the door.

"You go on. I shall lock up." Catherine still felt too upset to face the outside world for a while. He shot off – almost as if he didn't want to walk home with her, Catherine thought sadly. Did even he feel shame at the way she had made a fool of herself today? But he had seemed constrained last night, too, when he had finally turned up long after he should have been in bed, as well as when they were walking into Newlyn this morning.

The thought of going outside frightened her. Was this what Father had felt like, those years when he was afraid to leave his bedroom? She felt more sympathetic towards him that she had for weeks.

She looked round the room. Unlike when Gunter had been there it was untidy, with scraps of silk and thread on the floor where

Penny had cut out the dress. What would Gunter feel like if he was allowed out of prison by some miracle and saw his living quarters like this?

She cleaned them then moved out into the other buildings. It was no one's job to clean these rooms; presumably he did it himself after everyone had left. It made her feel closer to him to be doing the things he would have done.

She swept her way through the storerooms. They seemed to be getting low on dye. Where would they order more from, she wondered, and could they afford to buy it? She tidied as she went, stacking cans neatly, emptying the used water out of the great wooden bath in which the raw silk was washed, . picking up anything on the floor and putting it neatly back on to the shelves.

It was as she was tidying the last storeroom that she caught the glint of silver. A coin? She stretched for it, pulling it out from where it was caught in a crack between the warped floorboards.

Not a coin. A medal.

She turned it over in her fingers. It was Uncle Robert's Military Medal – the name R. W. Harrison glittered in the sunlight. Robbie was always getting into trouble for taking it.

It was typical of him that he should bring it here and lose it, she thought with mixed exasperation and affection. If Father found the medal was missing he would give Robbie a sound thrashing. Well, at least she had saved the boy from that.

She tucked the medal into her pocket, checked that the bars, which had been refixed across the broken window, were secure, and carried on cleaning.

Robbie was waiting for her at the bottom of the road that ran up Newlyn Coombe, his face so concerned that, despite her problems, Catherine's heart went out to him. "What's the matter, Robbie? Is something wrong?"

He gulped. "I've found your pictures, Katy. The ones you lost."

Her heart gave a single, huge thud that shook her whole body then settled into a fast patter that seemed to deprive her of breath. "Where? How?"

He was avoiding her gaze, looking at the trees that bent over the road, the ground, anywhere but at her. "An old rag-and-bone

162

man at Kerris has got them." Suddenly he raised his eyes and she was struck by the desolation in them. "I tried to get them off him, Katy, I did try, but he said" – his glance moved away from her again, on to the scuffed toes of his boots – "he said he would only give them up if you came to get them."

Horror and delight fought. To get her pictures back – but that man . . . She shuddered as she remembered his hands touching her hair, his hoarse voice, but it all made sense. He made a living by picking up the rubbish that other people did not want; he certainly would not be likely to leave behind paintings that had been abandoned to the wind.

She had to get those pictures. For Gunter's sake – for her own – as if Gunter's happiness didn't now lie entwined with hers. But to see that disgusting old man again . . .

"Where does he live?" Her voice came out sounding strangled. "I've got this afternoon free. I can see him today."

"Kerris." Robbie sounded completely wretched. He stared at the ground a second longer then burst out, "It's a horrid place, Katy. It's filthy and he's horrible and—"

She touched his shoulder lightly. "I know, sweetheart. I've met him before. But if he's got my paintings . . ."

How much would he want for them? She had already spent nearly four shillings on the stockings she had worn today with that awful dress. She remembered the small amount of money left in the tin in the silk factory. She could not take that.

"I'll go now. I have to have those paintings." She touched his cheek lightly. "Thank you for your help, Robbie. You go and enjoy yourself. You've worked hard all week and you deserve it."

Catherine turned and walked resolutely back to Newlyn. She knew where Kerris was – up the hill where she had first met the rag-and-bone man then inland.

Behind her, Robbie watched her retreating figure with a worried look on his face, then, suddenly, he began to follow her, keeping out of sight around the twists and turns of the road.

The shack was as noisome as Robbie had described, Catherine realised when she reached Kerris. Despite the urgency of her visit Catherine's heart sank when she saw the skinny donkey tied up to a rotting post. She had half hoped, despite herself, that the man would be out.

The door was dragged open as soon as she had knocked and the face that had haunted her dreams stared at her, wild white hair framing a sallow face ingrained with blackheads. "I knew you'd come here, my handsome." He pulled the door further open. "Come on in."

"No, thank you." She swallowed, trying not to gag at the miasma of filth that seeped through the open doorway, polluting even the fresh air in which she stood. "I – I came to – ask for my paintings." She would not mention money – not until he did.

His smile broadened, showing mossy teeth. "Then you'd better come in, my handsome. I idn't going to talk about they pictures outside." He stood aside. The door to the shack loomed like the door of a dungeon, or a trap.

Catherine hesitated, every instinct telling her not to go. But she had to have those paintings, she had to. She glanced desperately over her shoulder hoping that there would be someone near that she could call to in need – a farmer in a field, children with a dog – but there was no one in sight. She turned back. The doorway gaped.

"I'm waiting." The hoarse voice made the hackles rise on her neck but she had no choice.

With a final breath of clean air and a last, longing look at the open fields around, Catherine stepped forward, into the rag-and-bone man's shack.

Nineteen

Catherine felt a shiver of fear run down her spine as the rag-and-bone man closed the sagging door behind her.

Despite the bright afternoon sunshine outside, the interior of the hut was shrouded in shadow. No beams could penetrate far through the small windows, their thick, distorting panes crusted with the filth of at least a dozen years.

"I want my paintings." Holding her breath wasn't an option so she breathed through her mouth, trying to ignore the assailing smells. "You have no right to them."

"Finders, keepers," he reminded her, his voice rasping more than ever. "I found them and now they're mine. Until I decide otherwise. Which I might. For a – consideration." He reached out a grimy hand, pulling her wide-brimmed hat from her head with a rough gesture. "You've covered up your lovely hair, my handsome."

Catherine winced as her hat-pins were dragged out, moving away automatically, trying to put some space between her and the old man. She stared around the room, her eyes becoming accustomed to the dimness, appalled by the mess and chaos everywhere. Even if he still had her paintings, would they be any use to her after being kept here? But she had to try.

"How much do you want for them?" She had very little money, but what she had she would give him.

There was a surreptitious movement in the dark corner on which she had fixed her gaze. A rat? She shuddered, moving her eyes quickly away.

The hanks of hair trailed raggedly from the shelf. She swallowed, sickened. Even in the dim light she could see that the locks, once glossy, were now dull, tangled, covered with the all-pervading filth. Once they had been cared for, brushed, shone with health and youth and now . . .

165

They were all the hair of young women. None of the bunches were grey. How had he got them? she wondered, her attention fixed in horror. Did he dig up the dead? She could almost imagine it of him, so dirty, so frightening, so strange.

"Well, what about it?" She had been so preoccupied with the dreadful sight that she hadn't heard his question but now the hoarse voice quivered with a terrible eagerness. "What do you say?"

As she turned her head he saw what she had been looking at. "Admiring my trophies, are you? Brem lovely they are; brem beautiful." He moved across, stroking the hanging bunches with thick, grimy fingers. Even in the dimness she could see how the individual hairs snagged on his rough nails and skin, tangling and pulling. Eyeing her, he lifted the hank to his mouth, kissed it lovingly . . . She shuddered, looking swiftly away.

"Lovely." Her voice was no more than a croak. She gazed longingly at the irregular streaks of daylight that rimmed the drooping door. Two seconds and she could be out of here. Two seconds and she would be in the clean air, away from this place of filth and perversion, but she knew that she could not do it.

She had to have those paintings.

"So?" the hoarse voice asked, and it sounded more breathless, more excited than before. "What's your answer, my handsome? Do you accept? Eh? Eh?"

He came towards her, staring up into her face with bright rheumy eyes.

Catherine turned her head from the noxious blast of her breath. "I – I'm sorry. I didn't hear how much you wanted."

"I said it isn't money that I want for those there pictures." He reached out and she shuddered as his fingers touched the hair so carefully arranged by Penny that morning.

"I'll exchange you the pictures – for this."

Crouched against the hedge, Robbie stared worriedly at the closed door.

Catherine shouldn't have gone into the hut. He didn't understand why, but he knew, with the simple instinct of childhood, that the rag-and-bone man was dangerous.

What should he do? This was all his fault. If he hadn't told her . . . But she needed the paintings for Gunter.

The dilemma weighed down his eleven-year-old shoulders but, clear as a beacon, one thought stayed firm in his mind.

He had to make sure Catherine was safe.

The rag-and-bone man had told him not to come back but he could not obey, not with Catherine inside that place.

He took a deep breath and stood up, squaring his shoulders, then walked with steady steps and racing heart up to the door of the hut.

"My hair?"

Catherine took a step backwards, her hands rising automatically to protect her head. "Not my hair. You can't mean . . ."

Her glance again went to the shelf with its dreadful hanging ornaments and her voice died away. He did mean it, she realised. If she gave way to him her hair would hang there, alongside those gruesome trophies, to be fondled and kissed for his pleasure. The very thought made her feel as if her whole body was smothered in slime.

"Please." Her voice came out no louder than a whisper. "Please, not my hair."

Her hair. Her best feature. Mother had always said so and she knew it. She was not beautiful; she lacked the opulent curves that other women seemed to develop so easily. All she had to raise her above the mediocre was her hair, long and thick, gleaming like burnished chestnut in the sunshine.

And to leave it here, with him . . .

"No." Her voice was stronger now. "No. I'll give you all the money I have, but please – not my hair."

The door behind her scraped open and she swung round, her heart leaping. A well-known voice, quivering with fright but staunchly loyal, demanded, "D-d-don't you give him your hair, Katy. Don't you. He's got l-l-ots of people's hair as it is. He doesn't need yours."

"I told you to stay away."

The man was across the shack in two strides but Catherine had already moved, clinging to his arm to drag him away from her brother. "Leave him alone. He's only trying to help me."

Robbie stood his ground and Catherine's heart was lifted by his desperate courage. "Don't you do it, Katy."

The man grinned, showing his mossy teeth. "But if she wants

they pictures, she's got to do it." He swung back to Catherine. "And you want they pictures brem badly, I reckon."

She nodded dumbly. She had to have them. They might be sold to pay for Gunter's defence. She might even be able to show them to Augustus Farley. Her whole future depended on getting those pictures back.

"But you don't know if he's still got them," Robbie said shrilly. "He might have sold them – or they'll be all dirty or eaten by rats or something."

She hadn't even considered that. She broke into a cold sweat at the thought that she might have given up her hair to no purpose. "He's right." She swallowed, feeling her courage flow back in the boy's presence. "Before I'll agree to anything I want to see the paintings."

The rag-and-bone man cast the boy an angry look but walked to the corner where she had seen the rat and began to rummage through the untidy pile of papers and rags. She watched him, her heart in her mouth, torn between hoping the paintings were there and wanting them ruined. Unconsciously, her hand went to her head, smoothing the long, intricate locks, tucking a loose strand behind her ear.

"Here we are." He dragged something out from the depths of the pile and she saw that he had at least had the sense to put the paintings back in the portfolio she had dropped when she had fled from him all those weeks ago.

"I still want to see the paintings," she insisted.

He undid the ties and held them out for her to see, standing too far away to give Catherine a chance at grabbing the portfolio and running. In the increased light from the door she could make them out clearly and she blinked, remembering the happy times she had experienced when she had spent days at a time sketching and painting, when Mother was at home providing security and comfort and her future was mapped out and easy.

The memory of a child, she realised suddenly, not of a woman.

And now she was a woman and she had to make a decision.

"Those are my paintings." She could feel herself begin to shake as if she had a fever. The decision could not be avoided now. "Give them to my brother and I will let you have my hair."

"No, Katy!" She could hear the tears in Robbie's voice but she knew that she had no choice. Whatever it cost her, she had to get those paintings.

"I'm not giving anything to anyone until I got my payment." The rag-and-bone man propped the portfolio up on the shelf with the hair. "It'll stay there until I'm satisfied." He reached inside the dirty coat and pulled out a knife he wore on his cracked and straining belt. "Now then, my beauty, you let your hair down for me and you can have they pictures before the dog has time to lick itself."

Now that the moment had come Catherine felt as if she could not move. Arms, heavy as rocks, could scarcely be lifted above her shoulders. Fingers thicker than sausages fumbled and dropped the hairpins. Another minute, that was all she had. Another minute – and then all her hair would belong to this man. He would practise his strange pleasures over her crowning glory while she looked like a scarecrow.

The final pin came out and her hair slithered silkenly around her shoulders, covering her to below her hips. Automatically, she shook her head, sending the tresses dancing and shimmering around her in a scented dance.

"Beautiful." The hoarse voice was breathless and she saw that the man's hand was shaking as he reached out to touch the nearest locks with his filthy hand. "Beautiful. Now you just bend forward, my handsome."

Catherine could feel the tears starting in her eyes. She bent forward as instructed and the man brushed her hair roughly forward so that it hung in a chestnut waterfall in front of her eyes, trailing along the filthy earthen floor. Her crowning glory – her one good feature—

Be grateful you have something he wants, she reminded herself fiercely, trying not to shudder at the touch of the man's hands on her head. She felt him lift a section of hair, felt the knife press against the roots . . .

"Stop." Robbie's voice made her jump and she heard the man's panting suspended.

"What's the matter?" he muttered, sounding almost drunk with the shock of the interruption.

Robbie pointed to the hair on the shelf. "That hair is all a lot shorter than Katy's."

"So?" the man turned his back on him, putting a firm hand on Catherine's head. "Bend forward again."

169

"No. Wait." She turned in her cape of glory. "What are you trying to say, Robbie?"

He moved forward and reached up, gathering her hair together with unaccustomed hands at the nape of her neck. "If you cut it there it would still be longer than any of the other hair you've got."

And she wouldn't be bald. It was the fear of looking a freak that had been the worst thing of all. She turned eagerly to the man. "If you have some string and tie it together there it will all be held safe for when you hang it up. Not like that hair." She nodded at the shelf. It was obvious that the hair had been cut in separated hanks and tied together afterwards.

He considered this and she shook her head again, making her hair ripple and dance around her. She heard him catch his breath as he stared at her hair, as if hypnotised.

This was the way to do it, she realised. If she could play on his desire for her hair to such an extent that he did not think too clearly, then she might manage to escape with more than shaven scalp.

She tilted her head and ran her fingers through her tresses, lifting them back off her head, showing off their weight and texture. "All it will take is a piece of string and you will have the hair ready to hang up on your shelf." She turned around swiftly, so that it flew out around her body in a shimmering swirl. "That will be the best way, won't it, Robbie?"

She heard the man gasp once as a floating lock lightly touched his cheek then he was back in the corner, rummaging again. "Here." His voice was shaking with desire and impatience. "Here's the string."

She gathered the hair into a bunch at the back of her neck herself, bending her head forward and turning it from side to side in an attempt to work as much looseness above the string as possible. When he had tied the knot she adjusted it again herself, as if for comfort, edging it down another fraction of an inch. "You don't want to cut my head off at the same time."

The bunched mass of hair proved difficult to cut. He had to saw his way through it even though the knife was sharp. The sound of the steel rasping on the strands echoed through her head. The knife pulled and tore at the hair, bringing tears of pain to her eyes, but the pain of the knife was as nothing compared to the pain in her heart.

She would be plain now. Gunter would never look at her with admiration after this, whatever she did to save him. She would be rejected, ugly, unfeminine, a freak. She blinked, her teeth buried deep in her bottom lip, and stayed silent and motionless as the rape of her hair continued.

There was a last, painful yank, and her head was suddenly free. Disbelieving, she raised her face. Her head felt as if it would float off her shoulders at any moment. It seemed that only the heaviness in her heart stopped her from leaving the floor altogether, so unbelievably light did she feel without her cloak of hair.

"Get the paintings, Robbie." She bent to pick up her hat from the filthy floor, turning her head so that she wouldn't have to see the man caressing her shorn hair.

As the boy reached for the portfolio she crammed her hat on to her head. Without her hair it was too large, sliding down to almost cover her ears, and the hat-pins, with no long, interwoven tresses to pierce, would not do their job.

She did not care. She just wanted to get out of the place, out into the fresh air, into cleanness and life, away from filth and perversion. She caught Robbie's arm as he came up to her, holding the portfolio to his body as if it were the most precious thing in the world, and they made a silent exit together, head up, backs straight, dignified.

It was only when they reached the roadway that she began to run. Holding her hat to her head with one hand Catherine ran as if she could leave behind all the pain and heartache, as if there was a better world, a world where she had not had to lose her hair, a world where such things did not happen – a world she would reach if she ran fast enough.

"Katy. Katy, wait for me."

The plaintive voice from behind brought her to her senses. There was no running away from what had happened. She had had a choice to make and she had made it, but if it hadn't been for Robbie . . . She turned back, enfolding the boy in her arms. "Oh, Robbie. Thank God you came. Thank God."

"But I couldn't save your hair, Katy. And it was all my fault. If I hadn't told you—"

"I had to have those pictures, Robbie. We must get a lawyer for Gunter, whatever happens. And if you hadn't been there . . ."

She had visions of her hair, shaved off almost at the scalp, falling on to the filthy floor in a tangled mass. And afterwards – the man had only been interested in the hair he had cut off. What would have happened if he had cut it off and then refused to give her the paintings? She shuddered again.

"But your hair!" He reached up and pulled her hat off, touching the tendrils left with the sensitivity of a much older person. "Your hair was so lovely, Katy."

His sympathy was the final straw. She would not accept Robbie's pity. She sniffed, forcing a tremulous smile. "It will grow again. And I have a lot more hair than I would have done if you hadn't been there." She fumbled for a handkerchief, pulling it loose from her pocket, and as she did so something else came out with it, catching the sun with a metallic gleam as it fell.

"There you are. One good deed deserves another. At least I saved you from a hiding over this." She picked up Uncle Robert's medal and held it out to him.

He stared down at it blankly. "Where did you get this, Katy?"

"In the storeroom, when I was sweeping it." She shook her head. "You know Father has forbidden you to play with those medals. And to take one out of the house and lose it – he would have horsewhipped you if he had found out."

He turned it over and over, running his finger over the impressed letters that recorded his uncle's army number, his name – R. W. Harrison – and his regiment, then lifted his head and stared at her. "But I never took it out of the house, Katy. I promise you."

"What?"

He met her eyes and she could see only total honesty in his face as he said, "I have never taken Uncle Robert's medals to the works." He handed the silver medal back to her. "Father found me with it the other evening and he took it off me and I haven't seen it since."

"Oh, my soul and body!" Penny Pentyr stared with horror at Catherine's shorn head. "Whatever have you done to your lovely hair?"

Half laughing, half crying, Catherine almost fell into her arms.

"I had to sell it, and, oh Penny, it must look awful. I thought that you might be able to do something."

"Do something?" She pulled off the ill-fitting hat. "Why do you think I could do something? The only thing that will make you look anything like you did is a wig, I reckon."

"But you were a lady's maid," Catherine protested. "You know how to do hair. I thought perhaps if you could cut it or something . . ."

"Cut it?" Penny's voice rose in horror. "I didn't do that sort of thing, except perhaps a fringe or that." She walked round Catherine staring at her with amazed horror. "I never in my life saw anything that awful before."

There was a small mirror over the sink and Catherine moved to it. She had to agree. It had been Robbie's idea that a haircut might improve matters and, seeing the hacked mess of her hair, Catherine could understand why. Tendrils stuck out at odd angles, the hair in front was much longer than the hair at the back and flopped in an unregulated mass over her eyes. Robbie, at his worst, had never looked such a ragamuffin. "But what am I going to do?" she wailed. "I can't go out looking like this!"

She had finally covered the ruin of her hair with a knotted contraption of Robbie's and her own handkerchiefs. It had at least hidden the mess and enabled her to keep her hat on but she had had some strange looks as she had hurried through Newlyn to Penny's house.

She turned to Penny. Honesty was the only policy. "If I go home looking like this my father will kill me," she said. "If I can at least get my hair looking – styled – I can tell him that I had it cut deliberately."

"And why would you do that?" Penny demanded. "You with those lovely locks so long you could sit on them."

"Stop it." If she listened to much more of this she would start to cry. "It's done now and I must make the best of it. Please, Penny, can't you cut it for me?"

"No, I can't. And that's that." The other woman lifted a piece of hair, stuck it behind Catherine's ear, pulled it forward again. Finally, she sighed. "The only thing I can think of is a barber. They know how to cut men's hair and that's not much shorter than this."

"That will do." Catherine turned around and planted an

unexpected kiss on the woman's cheek. "So now, Penny, please could you find a barber and get him to come here. Please. Because" – her voice broke on a half-laugh, half-sob – "there's no way that I can go and look for a barber myself."

"Father."

Walter grunted, half asleep in a chair beside the range.

"Father," Robbie persisted. "C-c-can I see Uncle Robert's medals?"

Walter opened one eye. "No you bloody well can't," he snapped. "You're always playing with them. That's why I locked them away."

"Just to look," Robbie pleaded. "Just for a second. Before supper."

"There won't be any supper if your sister doesn't come in soon," Walter grumbled, but to Robbie's relief he rose from his chair. "Where is she, anyway? The fish factory doesn't usually open on a Saturday afternoon."

Katy was going to be in so much trouble when she came in, Robbie thought. She still hadn't told Father that she had been sacked and only had a couple of days' pay, and most of that she had spent on silk stockings – which even Robbie thought was a waste of money. They were so thin you could hardly see that she was wearing them, even when she was. And now there would be trouble about her hair . . .

Best to get the medal business sorted out first, he decided. "Uncle Robert's medals, Father?"

"Oh, very well. I'll get no peace until I show you."

He led the way into his spartan bedroom and unlocked the drawer to the bedside cupboard with a key hanging from his belt. With a rough hand he pushed handkerchiefs and socks to one side. "There you are. All present and correct."

Robbie craned his neck. "I can't see his Military Medal."

"It's there somewhere." Walter stirred the contents of the drawer with his hands while Robbie watched, his eyes darting from one corner of the drawer to another.

It wasn't there.

Walter stirred again, more and more irritated. "What does it matter, anyway? He had others more—" He stopped abruptly and Robbie saw the sudden look of panic that flitted across his face.

174

It was all the confirmation Robbie needed but, knowing his father as he did, he wasn't surprised when Walter turned on him. Walter would always blame him for everything, even if he knew Robbie was innocent.

"You've taken it, haven't you? You little rat!" He lifted a hand but Robbie was too quick for him.

"No. Look! There it is!" Robbie jumped forward as if reaching into the drawer and banged his hip against it. The drawer, already almost completely yanked out, tumbled to the floor, spraying socks, coins and medals all around the room.

"You clumsy oaf!" The slap was hard, knocking Robbie sideways. "Why don't you look what you're doing!"

"I-I'll help you pick them up, shall I?" Robbie offered.

"You get out of this room. And if I find you with those medals ever again . . ."

Robbie grinned secretly to himself as he left the room, rubbing his burning ear. Father was always able to put up a smokescreen if he was in any danger but Robbie had seen the look on his face.

Walter had known that the medal was missing – and that he was the one who had dropped it.

"I never cut no lady's hair before." The barber stared disapprovingly at Catherine as she sat, swathed in a towel.

"Just pretend I'm a man," she suggested. "You must be used to cutting hair this long."

"But not on a lady." He was a man with a one-track mind. He lifted a lock condescendingly. "Who cut this for you, anyway?"

"It was a joke." Catherine smiled at him in the small mirror that Penny had propped on the kitchen table. "Only it went a bit wrong."

"You don't say." But he seemed to have become reconciled to his unusual task. "What sort of cut do you want, then?"

She knew nothing of men's hairstyles; they all looked alike to her. "I don't want it cut too short," she said hastily. "Enough has been lost already." Then, as inspiration struck, "What about the sort of hairstyle you give little boys when they have their first haircut? Their hair is usually longer."

She could see that now he had something that he recognised. His comb came out, tugging her mutilated locks that way and this. "A fringe?" he suggested. "And longer at the sides?"

She couldn't envisage it but anything had to be better than what she had at the moment. "That sounds wonderful," she said firmly, and closed her eyes so that she wouldn't see her few remaining locks being shorn still shorter.

Twenty

"Where have you been?" Walter demanded.

Catherine's lips tightened. It had been a long day and she had hoped that her father would be out with his friends. The showdown would have been easier after a night's sleep.

"Why don't you fight?" Gunter had asked her. Well, now she had no choice.

She moved forward into the lamplight, pulling off her hat defiantly. "Getting my hair cut."

He stared at her for a long moment, as if he could not take in the sudden change in her appearance; then he was on his feet, his face a mask of anger. "You – slut!" The words echoed round the cottage and she heard a creak of the floorboards that warned her that Robbie must still be awake. "You whore – making a spectacle of yourself, parading yourself to the world like a woman of the streets. You – bitch."

A month ago such condemnation would have turned her into a quivering wreck but after her other experiences the words were no more than an irritation. "I've cut my hair," she said calmly. "That is not the end of the world."

"Yes – cut your hair. To make men look at you! To cut yourself off from your proper roots. Long hair was good enough for my mother and grandmother but not for you. You have to try to make a spectacle of yourself. But I won't have it, my girl. I won't have it. You're my daughter and you'll look and act like a respectable woman."

"Are you going to stick my hair back on?" It was rank insolence but she had to fight back as best she could. Her hair was only the first of the battles she was going to have to fight with him tonight, but it was the most easily won because he could do nothing about it.

He moved closer, waving a finger in front of her eyes. "Don't

177

you cheek me or I'll belt you like I used to when you were a child."

Again, the creak of floorboards. Don't come down, Robbie, she prayed. It would only anger him more and Robbie would suffer for it.

"Cutting your hair!" He was beside himself with rage. "A woman's crowning glory, the Bible calls it, but you have to go against the Good Book and get it all cut off for . . ."

He had not been to church for years and his hypocrisy sickened her.

Suddenly his face changed. "Your hair." He took a deep, satisfied breath. "You sold it, didn't you?"

It took her by surprise. "Well, I—" It had never occurred to her to sell her hair until the rag-and-bone man had suggested it.

"Fetch a lot, long hair like that would." His voice was calmer and she could see the calculation in his narrowed eyes. "Rich women are always ready to buy false hair pieces." Suddenly his expression changed again. "And I suppose you were planning to keep it all to yourself, weren't you?" Anger flamed in his face. "Planning to spend it all on gewgaws. Aping your betters!"

He held out a shaking hand. "Well, I won't have it. Hand it over at once. You're a working woman and my daughter and what you earn belongs to me."

Catherine's heart sank. This was the second battle – and one that she was afraid she would lose. And she still had to tell him that she had been sacked from the work he had found her.

She raised her head, taking a deep breath to steady herself, and found herself looking at him as if he were a stranger. His face was mottled with anger, his hand was shaking. He reminded her suddenly of a small boy having a tantrum – and she knew how to deal with that. There had been many such episodes in the small school in Affpuddle.

She gently moved his hand from in front of her face. "Don't be ridiculous, Father." She kept her voice down but instilled into it all the authority that she had acquired the hard way, trying to keep control of unruly classes when she was only another pupil, just a few years older than they were. "I am no longer a child and I have a right to do as I like with any money I earn."

She took another deep breath. She might as well get it all over with at once. "I have also stopped working at the fish factory."

He was on her, shaking her. "You bitch. I'll not keep any undutiful daughter here who doesn't earn her keep. I'll—"

The injustice stung. "I would earn my keep if all I did was wash your clothes, and keep your house clean and buy and cook your food and fetch your water and trim and fill your lamps and keep the fire in and—"

The litany of all that she had to do after her long stint in the fish-canning factory infuriated him.

"You're a woman! That's your job!"

Now her anger swelled. She had always hated injustice but this was the first time she had seen injustice in relation to herself. She worked as long hours as he did, walked further to work, toiled in the cottage to look after him – and he had denied her almost all the money she had earned, denied her also the consolation of painting in the few hours that she was at leisure. Even friends were denied her.

But he – he came home expecting the supper to be ready, the house clean. He spent more and more time out with his friends, drinking—

Drinking her money, she realised suddenly. How else could he afford it?

She placed her palms flat on the scarred wood of the rickety kitchen table which was the best he would "waste his money on".

"It is not you who are keeping me," she said quietly. "I am keeping you. And I am working in the silk factory." She took a deep breath. "If I have to earn money for you then I will at least do work I enjoy, amongst people I like – even if it does mean that I am doing work that you think is unsuitable."

She stood straighter, facing him down. "You might come from a family who worked on the land but what of my mother? She was educated and a gentlewoman. What right have you to say that I shall only take after your side of the family and not hers?"

"The right of your only living parent," he snarled.

She said quietly, "But not the right of an honest man."

His face was suddenly livid. His tongue flicked quickly across white lips. "What – I don't know what you mean." His voice was hoarse and shaking.

Catherine paused, her hand in her pocket. His reaction startled her. It seemed too strong for the relatively small hold she had over

179

him. Perhaps it was just the shock of her standing up to him, she reasoned as she opened her hand and let Uncle Robert's Military Medal drop on to the table top.

It spun in small circles, gleaming silver in the lamplight before coming to rest. The words "For Bravery in the Field" stared mockingly up at them.

"How could you?" Catherine demanded. "How could you deliberately plant a stolen watch on Gunter? I know you hate Germans, I know you don't like Robbie and I to have friends, but that is despicable."

Slowly Walter sank into a chair and stared at the small silver disc shining up at him. "I – you—" She noticed with astonishment that he could hardly get the words out. "How did you know I—"

"Who else could have dropped Uncle Robert's medal there?" Her voice quivered with disgust. "Robbie promised me that he had never taken it out of the cottage, and I hadn't – so there was only you."

"Robbie – you—" He still stared disbelievingly at the medal.

"I found it when I was cleaning one of the factory storerooms. It was caught in a crack in the floor where you had dropped it when you broke in to plant the watch." Suddenly her anger boiled over. "It was despicable! To take your revenge on an innocent man like that, just because he was a German."

Walter sat motionless, his eyes fixed disbelievingly on the medal. His stillness frightened her. There was something here she did not understand.

Catherine brushed the thought away. She had the upper hand now. He could no longer threaten her.

"I'm going to work there until he is released," she stated, her eyes fixed on her silent father. "There won't be any money but I shall still do my work here. But once I have got Gunter released I shall get other work, work I enjoy." She took a deep breath. "I shall teach, if I can get a post somewhere. I shall write to Dorset and get references. I'm not going to live this lie any more."

She stood up, staring down at him. "You were ill," she said more gently, "but you are well now. There is no need for all this secrecy. It is just a final symptom of your illness. That is why I am not telling anyone about you. But I won't stand for being bullied by you – and I am going to get Gunter released."

She pointed at the medal on the table. "I know you were there," she said, "but I couldn't prove it in a court of law. You would say that Robbie took the medal to the silk works and everyone would believe you. But I know. Remember that. I know."

With a swift movement she turned and walked out.

Walter sat silently, staring at the silver disc as if hypnotised though inside his thoughts raced in panic-stricken circles like rats in a cage.

It was worse than he had thought. Far worse. Not only was the man who he had held capture, who had witnessed his subsequent degradation, here in Cornwall, but he was friends with the two children. And Catherine had connected him, Walter, with the watch.

He began to shiver. On all sides exposure threatened. The firing squad was only a matter of weeks away. Catherine was right when she said that the medal by itself proved nothing, but if William-John Tredissick heard about it Walter knew that he would be in trouble. Or if William-John learned about his relationship with the German – or even of the German's relationship with his children . . .

He had made his hatred of the Germans so well known that no one would be surprised if they learned that he had deliberately incriminated a German who was friendly with his daughter.

And then there was Catherine. Catherine was the key to his danger, he realised. He was in her power. She could incriminate him in a dozen different ways.

But would she? Despite her rebellion today she was still a loyal daughter. She had not gone to the police with the medal but had brought it to him.

He remembered her final remarks about his illness. That was why she was so dangerous, he realised. If she had known he was a deserter, much as she would have despised him, she would never have given him away. Instead, because she did not know, she was a walking time bomb.

It was too late, now, to tell her the truth. He had seen the look in her eyes when she mentioned the name of the German. She was in love with the bastard, though he doubted whether she knew it herself yet. But, sooner or later, the realisation would come – and then what? If matters came to a

181

head, who would she side with? Her father – or the German?

No, he could not tell her now. But nor could he leave her in innocence – she was far too dangerous.

His shaking hand stole out and covered the silver meal that his handsome, laughing brother, Robert, had been awarded for courage.

He would have to do something about Catherine.

Catherine hefted the roll of silk and tried to ignore the glances.

It wasn't getting any easier. Today she had been all too well aware of what would happen when she went out wearing the dress. Knowing how awful she looked without her long hair just made it worse. It was kind of Penny to say that Catherine looked better in the dress with short hair, but Catherine knew what she really meant.

Catherine now looked, from head to foot, as if she were going to a fancy-dress party dressed up as a child.

She couldn't even hide, as she had before, behind the broad brim of her hat. With short hair it slipped down so far it hid her eyes and even she could see that the wide hat on top of her slender body made her look like an exotic mushroom.

The smaller roll of paintings, chosen from the portfolio that she had left with Penny for safety, was clutched carefully in her hand.

Catherine hesitated at the top of the terrace by the domed Market House that dominated the town. Post the paintings off to Miss Rose first, or try another shop? Posting the paintings would put off the evil moment when she would have to brave another furious manager. She had moved one step towards the post office when the voice echoed in her mind. *"Fight."*

It was all right for her, she reminded herself, ignoring the startled onlookers who walked past, their eyes fixed on her strange garment and shamelessly exposed calves, but posting the paintings would not help release Gunter.

She raised her head high, gave it a small shake to settle the strands of hair that the light breeze had blown out of place, and marched into Tancock's.

"Madam?" She did not blame the voice for sounding surprised as she peered round her roll of silk.

"I wish to see your buyer of ladies' fabrics." She spoke with her most self-assured voice, as if she were addressing a classroom of recalcitrant ten-year-olds. "I have here a roll of exclusive silk, hand-printed by experts, which will make up into dresses and blouses that will delight the most discerning of your customers." She attempted to add a slight spin to the words, inferring that Tancock's customers were unlikely to be discerning enough to match her high standards.

A black pillar of disapproval, the saleswoman stared at her frostily and Catherine hoped that she wasn't going to be thrown out of the shop instantly. It was always embarrassing and, despite the fact that it was early in the morning, she could hear the chatter of customers down at the other end of the shop. To be unceremoniously dismissed in front of an audience would be even worse. Her face burned as she remembered some of the terms that the last manager had used.

The pillar hesitated, swaying to and fro uncertainly as though caught in a strong wind, and then the sound of the other customers seemed to have its effect on her. She glanced distractedly at where they stood, fingering light, summer materials, and made up her mind. "I'll see if the buyer is available, madam."

Catherine breathed a sigh of relief. She was past the first hurdle. She balanced the covered roll of silk on a bent wood chair, glad to rest her arms for a few moments.

"You wanted something?"

She swung hastily round. There was no doubting that this was the manager – unless he was the owner. He was short and pompous and his little moustache bristled with self-importance. Hostility poured from him, surrounding her like a cold fog. She might as well leave quietly.

She might as well fight.

Catherine raised her voice to give herself courage. "I have here a roll of high quality, hand-blocked silk—"

"We don't buy from gypsies."

She gaped at him. "I am not a gypsy." She glanced down at her silk dress, the loose pleats of the skirt scarcely covering her knees, then forced herself to meet his eye. "If you don't recognise modern fashions when you see them then I am obviously not in the kind of emporium to which the creator of this design would wish his silk to be sold."

"You certainly are not." She could see that he was not to be taken in by such tactics. "As a matter of policy we never buy from itinerants."

Her eyes snapped. "That, sir, may well be slander," she told him.

"On the contrary, it is more than likely the exact truth."

They stared at each other across the roll of silk, held in her arms like a lance at rest. She was suddenly aware that all other noises in the shop had ceased and realised that their raised voices must have reached to the far end of the shop.

"You haven't even looked at the silk," she reminded him. "You may be missing the chance of a lifetime."

"It is more than likely that, once you have left, I shall find myself missing several items from around the shop." His eyebrows bristled. "Do you think I don't know the way you and your sort work?"

"My sort?" Catherine snapped. "Even if I were a gypsy I would expect to be treated like a human being and not simply judged by and condemned for my race alone."

"Of course you are a gypsy," the man retorted. "And if you and your confederates are not out of here within five seconds I shall call the police and have you arrested."

With her last hope of a sale gone Catherine jumped the silk up higher in her arms to make it easier to carry and smiled brilliantly at her adversary.

"I hope that by 'your confederates' you are not referring to the ladies at the far end of your shop," she told him sweetly. "It may just be that you have lost more sales than I have." She turned and marched out of the door, the bell jangling behind her.

Outside, she balanced the silk against the iron railings that edged the Terrace and leaned beside it, trembling with anger. How dare he judge and condemn her like that? Just because he thought she was a gypsy. She felt an unladylike urge to go back into the shop and kick him.

How could Gunter stand it? she wondered suddenly. He had to put up with that and worse all the time, yet he never seemed to lose his temper or even get upset.

The bell over the shop door tinkled again and she quickly jumped around. If that man had come to tell her to move along she would really lose her temper. This was a public place and she was doing no more than a dozen other loafers were doing.

The two shoppers came out and crossed to her straight away. "You were quite right." The speaker was a slightly older woman with a strange accent that Catherine suspected might be American. "That man has the manners and intelligence of a cockatoo. Condemning you like that, and without even giving you a chance to show him what you were selling."

"He could do with some new stuff, anyway." This was the younger girl, a pretty blonde with a delicious hat that Catherine would have loved perched on her ornate hair. "Most of what he has must have been bought before the war."

"Before the Boer War, probably." The American was looking at Catherine consideringly, her head on one side. "Is the material you were trying to sell what you are wearing?"

"It's the same pattern but a different colour. Pinks instead of greens." She glanced at them. "If you are interested . . ."

"I'm more interested in where you got that dress," the blonde admitted. "I've seen something similar in London but I never thought to see anything like that down here."

Catherine managed to swallow an amazed, "You have?" She had been firmly of the opinion that Gunter must have been suffering from a brain defect when he designed the dress, but the thought that there might be other, similar clothes around, even if only in London, was wonderfully soothing. She said quickly, "The pattern was produced by a trained dress designer specifically to show off this material."

"It does too," the American insisted, fingering the pleats as she talked to her companion. "You're only against it, pet, because despite your artistic pretensions you're like all blondes and make a beeline for the pink."

"The pink material *is* nice." Catherine pulled back a little of the covering to show one end of the roll. Of course, she ideally wanted to sell to the shops but if all she could sell was a few yards to one of these ladies that would be a start.

The American fingered it again. "Could your designer make it up for me in a dress similar to the one you're wearing?"

Catherine thought fast. Penny could probably adapt the basic pattern and do the sewing. It wasn't at all what Catherine had intended but there would be extra profit if she could charge for the making-up of the dress rather than just the material.

She smiled broadly. "That would be no trouble at all."

Elation at her first sale, even if it was a small one, made her unwilling to break the spell immediately by facing rejection in another shop. She made her way down the granite steps from the Terrace and across Market Jew Street, dodging the ponies pulling traps and a bustling, rattling charabanc full of visitors. Again she saw the heads, covered with veils that were tied over wide hats and under chins, move to follow her progress but she did not mind now.

Women in London wore clothes like this. The American lady, who despised the materials on offer in Tancock's, was going to have a similar dress made. She wasn't a clown or immoral, she was just fashionable. Revelling in her modernity, Catherine almost flew across the road and into the coolness of the granite-fronted post office.

She was just turning away, having paid the postage on her pictures, when a thought struck her. "You don't – there isn't a letter for me, poste restante, is there?" Foolish, of course. Miss Rose wouldn't write again until she had heard from Catherine but today was a magic day. Today anything could happen.

She saw the half-smile in the clerk's eyes as he turned away and knew that he was suspecting her of a clandestine correspondence but she did not care. Such a thing was allowed for someone who wore fashionable clothes.

He checked the pigeonholes, checked again, came back with a letter in his hand. "Your name again, miss?"

"Catherine Harrison." She smiled as she took it, struggling with her unwiedly roll of silk, smiled as she walked out into the sunshine, smiled as she slit it open with an impatient finger.

The contents brought her to an abrupt halt, her face white with shock. It took seconds before she could realise what she held in her trembling fingers.

A money order for eighteen pounds.

It was late for breakfast and Random was the only guest, but the hotel staff had accommodated him, seeming pleased that he was up and about again.

"Glad you're better today, sir." The friendly waiter poured

another cup of tea then moved away, bored, to stare out of the window.

Random stared at the toast and tea and his stomach revolted. But he had to eat. The pain and sickness were better today but he felt horribly weak and he was losing weight at a frightening rate.

He watched his hand as it reached for the cup. He had always been lean and brown but now his skin had a yellowish tinge and the tendons showed stringily with no flesh to hide them.

So little time. He did not want to think about it. Jenny was waiting, he believed, with the same absolute certainty with which he believed that God existed. Once he had longed for nothing but to be with her; now he desperately wanted time. More time. A few more weeks.

"Oh no!" The waiter's words were muttered under his breath but Random was grateful for any distraction from his thoughts. He stared out of the window, following the man's gaze. Across the Promenade, in front of the hotel, a thin, lop-eared donkey dragged a decrepit cart and in it—

Random rose to his feet as the waiter hurried over. "That tramp came to see you yesterday, sir, but you were ill and we knew that you would not want to see a person like him."

"But I do," Random insisted. After Grantham's news that he had bought Catherine's picture from the rag-and-bone man Random had gone to see him. He had promised him money for news of her. And now it looked, at last, as though he was to get the information for which he had searched for so long. He threw down the linen serviette. He had no appetite anyway. And if the rag-and-bone man had any information . . . "Send him in."

The waiter stared around the pristine room, taking in the paintings, the crystal glasses and silver cutlery. "In here, sir?" His voice was scandalised.

"I am a guest," Random reminded him fiercely. "I have a right to receive what visitors I choose."

When the rag-and-bone man finally stood before him Random wondered if he had been right. Even his smell . . . "You may stand over there, my man, and tell me what you know."

The rheumy eyes gleamed. "I seen the girl – and her brother. On Saturday."

So they were still in the area. Random felt a sudden jolt of

187

pain and sat quietly, breathing slowly while he assimilated the information. "You know where they live?"

The greasy cap turned and turned in the filthy hands. "Not that, no, but the boy should be easy to find. Small, thin little bugger with bright ginger curls. You can't miss him."

"You were told to follow them home," Random snapped.

"I couldn't, could I?" The man looked sheepish. "I had other things to think about at the time. Business," he added, as if that was an excuse no one would ever challenge.

But at least he had something to go on. Two descriptions. The boy, eleven years old, small, thin, with bright ginger curls and the girl – he remembered Miss Rose's description of her; slim with a mass of chestnut hair.

"Not any more."

Random jumped at the voice. He had not realised that he had been thinking out loud. These damn pills the doctor had given him! "What did you say?"

"The girl. She hasn't got long hair any more. Real short it is now. She doesn't look half so pretty." There was regret in the man's voice.

Short hair? A picture of the disgusting hut rose before him. The long hanks of tangled hair dangling from the shelf. He half rose, ignoring the stab of pain. "You cut it off, you—"

"She sold it to me." The rag-and-bone man's voice was hurt. "I made her an offer and she accepted it, cap'n. It were business, that's what it were. Just business."

Random felt sick. He reached into his pocket and tossed the man a coin. "Take it and go. Immediately." As the man left he sank into his chair, burying his face in his hands. Her hair. The girl had sold her hair. He remembered his Jenny, sitting before the dressing table at night, her brush sweeping, sweeping down the black curtain of her hair.

The girl had sold her hair – and it had been her best feature. And to that pervert. Random shuddered. She was seventeen – young for her age, Miss Rose had told him, kept sheltered by her dead mother – and she had faced that man alone . . .

"Oh God!" Suddenly he was filled with self-loathing. Despicable, childish tears came to his eyes and he dashed them quickly away, damning the pills he had to take. Selling her hair – a young girl like that. And he was trying to get her father imprisoned, possibly shot.

He could not do it. How could he face Jenny in a few months – weeks? – and tell her what he had done to that child? She would be disgusted by his actions. And to die with his heart full of anger and revenge – what way was that for a Christian man to go?

He would find those children, he vowed. He knew they were in the area, he knew what they looked like, they were strangers, it wouldn't take long. And then—

He had the message from their grandmother, he could give them money, make sure they were comfortable, safe. If necessary he would negotiate with their father. Random knew that if it came to bargaining he had a strong hand.

He could arrange for the children to move back to Dorset, give them an income, see the boy through school, make sure the girl was comfortable. He had money, and no one else to spend it on.

He rose from the chair feeling happier than he had felt for months. Even the constant nagging of his pain seemed less.

He would help those children, but . . .

If only she had not had to sell her hair.

"Harrison! What the hell are you playing at?"

Jerked back into the real world, Walter gazed blindly at the spring cabbages he was supposed to be planting. Instead of a nice straight line, his row of cabbages sagged and curved.

Angrily, he reached out and cuffed the boy beside him, whose job it was to place the cabbages in the holes that Walter had dug. "Why didn't you tell me, you little runt?" Now he had been made to look a fool in front of Billy Bennet, who was a hard taskmaster at the best of times and did not put up with fools gladly.

"You leave him be," Bennet intervened, slapping his arm down. "It weren't his job to tell you what to do." He stared inquisitively at Walter. "What's the matter with you today? You're looking sick as a shag and acting as plum as bun dough besides."

Walter lowered his gaze. "Sorry, cap'n." He knew better than to argue with Billy Bennet. He would be out of a job before he knew it – and out of a house as well.

He bent again, digging holes with his shovel so that the boy could put the spring cabbages in, then covering them over and leaving the boy to stamp the earth well down as he moved on to the next hole.

He knew why he wasn't concentrating. How could a man concentrate when his life was hanging in the balance?

Catherine and Robbie. He had heard one of the men in the Star Inn say once, in mock despair, "Children's tongues will cut your throat with a bar of soap and hang you with a yard of cotton." He had understood the meaning, of course; everyone knew that children would repeat the most damaging things in total innocence. He had laughed along with the others at the time but now he recognised the bitter truth behind the words.

His life depended on Catherine's and Robbie's silence but he was terrified that they might innocently blurt out the information that would be the death of him.

Either he would have to leave here, leave them behind, find another place where he wasn't known, where he could lie low, or else—

There might be another way.

Twenty-One

"I don't care if he is a Hottentot, the man has a right to bail!" Catherine sat back in her chair and breathed a sigh of relief. "So you think you can get him out?" This was definitely her lucky day, she decided. As a lawyer, Mr Pettifer was perfect. He was young, he was intelligent – and he was obviously finding the practice of law in Penzance boring after the excitement of fighting in France.

"I'll say I can get him out." He walked up and down the small back room rubbing his hands together, relishing the fight. "A foreigner who does not know our laws, not speaking English, unrepresented—"

"Actually, he speaks very good English," Catherine began.

Mr Pettifer waved an impatient hand. "For the purposes of the court he will need an interpreter." He grinned at her. "I'll have their guts for garters over this."

"And you can prove he's innocent?" Catherine was breathless with relief.

"Oh, innocent." He waved a dismissive hand. "That depends. We'll need more evidence than we've got so far but bail – a man with a business, of previous good character, employing old soldiers—" His face was alight with glee. "If I don't have him out by tonight there'll be magistrates' bodies lying end to end all the way up Market Jew Street and such a stink in the local paper that they'll want to emigrate to Germany themselves."

Catherine wanted Gunter found innocent but just to get him released was more than she had believed possible this morning. She smiled brilliantly at the young solicitor. "I think you're wonderful. Thank you."

His face reddened and he stroked his small moustache awkwardly. "Well, as a matter of fact, Miss Harrison—" he cleared his throat awkwardly then finished in a rush "—I think you are rather ripping yourself."

In her short dress, with her little boy's haircut! Catherine gazed at him with her mouth open with astonishment. Was there, could there be the faintest chance that Gunter might think the same?

"We'll need a looking-glass." Penny stared round the room. "And we'll need some more lights." She pushed Gunter's bed into one corner and hid it by stacking the completed rolls of silk on top of it. "And a screen for them to change behind."

Thank God for the money Miss Rose had sent. "There's a second-hand shop by the fish market. I'll buy it all there." Catherine turned to go.

"Not in that dress!" Penny exclaimed, horrified.

Catherine glanced down at herself. She had been so excited that she had forgotten her strange garb, and besides, Mr Pettifer had admired her in it, and the two ladies from the shop.

"I'll wear it," she said, laughing. "The shop can deliver the goods so I won't get it dirty and besides" – she twirled round, making the light pleats flare out round her and showing her garters – "I might actually sell another dress. You never know."

"Not in Newlyn, you won't," Penny said repressively.

"I'm ill." Walter could not bring himself to meet Bennet's eyes. "I can't work any more."

"The way you've been working today you might as well have stayed home anyway," he grumbled. "But you're not getting any wages for when you're not here."

"I understand." As if money was of any concern when his life was in danger! He just wanted peace, time to think, time to plan, to come to terms with what he had to do.

The cottage was empty. Without the children it felt cold and damp. The range was damped down to a bare glimmer, there was no water in the pail, the lamps needed filling. Catherine would do all these things when she came home – but that would not be for hours yet.

Walter sat at the scarred table. He pulled out the Military Medal that Robert had won and laid it down in front of him, then sat and stared at it until it blurred before his eyes.

Robert. How well he remembered Robert. The younger brother,

the favourite of their mother until her death and then the favourite of all the girls, admired by all the men. Brave Robert who would take on any dare for a laugh; clever Robert who had done well at his books; trustworthy Robert who the army had wanted to promote; wonderful Robert, who was the acknowledged leader of every gathering.

Walter brought his fist up and hammered it down again and again on the shining silver disc, as if, with his bare hands, he could erase the printing on it. "For Bravery in the Field."

Robert had won. Whatever they had done, Robert had been best. Even when Walter had tried to win by marrying a girl who might be plain but was far out of his class, Robert had still won. The money Walter had hoped for had not come; Elizabeth had been cut off from her family without the proverbial penny. Even when Walter had written a grovelling letter at the arrival of their first child there had been no response.

Only Robert had benefited. Elizabeth had insisted that he move in with them. He had had his food and a comfortable home and freedom to chase the sort of girls who would not have looked twice at Walter. He had even captured the hearts of Walter's own family; Elizabeth had insisted on calling their first son after him and the children had loved and worshipped him as they had never loved Walter.

What had he to set against all Robert's attractions? A party trick of being able to ape other people's accents and even their ways of standing and walking. Good for five minutes' amusement but of no real importance.

And now, for the first time in his life, he had achieved the sort of success that had come so easily to Robert. He was the leader of the small group in the Star Inn. They were despicable, he knew, but they were his. He had work and a home and no one was comparing him unfavourably with anyone.

He was his own man at last.

He could not bear to lose this by running away. He would not lose it by being trapped like a rat and shot as a deserter. Not after all he had suffered. Not now. He had paid for those moments of madness a hundred, a thousand times over. And even then, it had been Robert's fault.

Handsome, laughing Robert, with his face half blown away, crying with pain. Brave Robert, with his shining silver medals, cowering, tears and snot running down his face, mixing with the blood.

All his adult life Walter had played second fiddle to Robert. With such a heroic figure, what else could he do? But when your hero turned out to have feet of clay, when you realised that, all your life, you had been second best to a man who could cry and beg like a small child, what did that say about you?

If Robert hadn't died, Walter would have killed him himself.

He had tried to kill the German soldiers – it had been their fault that Walter had suddenly seen himself for what he was – but he hadn't even succeeded in that. He had had his revenge on the officer who had stopped him, though.

That was his one triumph in life: that, and the way he had got back across the Channel, using the officer's papers, adopting his stupid accent, affecting his swank.

And now, when he had reached his safe haven at last, he was in danger of being betrayed – by his own children. And all because of Robert's bloody medal.

"You weren't a hero." He scrabbled it up from the table and hurled it across the room. It hit the front of the iron range with a clang and ricocheted off.

"I'm braver than you." He was, too. Robert was soft. He always had been. He hated hurting people. He would be kind to his old girlfriends, feed stray dogs, comfort crying children. He would never be able to do what Walter knew he was going to have to do.

Robert could never get rid of Catherine and Robbie.

It was much easier trying to find a small boy with red hair than a man with a Yorkshire accent, Random discovered.

It was almost dark. He knew he should have gone back to the hotel for dinner but he was conscious that time was racing away from him. Anyway, why stop for dinner? He wasn't hungry now, hadn't felt hungry for days. Soon it would be time to go to bed, to toss and turn for more pain-filled hours, wondering, worrying.

He would sleep much better if he knew where the children were.

Newlyn. That was where all his enquiries led him. No one he had asked had known where the ginger-haired boy lived, but they all agreed that he had been seen frequently around or near Newlyn.

Now he was merely wandering the streets, the tap of his stick and his uneven footsteps echoing off the whitewashed walls of the cottages. There were few women and children around and the men he saw seemed to think that children were beneath their interest. They shook their heads at his enquiry and hurried on, to their suppers, to their boats, to the pub.

He would come back early tomorrow, Random decided. God willing, he would find them tomorrow.

He turned back the way he had come – and saw a figure he recognised.

It was one thing to decide what he had to do, another to do it.

Walter could no longer stand the cottage and its small, dark rooms. Everywhere he looked he was reminded of the children: Catherine's pinny hung on a hook on the stained wall, Robbie's old boots were jumbled into the corner, awaiting cleaning. Worse, in the neatly stacked saucepans by the stone sink he could almost see the hand of Elizabeth, almost hear her disapproving voice.

Strange that he had not been aware of her since her death, even in the Dorset house, and now he could feel her presence everywhere. It was as if she knew of his plans for her children and resented them. The thought made the hairs on the back of his neck prickle. If even the dead were against him, what hope did he have? But that was ridiculous. The dead were dead. Who could know that better than a man who had fought for more than two years in the trenches?

Walter moved around the kitchen restlessly, his feeling of unease growing.

Catherine and Robbie would be back soon and he knew that he could not face them. He felt that his decision was written on his forehead in blood for all to read. He could not see them and eat with them and talk with them, not when . . .

He felt sick but he knew that he had no choice. If they told what they knew he would be shot. His greatest safety over these years had been the fact that the authorities believed him dead. Catherine had only to hint to some official authority that he was alive and it would not matter where he went, how far or how fast he ran. They would hunt him down like a rabid dog and then, early one morning . . . He shuddered. The last cigarette, the blindfold, the white paper pinned over the heart. He had heard stories during the war of firing squads who had refused to shoot a young deserter, too young even to have joined up legally, but that would not happen to him.

They would be queuing up to volunteer after what he had done.

He had to get out. He snatched up his cap and was out of the house, running as if the police were already on his trail.

"We should be going home." Catherine lifted the first wine she had ever tasted to her lips and smiled apologetically at Penny over the rim of the teacup into which it had been poured.

"You stay here, my handsome, and celebrate," Penny said decisively. " 'Tesn't every day you make your first sale and sell your first frock, not to mention getting money for some picture and getting your young man out of gaol. That's right, idn't it, Da?"

"Damn right." Percy Pentyr was drinking beer with the quiet efficiency of a man who knows that the women in his life are likely to call a halt to the fun at any moment. "Not to mention we'll think you're too stuck up to drink our contraband."

Catherine, already flustered by Penny's reference to her "young man", choked and was walloped overenthusiastically on the back by Robbie. "Contraband?" she gasped with watering eyes.

"We're Cornish, m'dear," Percy Pentyr twinkled at her. " 'Tes one of our industries, along with mining and fishing."

Catherine took another sip. She hadn't liked her first taste but it was beginning to grow on her. "We don't know that Gunter will be let out of gaol." If they all thought that he was her "young man", it seemed pointless to continue calling him "Herr Steiner".

"That lawyer will get him out all right, you'll see." Penny refilled the cup. "Anyway, you can tell everything's going to be all right. Look at all the good things that have happened to you today. Anyone can see that things have turned the corner – for you and for the factory."

Catherine surreptitiously touched the wooden arm of the chair in which she was sitting. She wasn't really superstitious, but talking like that was asking for trouble.

*   *   *

Random caught up with Gunter as he was unlocking the door to the factory. "Herr Leutnant Steiner, if I am not mistaken."

"Wh—" Gunter stared at him, mystified, then memory swept back. "Major. I am sorry. I did not expect to see you." He pushed open the door. "Please. It is not smart but it is where I am living at this time. Will you not enter?"

He felt his way to his living quarters and lit the lamp that stood on the table, glancing around the room as he did so. It had changed out of all recognition in the few days that he had been away. His bed was hidden under rolls of silk, there was a cheval-glass standing in the corner beside a screen covered with an unfortunate chintz that he would never have allowed inside the door if he had been here and the table was covered with cut-out pieces of silk.

He started to laugh. "You must think that I am a very strange man, Major."

Random said dryly, "I have seen similar in some bunkers I have been in, but in this case" – he picked up a piece of silk and gazed at it critically before dropping it back on to the table – "I can only assume that you have taken up the trade of a ladies' dressmaker."

Gunter started to laugh again. "That is how it appears to me also. And to think, when I was arrested, I believed I was running a silk-printing factory."

"Arrested?"

Gunter shrugged. "It appears that anti-German feeling has taken a turn for the worse here. A man was hit over the head and his watch found in these premises. I assure you that I had nothing to do with it but I have had trouble convincing the Cornish. I have only just been released from prison – on bail is the term, I believe."

"Good God!" Random dropped into a chair.

With the lamplight falling more fully on his face Gunter could understand why it had taken so long for him to recognise the major. One of his eyes was covered by a patch and he was limping badly, able only to get about with the help of a silver-topped stick. His face was thinner than Gunter remembered it, the cheeks fallen in, and his single eye was darkly shadowed. Even his skin had a yellowish, unhealthy tinge.

Gunter moved to a cupboard and took out two bottles of beer.

At least some things hadn't changed while he had been away. "The last time that I saw you" – he kept his eyes on the beer he was pouring out – "it was I who was ill and in pain and you who were the healthy one. Now it seems as if it is you who are unwell."

Random took his glass with a grunt of thanks. "I'm well enough for what I need to do."

"And that is . . . ?"

Random stared at his glass. He was exhausted and the pain he had tried by willpower to keep at bay all day was lancing through him. It had been surprise at seeing Gunter rather than logical thought that had made him speak to him. He no longer had the strength to tell Gunter the whole story. It was too long, too convoluted.

He touched the black patch that covered his eye. "I am trying to find the man who did this."

Gunter's eyebrows raised. "It was done in Cornwall?"

"It was done in France," Random said quietly. "By the man who I stopped from shooting you."

Gunter took a deep draught then lowered his glass. "That I scarcely remember, as I think I told you at the time. It had been a long assault and we were weary and beaten long before the final attack. I was wounded and not in a good state. I remember that English soldiers wanted to shoot me, I remember that another soldier stopped them, but—" He shrugged. "If it had not been that you came to see me in the field hospital in the days after I was captured I would not even remember that it was you who saved my life. I certainly can remember nothing of the other men." He glanced up curiously. "Why are you looking for this man now? Was he not punished before?"

Random sighed. "I could not identify him at the time."

Gunter bowed his head gravely. "I can understand why you wish to find the man, Major, but I regret I cannot help you. That part of my life is not clear. I cannot recall it nor do I wish to."

Random drained his glass and struggled to his feet. "I don't blame you. It is just that I know that the man is around here somewhere and I can't put my finger on him."

He limped to the door and Gunter opened it for him. "The thing is" – Random rubbed a hand tiredly across his face – "Walter Harrison has two children and I want—"

"Walter Harrison?" Gunter's voice rose in astonishment. "Did you say Walter Harrison?"

Random swung round. "You know him?" He could not keep the eagerness from his voice.

Gunter stared him straight in the eye. "I have never heard the name before," he said deliberately.

Twenty-Two

W alter hesitated in the darkness. He could hear the approach of halting steps and he drew back into the shadows of a doorway, a dreadful suspicion growing in his mind. He was near the works where the Hun had lived; surely he could not . . .

The figure halted at the very door, fumbling with the lock. Even in the starlight Walter could see the glimmer of his fair hair. They had let him out! The fools had released him!

Volcanic anger burned in his veins. The Hun was out and Catherine and Robbie would see him the very next day. He could imagine their innocent prattle: words which could all too easily put a rope about his neck − or a bullet in his heart.

He had to stop them seeing him. He was about to step out into the street when the sound of other steps approaching halted him. Slower, uneven steps, supported by a stick − and a figure who had haunted his nightmares. He stared, disbelieving, as the two spoke; then the Hun called the new figure "Major" and any hope was over.

They were on his trail. He shivered, pressing the heels of his palms against his eyes, trying to block out the vision of the firing squad.

Run. Run. Get away. But what good would that do? Walter huddled into the shadows as the two men passed into the factory. His safety had always relied on the fact that everyone had believed him dead, but now they knew that he was alive. He imagined them in there, plotting together, planning to hunt him down. Even Catherine and Robbie would help. The girl could even draw them a picture of what he looked like; she had done many such drawings of Robbie over the years.

He did not know how long he stood there, his mind a churning whirlpool of panic. Only the opening of the door to the factory brought him back to the present.

Walter pressed back into the shadows, his heart thumping. The Hun and the major came out of the factory and stood on the threshold speaking together quietly. He could not hear what they were saying. Only two words drifted across the quiet street to where he stood hidden. "Walter Harrison." The Hun's voice was raised as if in surprise.

Walter felt the blood pound in his head. He was caught. He was dead. There was no escape.

Unless . . . His head came up as the thought struck him. Both these men had a vested interest in hunting him down. If it had been official there would have been men in uniforms, police, not just these two standing in the back street of a tiny fishing village against a faded, graffiti-covered door.

If he acted quickly . . .

He began to follow Random's halting steps as the major made his way back down the street.

Catherine's father was a deserter. Catherine's father was the man who tried to shoot him, the man who had attacked the major.

Gunter sat at the kitchen table staring blindly before him, struggling to come to terms with the information Random had let drop.

After Matilde he had sworn never to get involved with another woman, but Catherine had got under his skin. He half suspected that it had been Robbie who had done her wooing for her. Robbie had seldom mentioned his father; he had been a shadowy figure in the background, while the boy's every sentence was about Catherine: her hopes, her fears, the way she protected Robbie. Catherine herself had always seemed wary of him, however – until that moment in the police station.

And now it seemed that she was going along with his plan to make up a dress out of the silk he had printed. He reached out for a piece of material and frowned. Robbie had always said that she was artistic; surely anyone with an ounce of sensibility could have seen that the green print would look much better with her copper hair than the pink? But there was green silk there, also. He spread the pieces out across the table. Enough for two complete dresses, and one of them, surely, far too big for Catherine's slender figure.

Was Penny also going to wear his dress? He almost shuddered

201

at the thought. She had the buxom curves that the Edwardians had so admired. Her fitted blouse and skirt made the most of her charms but in his dress she would bulge like a sack of potatoes.

But even the green silk – automatically Gunter reached for a pencil – even the green silk was not perfect for Catherine. With her pale skin and green eyes and hair that shone in the sun like the coat of a glossy chestnut pony, she deserved something richer, brighter, to show off her looks, her personality.

He began to sketch, his pencil moving in swift curves, roughly trying to catch on paper the essence of the woman he had only just realised he loved.

There was a subdued creak of metal on metal from somewhere near but he took no notice, distracted by the composition of his first love gift to Catherine.

He knew that he might have to fight for her love. Except for those moments in the cellar of the police station, she had never shown her emotions for him. Perhaps she saw him only as an older man – almost ten years older in age and, thanks to the war and Matilde, a lifetime older in cynicism and experience. And it had been obvious that the young lawyer was also smitten by her. He had raved of her innocence, her courage, her charm – all the things that Gunter had tried to dismiss from his mind these last two months, when he had been determined not to get involved with a woman ever again.

Lost in his creation he indicated the colours in his pattern by different hatchings: green for her youth, cream for her innocence, red for her courage and, intertwined under the rest, the line of blackness that was her father. The pattern of her life.

The major was walking slowly, leaning heavily on his stick. Walter followed him, feet silent on the unpaved road.

He had not expected the major to survive the beating he had given him on their last meeting. Walter shivered as he remembered the thrill he had got from inflicting those injuries on the man – though they were no worse than he deserved. Random had stopped him killing the Hun. Random had stopped him destroying the man who had maimed and killed Robert, and who, in doing so, had shown him the emptiness and worthlessness of his own life.

Random had deserved death then and he deserved it now.

Walter stopped outside the next cottage he came to. Most cottages faced directly on to the street but this one had a minute front garden no more than three feet deep. A tiny path made from a mosaic of small pebbles picked up from the beach led to the door, which was bounded on either side by larger, whitewashed stones set into the earth. Walter pulled one out. It was rounded from the action of the sea, fitting his grasp perfectly.

Cradling his weapon he hurried after the limping figure before him. The street he was walking along ran down into the road that bounded Newlyn harbour and Walter knew that he had to stop Random before he reached it. There was always traffic along the road: traps bringing farmers back from an evening in Penzance, fishermen passing, early or late, to catch the tide, men visiting the pubs that clustered all round the harbour. Once Random was on that road it would be too dangerous to attack him.

He began to run. Speed was more important than silence now. Once he was around the corner Random would be in view of passers-by. Walter was behind him. He raised his stone.

Random swung around, warned by some instinct, and the blow that Walter had aimed at his head smashed into his shoulder. He heard the man grunt with pain, then jumped back as Random reversed his walking-stick, bringing the heavy silver knob around in a vicious swing that Walter only just managed to duck.

Walter saw Random open his mouth and hammered the rock viciously at his head to stop any shout. Again, he was blocked by Random. The stick was as much a weapon as an aid, Walter realised, feeling sick. Had Random realised that they might end up face to face and come prepared?

Now Random advanced. With the stick he could attack Walter while staying out of reach himself. It smashed painfully into Walter's side and he gasped under the blow, then used his arm to protect himself as Random brought the stick back the other way, aiming this time for his head.

He had to get closer. Seizing his chance Walter ducked under the swinging stick, aiming a vicious kick at Random's left leg. It should have cracked the bone but instead there was a dull thud.

He backed swiftly away as Random followed. "Bad luck, you bastard." Walter ducked as Random aimed another scything blow to the head. "That was the leg you got last time."

Walter backed away. He had the advantage of being uphill from his opponent but against the stick his rock was useless. If he threw it and missed he would be at Random's mercy. Running away was not an option. The police would find him before daybreak. He had to kill Random.

The stick swung again but he noticed that the older man was only using one arm to defend himself. Walter remembered that his first blow had landed on the man's shoulder. Had he broken Random's collarbone?

He began to move sideways, giving up the advantage of higher ground in an attempt to get on Random's lame side. Random swung round to face him and Walter saw, with a surge of pleasure, that his false leg made him less steady on his feet when he was standing sideways on the steep slope of the hill.

He was panting heavily, too, as if his strength was not what it had been. Had he been ill? Walter wondered, remembering how thin he had looked against Gunter's more powerful figure. Walter began to smile, baring his teeth. After working on the land for six weeks he was as fit as he had ever been. He moved closer, sensing victory.

Too soon. The stick came up again, slamming into his arm, and the rock flew out of his hand to clatter against the wall of a cottage.

Walter began to back away. Random was older than he was, thinner, a "toff" – a category for which Walter had nothing but contempt. It wasn't supposed to happen like this. Walter had beaten him once; he should be able to beat him again. He couldn't lose to a one-eyed man with a false leg.

Random followed him. His breath was hissing between his teeth and he was limping badly but his single eye shone in the dim light and the stick was held at a dangerous angle.

"You bastard," he gasped. "I'd almost forgiven you. I'd decided not to follow you any more. But you're evil. You deserve to die. To be put out of – your misery – like a mad – dog."

He lunged forwards, the stick swinging. Walter tried to back off but his foot caught against one of the stones that stuck out from the cottage behind him. He stumbled and Random's swinging stick passed over his head and shattered against the stone wall of the cottage.

Instantly Walter hurled himself at the man in front of him, his hands searching for Random's throat. The two went down in a tangle of legs, rolling with the steepness of the hill as they struggled for the upper hand.

Random was weaker than he had been when they had last fought, Walter realised; weaker and thinner. As Walter's fingers found his throat and began to squeeze he could almost feel the strength draining out of his opponent.

Joy swept through him. He was going to win. After all this time he would have his revenge on the man who had treated him like a dog because he had wanted to shoot a German prisoner. His fingers tightened. He could see the single eye flicker, bulge—

The broken-off end of the walking stick, sharp as a spear, lanced into his ribs. Walter gave a choking cry and his grasp loosened as, with an effort he had not believed possible, Random jerked up his good knee and caught Walter in the stomach.

With a convulsive twist Walter pulled himself away, rolling downhill, off Random's thin body, his arms flailing in an attempt to prevent himself from rolling further down the hill. His hand struck something smooth and round.

The stone. Walter's hand fitted around it as if it had been designed for him alone. His arm came up, over . . .

This time the blow was true. The stone hammered into Random's head with the soft sound of a knife cracking open an egg.

There was a moment when time stood still. Random did not move, did not wince. For a long, unbelievable second he still stared at Walter, his one eye bright in the darkness.

Slowly his glance shifted until he was staring over Walter's shoulder. The lips worked once, framed a single word – "Jenny" – then the eye clouded, the head drooped, there was a long, long sigh.

Random was dead.

Walter swung round, the hairs on the back of his neck rising, but the alley was empty. Whoever Random had spoken to could not be seen by human eyes. He swallowed, staring down at the shell on the ground underneath him, and reached out a trembling hand.

No pulse in the thin throat; none in the sticklike wrist. Random was dead.

He wanted to sing, to shout. He wanted, stupidly, to cry. He knew more about this man than any other except for Robert. He had stolen his papers, read his letters, acted his part.

Not just a major, he remembered, but the Honourable Francis Random MC, younger brother of the Earl of Loch Lour.

Suddenly the enormity of what he had done hit him. He must have been mad. This wasn't the war. A dead body meant trouble, especially one as important as this.

Walter began to shiver. He had done it now. Now it wouldn't even be a clean, soldierly death by firing squad. He would be stood on a trapdoor and choked to death like a dog.

Suddenly he wanted a drink. He wanted company. He wanted laughter and people and normality. Anything but to be left here with the dead body.

Voices brought him spinning round on hands and knees, panting, ready to flee, but it was only the sound of men walking along by the harbour, probably heading for the pub. He swallowed longingly.

Hide the body. If he hid it he would have time to think of something, time to plan. But where in this village . . . ?

A sudden thought made him choke with laughter. The Hun's place. Why not put the body there? He would give a week's wages to see the Hun's face when it was discovered. Let the bastard talk his way out of that one.

Bending, Walter struggled until he had lifted Random's body over his shoulder. Despite his thinness the old soldier was heavier and more difficult to manage than Walter would have believed possible. With difficulty, he picked up the pieces of Random's broken cane. They were too easily recognisable. Let them lie with the body.

It was only a short walk to Gunter's factory but it was all uphill and Walter was panting and sweating by the time he lowered Random's body into the shadows beneath the window at the back. The bar he had removed on the previous occasion was fixed firmly into place but there were other broken windows into the storerooms; broken, he guessed, by young boys showing their anti-German feeling the only way they dared. Well, he was a man. He could do far better than that.

He braced his foot against the wall and heaved with all his weight on the bars he had chosen. As he had suspected, the screws that held them in place were rusted through. With no more than a faint groan they pulled away and he could reach his hand through the broken pane and unlatch the window from the inside.

It had not been opened for years and groaned as he forced it open. Walter paused, his heart thumping, but there was no questioning voice raised, no footsteps coming to see what had made the noise. With a struggle he heaved Random's body over the sill into the quiet room and then stood, mopping his brow and trying to get his breath back.

In the dim light he could make out various crates and cans piled up in the room and when he ran his finger along the top of the nearest box it came away fuzzy with dust. Obviously not a room that was used much. A body could lie hidden in here for days, perhaps, until someone noticed the smell.

He stopped as a better plan came to mind.

Walter checked that the door of the room was unlocked. Despite his care the hinges squeaked slightly as he pushed the door open but, again, there was no sound from the Hun, though Walter could see a line of lamplight under one of the doors that opened off the central courtyard.

It took only seconds to find a room suited to his purpose; then he was back and carrying the body, as silently as possible, into the other storeroom that he had chosen.

Carefully he arranged the body, then left the building by the same way he had come, pulling the window down behind him and wedging the bars back into place so that, to a casual glance, they did not appear ever to have been moved. He wiped his hands on his trousers and smiled with satisfaction.

Time for the drink he needed so badly – and the second part of his plan.

Twenty-Three

T he noise from the Red Lion was audible from outside, swelling into a crescendo whenever anyone opened the door.

Walter needed a drink as he had never needed one before but, at the door, he hesitated. He had killed in the war but that had been officially sanctioned and at a distance; he had even been responsible for the death of Elizabeth, but that had been almost an accident, the upswelling of panic. To kill deliberately, at close quarters, even in a fight, was to put yourself apart from other men. He felt as if his guilt was written on his face for all to see. But if his plan was to work he had to go in. He needed other people. Lots of other people. He took a deep, trembling breath and threw open the door.

Thick, pungent pipe smoke wreathed and curled in the lamplight, catching in his lungs and almost hiding the far corners of the room. Behind the bar large barrels lined the wall under shelves of bottles. In the smoke-filled dimness only the brass and the mirrors advertising beer and Player's cigarettes shone with any lustre.

Walter ordered his pint and drank half of it in one deep draught, desperate for the comfort it could give. He had been mad. Mad. But it was done now. Now he had to keep his nerve, put the rest of the plan into action.

He raised his glass again and saw, over the tilted rim, a face he knew reflected in the mirror above the bar. He stopped, feeling relief wash over him. If *he* were here everything would be much simpler. He swallowed the rest of the glass and ordered another, feeling his confidence begin to grow again. Things were going better than he could have hoped.

"Slumming it, you?" He dropped into a seat beside Nabbo and stretched out his legs.

"My bloody head." Nabbo touched it tenderly. "I didn't feel like going into Penzance for a drink."

"He's better off here," the man the other side of Nabbo broke in belligerently, his flushed face indicating the amount he had already drunk. "We're real men here, not like they lot in town." He took a deep draught. "Stuck-up buggers, they are."

"They don't know how to drink properly, either." Walter led the conversation into the tracks he wanted.

"Too right. But then, what are they? Clerks and shop-workers half of them. What do they know about real work?" The words were over-loud and slightly slurred. He was already half-cut.

"Fishing?" Walter hazarded, then, looking round the room, "A good catch?"

"The best this season."

"Best since before the war." There was a chorus of agreement as more and more men round the table joined in the conversation.

"He's got a Military Medal, Jago," Nabbo broke in, pointing to Walter. "He showed it to me." He hiccuped. "Got to be brave to get one of they, I reckon."

Nabbo was only concerned that the fishermen should accept his friend, Walter knew, but the comment played right into his hands.

"What did you earn it for?"

"What happened?"

Walter stared thoughtfully into his glass. "Killing Huns," he said with a modest shrug. "I don't know why they give it to me. I was only doing my duty. They bastards deserved everything that was coming to them. The only good German is a dead German, I say."

There was a chorus of agreement. Walter let it die then went on, "Rapists and murderers every one of them. I tell you, we took their trenches in one place and they was stinking. Rats as big as dogs everywhere. And then someone moved a sandbag and they found out why. The walls of the trenches were built like Cornish hedges. They was sandbags each side but in the middle—" he paused for effect "—in the middle they'd piled all the dead Englishmen they could find! They was using the bodies of English soldiers to stop English bullets from hurting their filthy hides."

"Bloody swine." Jago threw back the rest of his beer as if to wash the taste of death from his mouth. "They must be animals to do a thing like that, I reckon."

209

"They did worse," Walter assured him.

"Nah." The man the other side of Jago leaned forward. "No one could do worse than that."

"You shut yer mouth, Willy." Jago cuffed the other man's shoulder hard enough to make him sway on the bench. "He knows what he's talking about, I reckon. He didn't get given no Military Medal for sitting on his backside all day."

Walter smiled at him, aiming for the sort of brilliant smile with which Robert could always win over strangers. "You the cap'n round here, then?"

"He bloody tells us what to do quick enough!" Willy muttered into his glass.

"I can tell," Walter said. "Seeing what I seen – men under fire and all that – I can tell who's got it in him to lead men and who hasn't. And you" – he slapped Jago on the back – "you're one of they what have got it."

Walter suspected that Jago was probably too intelligent to fall for such flattery normally but, drunk as he was, he was an easy mark.

Now he leaned forward and rested an arm around Walter's shoulder. "You're right, m'handsome. I'm the one they follow. 'Tesn't easy, mind." He held up a wavering finger in front of Walter's face. "You got to lead 'em right, but if you do" – he waved his hand in a swinging gesture at the men sitting round the table and almost overbalanced – "they're the best bunch of men anywhere."

Nabbo pushed Jago upright, still anxious to recount the credentials of his friend. "Walter knows what he's talking about."

"What other awful things did they Germans do in the war?" Willy leaned across Jago, his eyes bright with morbid curiosity. "I bet – I bet you seen some dead bodies, didn't you? Didn't you?" He was panting, his loose lips wet with excitement. "Go on, you. Tell us."

Jago pushed him back on to the bench. "He's a bit excitable, like." His eyes met Walter's with a message in them. "He's not very . . ." He spread his hands in explanation.

"You don't want me to go into all they details of what they buggers did in the war," Walter said to Willy. "It would turn your stomach. And not just to soldiers, either. Women, children, nuns – it were all the same to them."

210

"All the same?" Willy licked his wet lips. "Go on, 'he pleaded. "Tell us."

Walter stared down into his drink, trying to gauge the reaction of the men around the table. They were all interested, all listening, their imaginations working. If he could get this right . . .

He repeated the sentence he had spoken earlier. "The only good German is a dead one." From the corner of his eye he could see nods. Another round of drinks came to the table and he saw that he had been included in it. He lifted his glass in a toast. "To Nabbo. For introducing me to such a good lot of men." He grinned at the embarrassed Nabbo. "And all because you've got a sore head. First time I ever knew of any good coming out of something a German did."

"Bastard," Nabbo said viciously. "But at least he's out of the way. They won't let *him* out again in a hurry." He spat on to the tiled floor. "I reckon they should throw away the key. Hitting me like that and stealing my grandfer's gold watch."

Walter stared at him. "You mean you don't know? About that there Hun?"

"What? All I know is the swine is in prison."

"He isn't." Walter pitched his voice so that it would carry beyond the confines of the table. "The bugger's free and walking about without a care in the world."

"Free?" Nabbo was on his feet. "After what he done to me? They let him out?" His voice carried easily across the room and other voices hushed as faces turned to him.

"That bloke attacked him on his way home!" Willy protested. "Stole his grandfer's watch."

"The blasted foreigner attacked a *Cornishman!*"

Walter shook his head sadly. "It shouldn't be allowed," he agreed, "but there you are. They're so blasted cunning."

"I'll say it shouldn't be allowed." Nabbo hammered on the table with his fist, sending the beer slopping over the sides of the glasses. "I was minding my own business and he attacked me."

"Could be any of us next," Willy broke in, glancing over his shoulder.

"Could be your wives or daughters," Walter added quietly.

There was a long silence as they took in the implications of his remark and he could feel the mood of drunken good humour turning sour, like air before a thunderstorm.

"The bastard." Jago spoke quietly but there was an intensity in his voice that made the words drop like icicles into the stillness.

"And he sits there in that great building of his, twice as big as what any of you have, I reckon. An enemy of the country living high in the hog when there are honest patriots who fought for their country who can't get jobs or houses to live in." Walter added extra digs. "He attacks Nabbo and he gets let out. What will happen to him if he attacks your daughter as she's walking home one night? And not just with robbery in mind, neither."

He leaned forward, pitching his voice so that the silent, seething men around could hear every word. "I heard stories about what they Germans did to women in the war. Animals and worse than animals. He's laughing at us now, I bet. He's got away with robbery and hitting Nabbo over the head – isn't he going to think he can get away with more than that now? Housebreaking, perhaps? Murder? Rape?"

"He idn't going to rape my wife!" Willy was on his feet, eyes wide. "He idn't going to touch a hair of her head. Nor my little maid's, neither."

"But who's going to stop him?" Walter asked quietly. "He's got away with making fools of honest men. All he's suffered is a few rude words scratched on his door and a couple of windows broken. What punishment is that for a man who's attacked Nabbo here and robbed him?"

"The man who's going to attack our little maids." Willy was on his feet, his face alight with excitement. He pulled urgently at Jago's arm. "We can't let it happen, Jago. It idn't right. Not a man like that. He's dangerous."

Jago was the key, Walter knew. If he took the lead the others would follow. Already there was a rising rumble in the pub. No voice that you could put a name to, no words that you could understand, but a low, rumbling thunder of anger, a ground swell of hatred.

And still Jago sat there. Walter could feel the sweat running down his back. Jago had to move. He was their leader. If he didn't say the word all this emotion would simmer slowly down, die away into a few catcalls and broken windows. If he didn't say the word then Walter was a dead man.

Through the panic that clutched his throat Walter forced out the words, "The authorities have done nothing. The authorities have let him go. A criminal, an enemy – and they let him free to strike again."

There was a rumble of agreement, louder, deeper. Most of the men were on their feet now, their drinks forgotten. And all their eyes, Walter could see, were fixed on Jago.

Speak, Walter urged silently, through the fear that gripped him. *Speak.*

Jago rose.

"I reckon," he began, his voice so quiet that Walter feared the worst, "I reckon that this sort of thing is up to the authorities. I reckon the police and the magistrates should be dealing with this sort of thing."

Walter sagged in his seat. No hope. No life. Nothing.

"But if they don't know their duty," Jago went on, raising his voice above the murmurs of discontent that flowed through the room, "if they don't know their duty then I reckon it's down to the likes of us to see that justice is done."

He pulled his cap out of his pocket and jammed it on to his head. "Come on, lads."

There was a cheer that made the furniture vibrate and much pushing and shoving as men tried to be the first to follow Jago out of the door.

Walter sat for a second, shaking with relief. He had done it. Better, he had made someone else act as ringleader. Someone else would take the blame afterwards. He swallowed, rubbing his hands over his face, trying to wipe away the fear that had gripped him for those few dreadful seconds.

But he couldn't sit here, he knew. He had more to arrange if this was to go according to plan.

He took his cap and ran to catch up with the shouting, marching gang as they headed for Gunter's factory.

"We really must be going."

Catherine had said it three times before but this time she knew that it was true. She and Robbie had already stayed far too long. They had drunk the wine and eaten the supper of fish and potatoes that Penny had insisted they share with her and her father, laughing and happy in the relaxed family atmosphere that Catherine hadn't enjoyed since her mother

213

died – or was it since her father had come back from the war?

"'Tesn't every day we've got so much to celebrate," Penny had insisted, talking down Catherine's polite objections.

"But we still don't know if Gunter has been released." Catherine had felt that it was bad luck to celebrate in advance.

"'Course he will be. Brem clever that lawyer, from what you tell me. And there's the money from your picture and the orders for the two dresses – there's enough there to celebrate till Christmas come."

But those achievements were meaningless if Gunter wasn't released, Catherine knew. She took a deep breath and stood up, smoothing down her old grey skirt, so different from the light silk of the dress. "We really must go, Penny. Robbie should have been in bed long ago."

"Oh, Katy—"

She smiled at him, pulling him to his feet, dragging his sweater over his ginger curls. "Come on, sweetheart. It's late. And there is a lot of work to do tomorrow."

Robbie stamped to the door after her, dragging his feet. "It's your haircut," he announced. "You're like that person in the Bible. Only when he had his hair cut he went all weak but you've gone strong."

Had she? But Catherine could see, looking back, that her strength had been growing, little by little, ever since the day she had found her mother lying at the foot of the stairs. Or had the strength always been there, but it was only when she needed it that she had discovered she possessed it?

Robbie waved a brief goodbye to the Pentyrs and followed her out of the door. "I wish your hair was still long," he said crossly. "Then you wouldn't be so bossy."

Catherine smiled. "You always told me I was like a teacher," she reminded him.

"You were. But now you're—" He waved his hand, trying to explain his feelings. "Then you just hoped I'd do what you say and now you expect me to," he complained.

"That's because I've been telling you what to do in the works." For the first time Catherine realised how much she had enjoyed working there, even with the responsibilities that it entailed. Of course she couldn't wait for Gunter to come back, but she would miss the excitement of making decisions. It had been even better than acting as a teacher in school.

"Why don't we go and see if Gunter is back?" she suggested. "It is rather rude if none of us are there to welcome him. And if he isn't we can check that everything is still locked up safely." Since Gunter's arrest windows had been broken every night, even though the men replaced the broken glass each morning.

"Yes." Pleased with the idea Robbie ran on ahead. Catherine followed more slowly. Suppose he wasn't there? The disappointment would be terrible.

What if he was there and he disapproved of her foray into dressmaking rather than silk printing? What if he was angry with her for taking over in his place? What if she had unwittingly allowed the men to do something wrong and all the rolls of silk they had printed since his arrest were ruined?

What if he didn't like her hair?

"I can see a light, Katy. He's back." Robbie began to hammer with his fists on the scratched and peeling door. "Gunter. Gunter. It's us."

"Hush, you'll rouse all the village." Her heart pounding, feeling as if she was suddenly short of air, Catherine hurried after him.

Then the door was opened and the soft lamplight shone out, illuminating the tall figure, the broad shoulders, the fair hair.

And she was in his arms, crying on his shoulder, stammering, as he aimed kisses at her averted face.

With his free hand Gunter pulled Robbie inside and shut the door on the quiet street.

Twenty-Four

C atherine thought, I have never been so happy.
   She smiled at Robbie's glowering face. "I know you
found him first, sweetheart, but it doesn't mean that I can't like
him too."

Robbie swung his booted feet violently against the legs of the
table. "You don't have to go round *kissing*," he said disgustedly.
"I thought Gunter was a proper man and then he starts to
hug you."

"But that is the sign of a proper man. As you will find out
when you are only a little older," Gunter explained.

The scowl did not shift. "I might find out but I'm not going
to do it. Not ever." Their laughter infuriated him and he climbed
to his feet. "I'm not going to stay here with you. I'm going to
check that everything is secure," he announced grandly and
stormed off.

Catherine turned to Gunter, words of amusement quivering on
her lips, but they died away as she saw the look on his face.

He was staring at her hair. Her heart plummeted. In the dark
street outside he might not have been able to see her clearly but
now . . . What if he hated it? She swallowed the lump in her
throat, scarcely able to breathe.

Slowly his hand came out. He stroked the soft, short sweep of
her hair from crown to cheek, adjusted her fringe where he had
disarranged it when he had embraced her.

She watched his face, saying nothing. Afraid to say anything.

"Your hair." He touched it again, tucking the sides behind
her ears, pulling the hair forwards again, his face intense in the
lamplight.

She swallowed again, struggling to be able to speak.

"You don't like it, do you?" She could never tell him why

216

she had done it, what she had sacrificed for his freedom, but she wished he could have tolerated the result.

He adjusted her hair again, his eyes never leaving her face. Finally, he spoke, his voice low. "I never knew you had such beautiful eyes."

"Me?" She gave a laugh of astonishment. "No, I don't."

"You do. And your hair—"

"It's dreadful, isn't it?" She glanced down at the table, gathering her courage before she could raise her eyes to his face again. "But it grows very quickly. That is why it was so long, I expect."

He did not answer, simply jumped up and started rummaging amongst the mess on the table.

Catherine felt a stab of guilt as she saw the scatter of papers and pieces of silk. He had even had to move the finished rolls of silk to uncover his bed. I should have tidied his room, she thought wretchedly, but I was so delighted he was coming back.

"Look." Gunter had found the piece of paper he was looking for. "Look, Liebling." He seized a pencil and began to draw with firm strokes.

Catherine saw that it was the sketch he had done of her wearing the silk dress. When he had originally drawn it he had been concentrating on the dress and though the hair and features were obviously hers they had only been sketched in very lightly.

Now, with new, heavier strokes, he was blocking in her new hairstyle, the fringe down to her eyebrows, the short sides curling round to her cheeks in the style worn by so many young boys once they had had their baby curls cut off.

"See. It balances so much better. All that hair – it was too heavy for the silk."

"You mean you like it?" It was more than she had dared to hope for, though a small corner of her mind wondered if he thought she could grow her hair long again in time for the heavier winter fabrics.

"Gunter. Gunter." Robbie skidded through the door, his heavy boots clattering on the stone floor. "Gunter, something's happening outside. There's this strange noise."

Gunter glanced up from his drawing. "Not now, Robbie. I am—" He stopped, his face suddenly alert and listening.

Now Catherine could hear it. It was half rumble, half shout, and there was something menacing about it. And it was coming nearer.

Gunter was on his feet, his face expressionless. "It is time you were both at home."

"But we've just arrived," Robbie wailed.

"You will go home. Now." It was the voice of a German officer, giving orders to his men. It was a voice Catherine had never heard him use before.

She rose to her feet, suddenly frightened. "What is it, Gunter? What is that noise?"

"I cannot be certain – but I have heard people sound like that before."

"People?" But she could tell now that it was people. There were men's voices, loud, angry, frightening.

"Go." He caught her and Robbie in his arms and started to hustle them out of the room. "Go now. Before it is too late."

Catherine pulled back. "You think they are coming here?" She stared at him. "But what about you?"

Gunter looked around the room. "This is my livelihood," he said simply. "I must defend it if I can."

"I'm staying too." Catherine shook off his grasp. "Do you think I would leave you to face them alone?"

"Do you think that they will stop just because of you?" Gunter sounded exasperated. "Go now, you and Robbie, before it is too late."

"I'm not running away either." Robbie lined up beside Catherine, his young face set.

"But you can do nothing—"

There was the sound of running feet outside, of raised voices. Gunter caught them by the arm and dragged them through to the back of the building but there were voices there, too.

They were surrounded.

Gunter swung them around. All he could do now was keep Catherine and Robbie out of the way for as long as possible in the hope that the mob would have slaked their blood lust before it discovered them.

"Get upstairs," he ordered. "Try to get out, get help."

"But you?" Catherine objected.

"I shall try to reason with them." He saw the disbelief in her eyes as the noise rose to new heights. There was a series of

218

crashes and the tinkle of breaking glass. Desperation made him resort to an appeal he knew she could not refuse. "Get the boy somewhere safe, for God's sake. Get him out."

For a second he thought even that would not work; then she gave a brief nod and dragged Robbie away, pulling him almost bodily up the steep, narrow stairs to the upper room where the silk was printed. Gunter gave a sigh of relief and began to search around for weapons. Not that anything he could do would halt the mob for more than a few seconds, but he had his pride.

Another crash of breaking glass. Someone had pulled away the bars that guarded the back of the building and had kicked in a whole window. He picked up the flatirons that Penny had left under the table and smiled as he felt their weight. They would do as a last resort but he needed something with more reach in it first. If he could hold them at a distance he might have a chance to reason with them.

He picked up the heavy broom with which Catherine had swept out the storerooms and moved to the back of the building.

He had been right. There was a body half-way through the window already. Gunter swung the broom hard, aiming for the man's chest. The force of the blow lifted him upwards so that he banged his head on the top of the window frame before disappearing backwards into the dark street.

The noise outside dropped abruptly.

Gunter smiled grimly to himself. They hadn't expected to meet opposition so quickly.

He took advantage of the lull to shout, "Why are you doing this? What have you got against me?"

"You bloody attacked me," a Cornish voice shouted out of the darkness. "You stole my watch and I'm going to get you."

"I am going to stand trial in your court of law. If I am guilty then the law will punish me."

"'Course you're flaming guilty." It was the same voice. "They found my watch here where you'd hidden it."

"If that is the case then I will go to prison." Gunter tried to make his voice as reasonable as he could. "Until then, like any Englishman I am innocent until I have been found to be guilty."

"But you aren't no Englishman – you're a German."

"A foreigner."

"A rapist."

"The bloody *enemy!*"

The angry response came from a dozen different voices at once, rising in fury.

He made one last appeal to their good natures.

"I have in here with me two English people. They, at least, are not guilty of any crime. Will you not let them go? If you will allow them to leave the building then I will go with you gladly to the police station or anywhere else you wish to escort me."

Again a jumble of voices, but he could sense the uncertainty in them now.

"It's just a ruse."

"He might use them to try to escape."

Then another voice, more sober, less slurred. "But if he has got other people in there with him, we don't want to hurt no one else."

If he could only get Catherine and Robbie out. "Believe me, it is no plot. If you will give them safe conduct I will come with no trouble."

He knew that it wasn't what they wanted. They wanted to get him, punish him, smash him and his belongings, but if he could stop them before the blood lust took too great a hold . . .

There was a crash behind him as the front door of the building was smashed in and he knew that he had lost his chance.

Holding the broom in front of him, with the flat irons weighing down his coat pockets, Gunter retreated swiftly to the bottom of the stairs.

He had failed to get Catherine and Robbie released, but at least he would die trying to protect them.

"P-p-perhaps someone will hear the noise and come to h-h-help." In the starlight that illuminated the room through the long line of windows Robbie's face was white and frightened.

"Possibly, sweetheart." Catherine knew that it would not happen. These were local men, probably the ones who scrawled on the doors and broke the windows on a regular basis. Now they were a drunken mob and no sensible person would even try to intervene. At best they would try to get the police from Penzance but that would take too long. How long could a building defended by one man and a girl hold out against a mob?

220

It was all her fault. Why hadn't she realised that Gunter would be safer in prison? The villagers all believed him guilty of attacking and robbing one of themselves and still saw him as the "enemy". Why hadn't she left well alone?

There was Robbie too. Gunter had told her to get him out if she could. She certainly could not hide him here. Apart from the tables there were only the trolleys used by the wipers and some rolls of silk that had been cleaned of gum and which were being stored in the corner before being printed.

She had to save Robbie.

Her glance swept the room, searching for a way out. No handy trapdoors in the ceiling, no doors through to the next building. She had to save Robbie. He was her responsibility. Once he was out of the way she could go down to Gunter, be by his side.

She moved to the windows. The room was at the back of the building with a view over the grey slate roofs descending in unequal steps to the peace of the harbour. The street below was crowded with shouting men and, as she eased up the window frame, she heard the crash as another window was smashed in.

She had to save Robbie.

Catherine dragged her eyes away from the scene below, praying that the men were too occupied with what they were doing to look up. By leaning out of the window at a vertiginous angle she could see up to the roof but she would never be able to get Robbie up there.

She had to save Robbie.

There was another crash, this time from the other side of the building. The mob had broken down the front door. Catherine fought with the terror that threatened to overwhelm her. She had to save Robbie.

The animal roar of the mob rose again and she could see that the numbers in the street below were thinning as they forced their way into the building. She had so little time.

"Robbie, you're going to have to get help." She saw his mouth open and went on in her best schoolmistress way. "Don't argue. The men are coming in the building so I'm going to let you down out of the window. When you get down—" She paused. "Go to the Pentyrs. Tell them what is happening." Catherine knew that the most Penny could do was send someone to call the police but she could trust her to have the sense to keep Robbie safe.

She ripped the half-printed silk from the table, sending the pins that held it to the calico skittering around the room. "Come here."

Robbie stared out of the window at the drop. "I can't jump that far." His voice quavered.

"You won't have to." The men had all gone from the street now, though she could hear from the crash of smashing furniture and shouts below that this was because they had all entered the building. Amongst the noise she could hear Gunter's voice raised in anger and her heart twisted – but she had done enough harm today. First she had to save Robbie.

She hurriedly doubled the long expanse of silk lengthways. "Get on to the window sill. I'm going to lower you in this."

"W-will it hold?"

"It will hold," she assured Robbie shortly. She wasn't worried about the silk. Was she strong enough to hold his weight in it? To lower him that far? "Get in. You'll have to fend yourself off from the wall as you go down."

She saw refusal in his face. "Now, Robbie." It was the voice that had enforced obedience on whole classes in the past. "Remember, you have to get help. Go to Penny." She placed the centre of the length out of the window like a cradle, wrapped the loose ends of the silk once around her arms and placed her feet on the silk on the floor for more purchase. Pray God she didn't drop him.

He sat on the window sill staring at her, his face white in the starlight, then he swallowed and edged forward. The silk took his weight, sliding for one dreadful second through her palms before it tightened around her forearms and her feet stopped the remainder from pulling any looser.

She had to be quick.

She opened her hands slightly, letting the silk pull through them under Robbie's weight. Although he was so slight he was surprisingly heavy. The silk slipped through her hands faster and faster. It burned her palms and fingers, wrapping her forearms in fire.

He was dropping too fast. She gritted her teeth, ignoring the pain in her arms, forcing her fingers and palms to clamp shut on the slippery, burning fabric.

"Are you nearly there?" She wasn't sure if he would be able to hear her gasped question over the noise from the mob but there was an answering cry.

"I can jump from here." There was a last, agonising jerk on the silken fabric that had her biting her lips to suppress the cry of pain then the material was dangling free.

Catherine rushed to the window, trying to get her cramped hands to unclench. Robbie was standing on the ground, unhurt.

"Get away from there," she hissed urgently, terrified that one of the men inside the building would see him and realise what was happening. "Go to Penny's. Run and get help. Quick."

He looked up at her for what she realised might be the last time, his face a white blur in the darkness, then he waved his hand and was gone.

Catherine breathed a sigh of relief then turned and raced for the stairs.

She had saved Robbie. Now her place was by Gunter's side.

Twenty-Five

The broom made a surprisingly good weapon. It was long
enough to keep the men at a distance and heavy enough
to hurt when one of his scything sweeps caught one of the mob.
Even the bristles made the men wary after one had retired after
being almost blinded by a fierce jab in the face.

From a few steps up the stairs Gunter was in a commanding
position. Three doorways faced him but he was able to keep the
men from the foot of the stairs themselves. Beyond, he could hear
the smashing of furniture and the crash as the steaming equipment
was overturned but he did not mind. All that mattered was to keep
Catherine safe for as long as possible.

It was difficult to remember that he had sworn he would never
fight again. Now he was not only fighting for the woman he loved,
he would gladly kill for her. He knew, swinging the heavy broom
around to hammer into the side of a man unwise enough to step
beyond the sheltering doorway, that he could not hope to hold
out for ever. The men were half drunk and disorganised, they
had not expected opposition. But every injury he inflicted only
antagonised them further. It was only a matter of time before they
rushed him in a mass and overwhelmed him by sheer strength of
numbers.

"Why do you not stop now?" he panted, eyeing them as they
hesitated just beyond reach of his broom. "No one has been hurt. It
will be dismissed merely as a drunken brawl that got out of hand.
Go now and let the law of England deal with me as it will."

"I say, kill the bastard." It was the man who had received a
face full of bristles. He stared up at Gunter from the protection of
the doorway, his face swollen and scratched, both eyes red and
sore. "He nearly blinded me."

"I wish no harm to any of you." Could Catherine get out of
the window? There was silk up there, and she would be able to

climb down if she could find a way of tying the slippery material so that it did not unknot and let her fall. He watched the doorway, trying to calm the men with his voice, but his whole concentration was upstairs with the woman he loved. *Mein Gott*, let her get out safely. Let her be unhurt.

He tried again. "Why do you not take me to your police and hand me over? They would lock me up again, I am sure. They will not be happy to be called out to a riot like this in the middle of the night."

Was there just the smallest hesitation at his mention of the police? He pressed home his advantage. "I will surrender myself to you now if you will just take me to your police." That would be the safest thing for Catherine and Robbie. If the mob knew that the police were involved they would not torch the building. That was his greatest fear: Catherine and Robbie upstairs and trapped with the flames licking around them. He would do anything to save them from a death like that.

"Please? I will give up now." He could see from the uncertain looks on the faces nearest him that they were considering it, that he was winning. He lowered the broom so that it was no longer protecting him, walked down a couple of steps, his heart rejoicing. They weren't bad men, just drunk and excited. If they accepted his surrender they would do no more than give him a good beating before they handed him over to the police.

He was on the bottom step, certain that he had got his way and saved Catherine and Robbie, when there was a shout at the far side of the building and the sound of running feet. Two men pushed their way excitedly through the crowd that had gathered in one of the doorways. "Jago." One of them shook the arm of a big man who was at the forefront of the group. "Jago. We just found a body in there, the body of a man with his head smashed in."

He turned and pointed at Gunter. "He idn't just a robber, Jago. He's a murderer as well. That bastard has killed an Englishman."

Walter had intended that someone else should find the body.

He had already played a greater part than he had planned, leading half the men round to the front of the building so that the German should not escape that way. In the aftermath of this riot Walter did not want anyone pointing to him as a ringleader.

He had come along merely to prod things along if they didn't seem to be turning out the way he wanted.

Already he could sense that his plan was failing. He had hoped that the German would be attacked immediately, that the place would be smashed and burned, that the dead body would provide ample justification for the death of the Hun.

But the fools seemed blind. They were overturning tables and kicking tins of dye with abandon but there had been no outcry as someone found the body. Worse, the noise level in the centre of the building was beginning to die down.

Walter hesitated. Jago was the leader and intelligent, in spite of the amount he had drunk. There was a real danger that he might realise the folly of what they were doing and then the whole plan would fail.

He dared not let the impetus slacken, even if it meant involving himself more that he wanted.

Walter moved to the room that Gunter had set up as his living quarters. This had been comprehensively ransacked, the table thrown on its side, the drawers emptied on to the floor, foodstuffs thrown wildly at the walls. As he entered his feet crunched over broken crockery and cutlery that had been thrown on to the floor. Most of the men had moved to watch the stand-off at the foot of the stairs. Only Willy was still here, emptying soap powder out on to the overthrown bed, laughing wildly.

As he moved forward Walter's foot knocked against a knife. It was an old one, its blade whetted so often that it had worn away into a curve, but it looked sharp and serviceable. He thrust it into his belt, under his coat, then caught at Willy's arm, "Come on. There's a room no one else has looked in yet." He almost dragged the man into the storeroom where he had hidden Random's body.

Even then the fool took precious seconds to find it and all the time Walter could hear the noise in the centre of the building growing quieter and quieter. Something was going wrong, he knew.

Desperation set in. "What the hell's that?" He pointed at the body lying in the shadow at the foot of the wall.

Willy moved forward, mouth slackly open. "Here, he's killed someone. He's killed a man." He looked up, eyes staring wide with horror. "He'll be raping our wives next, just like you said."

"He deserves to die," Walter prompted.

"He bleeding does!" At last Willy acted. He raced through the house, shouting for Jago, Walter right on his heels. Inwardly Walter's heart was leaping. There would be no holding back now.

Although there were still crashes from the outbuildings, the group in the centre of the works was ominously quiet. For a moment Walter hoped that it might be because the Hun was dead already: then he saw him, tall, fair, unhurt, walking down the stairs towards the Cornishmen as calmly as if he were welcoming expected guests, completely master of the situation, dominating even Jago.

Hatred surged through Walter's body. The man was an enemy. He had killed Robert, destroyed Walter's own life. He had no right to be so at home here. And if he lived—

He must not live.

"He weren't one of us," Willy was telling Jago excitedly. "He were a stranger."

Jago was looking wary and Walter understood why. Willy was not the most reliable man in the group.

"He were a thin man in a good suit of plus fours," Walter broke in, supporting Willy's evidence with his own. "He had a silver-topped stick."

"That's right." Willy confirmed. "Walter Harrison here found 'un."

Walter felt the attention of the German shift from Willy to himself. A hand caught his shoulder, spun him around. Icy blue eyes stared at him and he could see the recognition growing in them.

"You bastard, Walter Harrison." Gunter spat at him. "You've killed the major."

And Walter knew that his life was in the balance.

Robbie raced through the darkness. The quickest way to Penny's was down the main road that ran along by the harbour. Feet pounding, arms pumping, he raced with all his strength.

Catherine and Gunter depended on him. He had to get help. He reached out an arm and caught at the rough stone of the corner house, using his momentum to swing himself around into the small street that led up to the cottage that the Pentyrs rented.

His swinging body collided with another with a thump that knocked the breath from his lungs and sent him sprawling. And a voice he had not heard since his fight in Penzance said viciously in his ear, "I've got you now, you red-haired little runt. You haven't got no sister to rescue you now."

Fury burned along Gunter's veins. He would not have recognised Walter if Random had not jogged his memory but now he could see again the man who had held a gun to his head when he had been lying in the mud, injured and helpless.

And now the man had killed Random – Random, who had been Gunter's ideal of an honourable Englishman.

Gunter caught at Walter in case he should try to get away – but the atmosphere had changed.

"He's trying to strangle Walter now," the thin man who had announced finding the body shouted shrilly and there was a sudden deep-throated roar of anger from the other men.

As one, they surged towards him, no longer a collection of humans but a pack hunting their prey.

He had no chance of arguing with them now. Gunter lashed out with his feet, trying to clear a way back to the stairs where he could use the broom effectively, but they were on him. Hands grabbed at his neck, his coat. He pulled free, retreating up the first few stairs, but the broom was wrenched from his hands.

Backing towards the steps, using his feet as weapons, Gunter began to climb desperately up the stairs to the limited safety of the room above, praying that Catherine had managed to escape with the boy. He did not want them to witness this battle – or its inevitable outcome.

Jago was after him, his long arms reaching higher than the others, the grip of his strong fisherman's hands almost unbreakable. For a moment Gunter thought that he was going to be dragged from the stairs into the mob below. He half turned, clinging desperately to the flimsy rail that guarded the side of the flight of steps, and one of the flatirons that he had stuffed in his pocket banged against the wood.

He had forgotten the irons. He clung to the rail with one hand, kicking out with his feet at the grasping hands beneath him while he struggled to free the iron with the other.

It came free with a jerk that almost overbalanced him. Jago

228

dragged swiftly at him, trying to take advantage of his momentary instability, and Gunter swung the iron in desperation.

It connected with the side of Jago's head with a dull thud and the big man dropped without a sound, his slack body instantly swallowed up by the surging men around him.

Gunter took advantage of the shocked stillness that followed the man's fall to back further up the stairs. His head was almost level with the ceiling now. For the first time since the discovery of Random's body he could hope that he might win through to the room above. Once there he would be in a stronger position, able to hold off the men below for hours if need be. Unless they set fire to the building he might even be able to stay there until the police arrived, as they surely must. Even in a close-knit community like this there must be someone who would send for help.

He backed up another step, a second.

Walter came rising out of the mass of people beneath him like a trout leaping up a waterfall. Even as Gunter fought to make his way up the last few steps the man was at his throat, nails clawing at his eyes.

With a final effort Gunter forced his legs straight, bearing them both back up the steps, into the room above.

The weight of the man overbalanced him and he fell backwards on to the bare floorboards of the print room, leaving the staircase unguarded.

Her hands on fire from the burn of the silk as it had run through her clenched hands, Catherine hurried to the stairs and peered down them.

All she could see was Gunter as he stood on the lower part of the rickety staircase, the heavy broom in his hands. There was still the sound of crashes and breaking elsewhere downstairs but the angry voices that had frightened her so had died down to a subdued muttering. Nevertheless, there was still an undercurrent of violence that sickened her.

She waited, her heart thumping, praying that Gunter would be able to talk sense into the mob. They were not evil, she knew. It had been a long and a hard war and there was no family in the land that had escaped without loss. It was understandable that there should still be anti-German feelings. But to take it out on Gunter who was providing jobs for old soldiers when, in the rest of England, there were riots and strikes because even able-bodied men were being thrown out of work, was unfair.

She hated unfairness.

She stayed silent, stretching and relaxing her hands to try to get some use back into them as she listened with increasing hope to the negotiations below. Then, just when she thought that he had won, there was a sound of rushing feet, voices shouting again and, in seconds, the watching crowd beneath her had turned into a mob.

Gunter was fighting his way back up the stairs. Catherine swung round, her eyes raking the room. She had to help him. The tables were too heavy and well made for her to move but the wiper's trolleys were on wheels and she knew from bitter experience how heavy and unwieldy the rolls of silk could be.

The shouts rose to a crescendo but she ignored them, dragging the nearest trolley to the top of the stairs. With a sudden rush Gunter catapulted backwards out of the stairwell, another man at his throat, and there was a roar as the men below tried to rush, jostling, up the undefended stairs after them.

Catherine gritted her teeth against the pain in her hands and pushed the trolley hard.

It teetered for a second on the lip of the top stair then fell, crashing down the stairs, scattering pots and brushes as it went, smashing into the leading rioters and hurling them, arms and legs flailing, back on to the heads of the men below.

The cries of the injured men almost drowned the final thud as the trolley came to rest on the sprawled bodies but Catherine dared not wait to see the result of her actions.

She was already hurling the long rolls of silk, still wrapped around their central core of thick board, across the entrance to the stairs, jamming the ends between the rudimentary banister rails that surrounded it. Then she set her teeth and braced herself as she pulled a second trolley across. It was difficult to get it to lie on top of the silk to reinforce the flimsy barricade but she managed it in the end, tipping it over so that it lay poised over the stairwell, holding down the rolls.

It would not take long to dislodge the barricade, she knew, but the first person who did so would be knocked off the stairs by the trolley and that would give her a small breathing space.

Catherine turned and ran across to the bodies struggling on the ground and stopped.

Gunter was struggling with her father!

Gunter seemed for the moment to have the upper hand but, even as she looked, Walter made a supreme effort and brought his knee up. Gunter jerked backwards and Walter twisted sharply, throwing him on to the floor and rolling on top of him.

"Father, stop it." Catherine bent over the bodies, pulling at her father's shoulders, trying to drag him off.

Walter swung his elbow back viciously and it caught Catherine in the stomach. She doubled over, her lungs searching desperately for breath, unable to move.

"Catherine!" Gunter's startled cry told her that until that moment he had not realised she was there. He reared back, staring at her. "Catherine—"

Walter's fist came up, taking advantage of Gunter's slackened hold. It connected with the German's chin with a dull crack and his head snapped back. Horrified, fighting for breath, Catherine saw her lover slump to one side, his eyes dazed.

Walter pulled out a knife.

"No!" Catherine flung herself on to Gunter's semi-conscious body, trying to protect it with her own. "No, Father. You mustn't."

"He'll be the death of me." Walter caught her shoulder with his free hand, trying to drag her away. "Do you want me to be hung? Or shot?"

"No! Why should you? Leave him alone. He won't hurt you, I promise!"

Catherine was sobbing with fear, struggling against the greater strength of her father with hands that were already sore and weak.

"Why? Because I'm a deserter. And he knows it."

Shock paralysed her for a brief second as she tried to comprehend what he had said. "But – but—"

While she stared at him, her face blank with shock, Walter moved. With one strong pull he dragged her from Gunter's body and sent her sprawling on the floor.

"Wait. This won't help." But he was beyond reason. Catherine could see the terror in his eyes. He couldn't listen to her, she realised, he couldn't understand. All the hatred and the fear that he had clutched to him, brooding for all those months in the tiny bedroom in Dorset, all that had swelled up and broken the dams that held it back, had come flooding out, swamping his reason, his intelligence.

And before him, in Gunter, he saw the embodiment of all that he had hated and feared. Gunter was every German and Gunter deserved to die.

Even as Catherine stared at him, her mind racing, Walter moved. The knife came up, poised over Gunter's unprotected throat, came down—

Catherine hurled herself at the men. She had to stop this – for both their sakes. The knife came down, down – but she would never be in time, would never have the strength to push her father off balance so that the knife would miss Gunter's neck.

Inside her head she screamed words she had never spoken in real life. *Gunter. My love.*

Without conscious thought she took the only action that would save Gunter's life.

She thrust out her right hand, her painting hand, between Gunter's neck and the knife.

Twenty-Six

"Stop. Stop." Robbie wriggled and kicked desperately in the other boy's grasp as the two of them rolled on the ground. "Let me go. It's a matter of life and death."

"A brem likely story. You're just a coward." The boy's hands tightened on Robbie's shoulders, holding him down.

"My sister's in danger." Robbie balled his fists and thrust them up between the boy's arms, breaking his grip. With a sudden wriggle he broke free and was on his feet, running up the road towards Penny's.

A hand caught at his ankle and brought him down on his face with a bone-jarring thud. He lashed out with his foot and hit the other boy's hand. "Let me go."

Time was racing by. In his imagination Robbie could hear the shouts of the men, the smashing of windows. What would they do to Catherine? To Gunter?

The grip on his ankle slackened and he got to his feet. He was smaller than the other boy and less strong. He knew that he would not be able to run away fast enough to get to Penny's before the boy caught him again and he could not waste time. Catherine's welfare depended on it.

His only chance was to get the fight over with quickly, whatever it cost him. He turned to face his enemy, fists clenched.

The boy was on him instantly, his knuckles hammering into Robbie's face. Robbie hit back desperately, ignoring the blood that spurted from his nose. The pain was lost in the frantic message racing through and through his head. *Get help, Robbie. Get help quick.*

He could hear nothing but his breathless gasps and the sound of blows. He knew that he could not win but he had to fight. He had to finish it quickly.

A lucky blow sent him reeling back – into the arms of a stranger.

233

He gasped, swivelling round in the man's hold, and realised that his opponent had been captured also.

"Well." The man who held him had a high, drawling voice. "Plenty of bottom but not much science here, wouldn't you say, Farley?"

Grown-ups, and English at that. Robbie grabbed at the man's tweed jacket. "Please, sir. Please. There's a fight and m-my sister and—"

"My God." Another voice – and one he recognised this time. Robbie gaped at the pony and trap that had come up, unheard, behind him, and at the man who sat in it. "My God. It's the apple boy."

"Please." Robbie flung himself at the trap. "Please, sir. My sister is in danger from all these drunken men and—"

"Your sister?" Grantham interrupted. "The girl who painted my picture?"

"Yes, she—"

A strong hand reached over and hauled him into the cart and the other two men flung themselves bodily in after him.

"Damned if we're going to let people get away with hurting artists. Tell us the way, lad!"

"B-back there." He could hardly believe that the situation had changed so fast.

Grantham turned the cart, the pony backing and swishing its tail angrily, then set off at a canter. "A bit of sport at last, fellows."

"And I'm ready for it." The man who had held Robbie reached under the seat and pulled out a shotgun. "We haven't had any sport all day."

Robbie was impressed but Grantham said angrily, "You can't shoot people, Birch. It isn't done."

Lamorna Birch pointed into the darkness at the blacker shape of Newlyn Quay. "I spent the whole bloody war in the volunteers guarding that damn thing and never fired a shot in anger," he said crossly. "I'm owed one."

The pony and trap bucketed over the rough road with Robbie urging it on with every bone in his body.

Kill the German. Kill him.

Walter gave no thought to anything else. Catherine was a

distraction, irrelevant. All his thoughts were concentrated on the German.

The German knew he was a deserter. The German knew that he had killed Random. The thoughts ran round and round in his mind. Walter could think of nothing else. For two years all his conscious thoughts had been concentrated on hiding the fact that he was a deserter and now he could not adjust to the fact that circumstances had changed.

Kill the German.

The sharp knife glittered in the starlit room. The German's throat was open, uncovered, vulnerable. Nothing could have stopped Walter.

His lips bared in a snarl, he brought the knife down.

It was stopped inches from his enemy's throat.

The world stood still. He blinked stupidly at the sight, trying to understand what had happened.

And Catherine's blood sprayed in a scarlet fountain.

It spattered his face, blinding his eyes and even finding its way into his mouth. It dyed the face and clothes of his enemy. Red, red blood.

Behind him there was a dull thud and a yell and Walter was suddenly back again in the trenches, back again with the crunch of mortars and the screams of wounded men. He saw before him the shattered, ruined face of Robert and, under him, white and bloodstained, the face of the man who had killed his brother.

It was as if the last two years had never been.

He could smell the stench of death. He was there. Terrified, lonely, bewildered, *there*.

He lifted his head, breathing deep. He would kill the bastard. Now he would kill the bastard.

But there was something in his way, something that did not belong to the ugly, frightening scene. A woman's hand. A hand that reminded him of Elizabeth's. Slender. Long-fingered.

Bleeding.

The present slid back into place with a physical jolt that took his breath away. Walter blinked slowly, taking in the man lying dazed underneath him, the girl kneeling beside him with blood dripping from her pierced hand.

"Katy. Katy." He was shivering, tremors wracking his whole body. "Katy, my God! What have I done?"

She could not speak, could not look at him. White-faced, she knelt motionless at his side, her green eyes wide with shock as she stared at the knife implanted in the palm of her hand.

"Katy." He would have given anything not to have done it. He must have been mad. Mad. He looked at the man beneath him. Good-looking, pleasant-faced. Ordinary. Not a monster. Not a fiend. A man.

A better man that he was.

"Oh, Katy."

What could he do for her? How could he ever make it up to her?

The knife gleamed gently in the starlight. That, at least, he could do. His hands reached out.

"Do not touch it."

The sharpness in Gunter's voice made Walter jump. "I was only—"

"No. You may do more harm by pulling it out. Leave it there until we can find a doctor."

Gunter pushed Walter off his body and stood shakily up, rubbing his head. He leaned over Catherine, stroking her hair. "It will be all right, Liebling. Do not worry. You will be all right."

Shouts from downstairs caught his attention and he turned to the stairwell. "I do not understand why they are not here."

Catherine spoke. Her eyes were still on her wounded hand and her voice was dull with shock. "I tried to stop them."

Gunter turned to look at the rough barricade she had erected and grinned. But no barricade would last unmanned. If he had been able to guard it they might have been safe for a long time. But already the men below were dismantling it. There was a space at one end as if one of the rolls of silk had already been removed and even as he looked a second roll was dislodged and fell down the stairs accompanied by curses and thuds.

Already hands were working to loosen another roll. One of the rolls, Gunter realised, that supported the weight of the wiper's trolley.

He began to run towards it. "No, no. Wait. There is danger. You will get hurt—"

The roll of silk moved, hung for a moment on the very lip of the stairwell – and fell.

The whole rough barricade collapsed taking the heavy trolley with it. For a second the noise was deafening: the crashing of the trolley and thuds of the falling rolls, accompanied with screams and shouts.

Then there was silence.

Walter's eyes met Gunter's. Across the barriers of race and allegiance they were both soldiers. They both recognised the silence that follows a disaster, a silence all too often followed by an irrational reaction.

From below a single voice rose in a horrified wail. "They've killed Nabbo! The bastards have killed Nabbo!"

Walter glanced at Catherine, still kneeling where they had left her, rocking, over the ruin of her hand, and he took a deep breath and moved to Gunter's side.

The single voice had been joined by others. Harsh, raucous, the roar of a hunting pack. Walter shivered. Before now the crowd had been drunk and angry, ready for trouble but equally ready to be talked out of it if something better turned up.

This was different. This was personal. This was the sound of a mob after blood.

"Kill." The cry was taken up by other voices. "Kill. Kill. Nabbo's dead. Kill."

The sound swelled.

Walter moved to the top of the stairs. "It were an accident." His voice was almost drowned by the roar below. "Jago. Willy. It were an accident."

"Kill." They were like a single beast now. The crowd moved to the stairs in a concerted rush that bore the leaders half-way up the steps even as Walter was speaking.

They wouldn't listen now, he knew. They were after blood and nothing else would stop them.

He glanced behind him at Catherine's slowly rocking body and for the first time in two years he was suddenly overcome with love for her, for Robbie.

Had he been mad since the shock of Robert's death? Everything he had done, everything he had thought, seemed suddenly skewed, off balance. He remembered Elizabeth, he remembered her fall, he remembered that he had intended to kill his own children. It was as if it had all happened to another person.

Had he really thought that his life was worth more than their own? That he wouldn't die to defend them?

The first men were nearly at the top of the ladder now, their faces contorted with fury and hurt. One of their own had died and they did not care who paid for it.

Walter had seen men in the grip of blood lust before. Had he not been a victim himself the day that Robert died? He remembered how he had even turned his gun on a friend who had tried to stop him killing the German, as well as on to Random.

Men like that would not stop at one death. None of them was safe.

He turned to look at Catherine for one last time, his eyes filling with tears of love.

Gunter knew as well as Walter what to expect once the rioters reached them.

If Catherine had been unhurt he would have forced her through the window, believing that even though she would hurt herself she would, at least, survive the fall. Now, looking at her rocking in agony, her hand transfixed by the knife, he thought she was too shocked either to realise what was happening or to get herself through the window.

There was only one way to save Catherine. If he could offer himself to them as a willing sacrifice they might be satisfied by him alone. Fight, and he knew he would rouse them to new heights; hurt them and their anger would increase, feeding on itself until they were no more than wild animals.

For Catherine's sake he had to sacrifice himself. The bitter irony choked him. For months he had believed in non-violence and now he had to practise it in its ultimate form, for the sake of the woman he loved.

Gunter moved forward towards the head of the stairs. At the sight of him the mob's shouts rose to new heights. These were no longer men, they were a hunting pack of animals, and they would stay that way until something – probably the sight of his dead and bloody body – shocked them back into humanity again.

Gunter stood upright, hands by his side, offering no resistance. He would descend to them, let them deal with him downstairs. That way Catherine, even if she roused, would be spared the terrible sight. It might even be enough to stop them ever coming up to this room. It was a small chance, but it was all he could offer her.

He stepped forward another pace – and Walter pushed past him.

"No!" It was the worst thing he could do. He would rouse them further, excite them, increase the risk to Catherine. "No. Stand back."

Walter was deaf to his command. He stood at the top of the stairs, staring down at them. "Th'all not coom oop here." There was no trace of the Cornish which he had spoken these last weeks; now his accent was pure Yorkshire, the accent of his youth. "My lass is hurt. Tha'll not coom oop."

"Out of the way, Harrison." Jago was at the front of the column of men. "We're after the German murderer and we'll not let you stop us."

"The German didn't kill nobody." Walter leaned forward. "I'm the one killed the major, and it were my lass who—"

"No!" Gunter moved fast, jerking Walter back before he could say any more. "It was me that set the trap that killed your friend. Take me and have done with it."

Walter turned and faced him. For a second they stared at each other eye to eye then Walter spoke. "They won't be satisfied until they have a body."

"My body."

Walter shook his head. "They want the murderer and I've got enough on my conscience. But—" He stared at Gunter from suspiciously bright eyes. "This is for Katy, see, not for you."

"No. Wait."

But Walter had moved forward and was addressing the crowd. "I killed the major." The low mutter rose. "I killed Nabbo." The lie came out as calmly as had the first confession and Gunter could sense the astonishment and the anger rising like a wave up the stairwell. "And I attacked him and stole his watch."

The rumble of anger was louder now. Hands reached up, clutching at Walter's legs, dragging at him.

For a second he teetered on the edge, screaming out his last, terrible confession. "I murdered my wife."

And, arms wide, he launched himself head first down the staircase. His body took the first man, the man Gunter had already marked out as the leader, full in the face and the two bodies hurtled on to the heads of the men below, taking the lower men with them.

239

The sea of faces at the foot of the stairs heaved and swelled as the bodies disappeared into its depths. The roar of angry voices grew to a crescendo, interspersed with the terrible gut-wrenching screams of a man in torment.

The screams stopped.

All movement in the crowd below stilled.

For a second Gunter allowed himself to hope. These men were not killers. If they had been shocked to their senses by what they had done . . .

They moved towards him.

They moved in a human tide, only one thought in their minds, flowing up the stairs towards him and with every step they took, the sound of the mob grew louder, swelling from a mutter to a roar in seconds.

He could not stop them now by sacrificing himself. All he could do was buy Catherine a few more precious seconds.

As he stationed himself at the head of the stairs his coat banged against his hip. He still had one flatiron left.

The mob were too angry to think clearly. They had no weapons. Driven by fury alone they surged upwards.

Gunter swung the iron, the flat surface connecting with the side of the first man's head then back again, catching his colleague on the side of the face. The first man swayed against the flimsy banisters and, weakened already by the battering they had received, they collapsed, and he fell, his body swallowed by the crowd below.

Even at the head of the narrow stairs Gunter knew that he could not hold them for ever. Already more men were pressing forward, hands reaching out to drag him down, and he could see the hate and fury in their eyes.

Horatio at the bridge. His mind threw up the image. But Horatio had the River Tiber to carry him to safety when he was finally overcome. He swung the iron again and again but there was no end to the men climbing towards him.

One man ducked his iron. A hand caught at his trouser leg. Gunter kicked free but he had lost a vital half-second. They were nearer, higher.

Another hand caught at his leg, held on. He saved himself only by catching at the remaining newel post. The men climbed another step higher, were on the threshold of the room itself . . .

240

The roar of the twelve-bore was deafening in the enclosed space.

The gun had been fired at the ceiling but some of the shot must have hit nails or the walls because they ricocheted like a swarm of bees whining and stinging.

Clinging to the post for support Gunter stared down at the sight below.

The mob was silent, shocked by the unexpected noise back into their individual personalities. Facing them – in other circumstances he would have laughed – was a man like a bank manager, a man dressed so flamboyantly that he looked as if he was in fancy dress and a third man, the man with the gun, his plus fours and twelve-bore at odds with his scholarly, round, gold-rimmed glasses.

And beside them, foreshortened by the view, the ginger curls that he would recognise at a mile's distance.

"Robbie." Gunter's voice was a croak in his dry throat.

Robbie looked up and saw him, and began forcing his way through the silent crowd. A minute ago they would have ripped him apart; now they moved aside under his pummelling fists as he fought his way through them to the top of the stairs.

"Katy? Is Katy all right?"

Gunter reached down and dragged him up the last few steps, clutching the small body to him in an agony of relief. "Catherine's alive," he said shakily, "but she's hurt. She needs help."

Twenty-Seven

The cottage had never looked so bright. Flowers blossomed from every available container, scenting the air with their fragrance.

And the visitors – Catherine could not remember when they had last had visitors in a cottage she had lived in. Now they crowded round the kitchen sitting on chairs, stools, old boxes, or, in the case of Robbie, proudly on the table itself. She leaned back against the comfort of Gunter's shoulder and took a deep breath.

"They think" – she managed to keep the quaver out of her voice – "they think I will get back some use of my fingers."

"But painting." Grantham leaned forward. "Will you be able to paint again?"

She could not meet their eyes, shook her head, staring down at her bandaged hand.

Gunter took her good hand as it lay on the bright silk of her dress, stroked her shining chestnut cap of hair. "They cannot know for certain, Liebling, they only think that will be the case."

She raised her head and met his concerned blue eyes and her mouth trembled into a smile. Once this would have been the disaster to end all disasters but now . . . Not with Gunter here, in the cottage where she had never thought to see him, not when he was holding her hand, comforting her as he had, day and night, since that dreadful time.

Augustus Farley slammed one hand into the other palm. "It's a damn shame. The best new talent we've had down here for years—"

Catherine stared at him. "Talent? You think that? But your wife said . . ." Her voice trailed away.

"Oh, you spoke to her, did you?" Grantham snorted. "I've told you before, Farley, you should do something about that woman.

242

Not that it isn't your own fault. If you didn't make up to every young woman in sight she wouldn't be so jealous."

"Jealous? Of me?" Catherine was amazed.

"Looking like you do, talented. No wonder she did all she could to keep you away from her husband." Grantham snorted again, making his moustache flutter. "I wouldn't advise you to see him alone, even now, even if you are engaged to bold Horatio there."

"Yes, but this is going too far." Farley was walking round the table, hands thrust deep in his pockets. "Keeping an eye on me is one thing but to be rude to a young artist like this . . . I'm going to have to put my foot down this time."

"'A wife, a dog and a walnut tree,'" quoted Grantham.

"Oh, I'm not going to hit her." Farley rubbed his hands. "I'll send her home to her mother for six months. That will teach her a lesson."

"And in the meantime you will . . ."

Farley laughed. "That's her problem. And mine. But this young lady . . ." He came over and stared at her. "I am more sorry than I can say, my dear. Especially if my wife had any part to play in all this."

Daubs, Mrs Farley had called her paintings. But it no longer mattered. If Mrs Farley hadn't upset her so, she would never have lost her paintings and she might never have got to know Gunter, never helped to get the factory working. She looked at her bandaged hand. Some movement, they had promised her. Enough to be a wife, at least. And, given the choice between painting and Gunter . . .

"My God! Her paintings!" Birch was on his feet. "If they're as good as the one Grantham has, and with this story behind them, they'll fetch a mint." He came across to Catherine. "You *do* have others, my dear?"

"About ten with Penny but there are others which I sent off to the man who sold my first painting." She looked from one to the other, knowing that she was in the presence of men who could ask hundreds of pounds for a single painting. "I got twenty guineas for it, though he kept some as commission."

"Twenty guineas. Fiddle!" Birch snapped his fingers. "I can get you five times that."

"You believe what Birch tells you, my dear," Grantham advised her. "Never knew such an artist for knowing how to turn daubs into money."

"Even artists have to eat. And I like to eat well." Birch preened himself at the compliment.

"A hundred pounds for a painting." Catherine's heart beat fast. "We need the money to rebuild the silk factory."

"You will *not* need the money for that." Pettifer, the young solicitor, had been silent in the presence of so many well-known artists; now he pushed himself off the wall where he had been leaning. "A riot like that was a breakdown of law and order and the council should have foreseen it."

"Oh, come on!" Even Lamorna Birch was taken aback by that.

"It's true," he insisted. "This sort of thing has happened in other areas – and the council has been held responsible. Especially—" and he grinned mischievously around the assembled company "—especially when the mayor is chairman of the Bench, as he is here, and has released an alien who might well be the target for anti-German feeling." He rubbed his moustache. "He won't have a leg to stand on."

"But – it was you who got Gunter released," Catherine protested.

He stared at her. "But I was only doing my duty for my client. It is up to the Bench to take into consideration any implications their actions might have for the peace of the community."

"And it was my father who started it."

Gunter took her hand. "He was ill, Liebling. I was there that dreadful day. I know what he went through, what he had been through week after week, month after month, for years. That war – it was enough to send any man mad. And in the end" – he reached out and wiped a tear from her cheek – "in the end he died a brave man, Liebling. He died trying to save you."

"But you—" She looked at him, trying to be convinced. "You went through it, too, yet you—"

He stopped her with a kiss. "I thought I was sane, but when I look back – I was denying life, I was denying hope. It was you who brought me back, who gave me a dream, who taught me to care enough to fight for what I wanted."

"Me? But—" Catherine looked startled. "But I was afraid to

fight for anything – until I met you. I never had the confidence to fight."

"So we have healed each other. We have each made the other whole again." He smiled into her eyes. "Isn't that the meaning of true love? That together we can conquer the world?"

Locked in his embrace Catherine closed her eyes. She had no need to conquer the world.

All she could ever want was already in her arms.